# SUMMER HUSBAND

## Praise for *Summer Husband*

"Feminist, flirty, and fun! *Summer Husband* is a coming-of-middle age delight."

—Meredith Schorr,
author of *RoomMating*

"Bunk in with *Summer Husband, an* engaging first novel about an engrossing second chance."

—Marilyn Simon Rothstein,
author of *Who Loves You Best*

*"Summer Husband* will make you laugh out loud, cheering Lori Kramer on through an emotional, challenging, and transformative summer. As her marriage is falling apart, Lori's gutsy approach to taking life into her own hands shows readers that dreams can come true—even the ones you never knew you had."

—Lisa Smith,
author of *Girl Walks Out of a Bar*

"Like protagonist Lori Kramer, I never made it to summer camp as a child so I was swept away with Amy Lorowitz's fun, nostalgic and romantic debut novel. *Summer Husband* is a warm, hopeful story of friendship, love and rediscovery."

—Nicola Harrison,
author of *The Island Club*

# SUMMER HUSBAND

A Novel

Amy Lorowitz

SHE WRITES PRESS

Published in 2026 by
She Writes Press, an imprint of The Stable Book Group

32 Court Street, Suite 2109
Brooklyn, NY 11201
https://shewritespress.com

Library of Congress Control Number: 2025926955
ISBN: 979-8-89636-078-0
eISBN: 979-8-89636-079-7

Interior design and typeset: Katherine Lloyd, The DESK

Printed in the United States

I dedicate this book to the two most influential
women in my life, my grandmother, Jennie Kramer
and my mother, Esther Lorowitz.
And to Daryl Kunesh, a giant gentleman.

May their memories be for a blessing.

# Contents

# 1
# Welcome to Woodlands

I placed my iced coffee in the cup holder, glanced at the directions one more time, and checked the side-view mirror. I clicked the blinker and pulled out into New York City traffic—ready or not. I was certain I was more nervous than my kids, who would be joining me next week. Even though I was thirty-nine, I felt unprepared for my first ever sleepaway camp experience.

An hour later I pulled into a gas station and filled the tank. As I waited to pay, I stared at the cigarette display behind the cashier. I hadn't smoked since before I married Ronnie, but I had a sudden urge to buy a pack. A cigarette would calm the nerves I felt driving into the unknown. I looked around the store. No Ronnie, no kids—no one I knew was there to judge me. I shifted my weight from one foot to the other just as I had when I was a child and couldn't make up my mind. The woman behind the counter looked at me expectantly.

"Can I have a pack of Winstons?"

"Anything else?"

I grabbed some Trident gum and tossed it on the counter. Back in the car I stared at the cigarettes, but instead of lighting up I reached over and shoved them into the glove compartment. It was enough knowing they were available, if needed. I popped a piece of gum in my mouth, rolled down the window, and felt the wind on my face. I turned the radio to my favorite station and belted out top forty hits off-key, with no one back seat complaining about my singing—or my driving. My definition of freedom.

Two hours later, as I made a left turn onto the dirt road leading to the camp, Cyndi Lauper and I were singing "Girls Just Want to Have Fun."

I passed under a rustic sign hanging between two ancient oak trees.

CAMP WOODLANDS
ESTABLISHED 1929

I continued up a narrow craggy lane shadowed by towering trees. When I reached the top of the last hill, rays of sun broke through the canopy of leaves. I pulled over to a welcome banner flying above a log fence that overlooked an expansive, lush lawn. A path led down the hill to a lake that glistened in the late June sunshine.

The aroma of fresh-cut lawn and the crisp, clear air brought me back to my childhood at the bungalow colony in the Catskill Mountains. I smiled, remembering, *Summer camp for families.*

The colors—greens, blues, whites—were vivid. The sun, high in the cloudless sky, made the powdered lines on the baseball and soccer fields shimmer.

I parked across the road from a blond-wood log cabin. An old-fashioned placard that read OFFICE hung above the door and swayed in the breeze.

This would be my home for the next nine weeks.

# 2
# Over the Hill

Inside, the foyer was piled high with duffel bags that I sidestepped to reach the three women sitting at desks crammed together in a small room.

They were so intent at tapping away on computers while talking on phones that no one noticed me. Everyone wore a uniform, white polo shirts with Woodlands stitched over their hearts and a name tag pinned above the embroidery.

Nicole, one of the women, introduced herself as the executive administrator and said she'd be right with me.

While I was waiting, an attractive, tall man with shoulder length, wavy brown hair walked through the door. He was about my age and decked out in Camp Woodlands garb: white and green hoodie, shiny green soccer shorts, and green and white Converse All-Star sneakers—no socks.

"Good day ladies, always a pleasure to see your cheery faces."

The ladies were far from cheery, but they stopped what they were doing, looked up, and gave him big smiles. He had a British accent.

Nicole said, "Good morning, Sir Theodore. I'm processing our new division leader, Lori Kramer. This is Theodore Mooney, the head soccer coach and assistant director of Boys Camp. Can you load her bags into the cart?"

"Sure, Lori, was it? This way." He led, holding the door open.

"How does a Brit find his way to a camp in the States? Is it because it's in New England?" I thought I was being clever, but as I said it, I heard how ridiculous I sounded.

He stopped and a wry grin crossed his face. "Heh, heh, haven't heard that one in a long time."

"But seriously, I'd be interested in hearing how you ended up here, Theodore."

"Oh, no, that will not do. Please call me Ted."

"But didn't Nicole just call you Sir Theodore?"

"She thinks because I'm from the UK that I'm posh and likes to tease me. I told her if she ever curtsied, I'd thump Bob, her husband, even if he is my best mate." He broke into a cockney accent. "But the truth is, well, I'm just a regular bloke." Then he threw out his arms. "Look around you, it's breathtaking. I can't think of any place else I'd rather be at this moment."

His exuberance was contagious. I smiled, looking around. Everything was green and lush, and the scent of pine trees and freshly cut grass filled the air. It was a stark contrast to the drab, dirty streets of the exhaust-filled city I'd left that morning. I could just make out the shimmering water of the lake below the hill and beyond the trees.

"You're right, it is beautiful."

"What brought you to my little slice of paradise?"

"I wanted my two daughters to come here. Zelda's eleven and Hazel's nine. It'll be the first time at a sleepaway camp for all three of us."

"We have something in common. I'm here with my ten-year-old son, Max. Let's get your bags on the cart."

Ted went to my car to lift the enormous camp-issued duffel out of the trunk, grunted, and dropped it. He stayed bent with his hands on his knees. "What've you got in there? You know you didn't need to bring all the sporting equipment—they do supply it."

"I guess I must have packed too . . ."

While I spoke, he picked up the duffel and tossed it onto the back seat as if it were a feather. "I'm just giving you a hard time." I probably didn't look amused because he said, "Lori, lighten up, you're at camp now. Remember to have fun, be campy. That's my philosophy when I'm here."

"You don't strike me as the philosophical type," I said.

"What type am I?"

I eyed him up and down. "Charming rogue."

Ted laughed loudly.

"Are you laughing because I'm on the money or because I'm way off?"

"I guess you'll just have to find out for yourself."

"What about me?"

"Easy. Anxious New York City overbearing helicopter mum," he said.

"You just piled every stereotypical motherly adjective on me."

"Shall we agree to let our first impressions go and figure it out as the summer unfolds?"

He stuck out his hand and I shook it. I was pretty sure my assessment of him wouldn't change. "Fair. Do you have any survival tips to share with a newbie?"

"Hmm. Get as much rest as you can because you're constantly on your feet. The campus is massive. I think everything else would be better for you to find out yourself. I don't want to influence your experience, but ask me a direct question, and I'll do my best to answer."

"Okay, where do I live?"

A woman with long, frizzy brown hair who looked sixtyish walked out of the office holding several keys swinging from her wrist and a clipboard held to her chest.

"Welcome Lori. Jack and I are happy that you're joining us this summer." Happy? She was expressionless. "I see you've already met Ted. I'll drive you to your cabin."

We'd spoken on the phone back in February, and I'd seen photos of Marilyn on the camp's website, but this was the first time we were meeting. I was put off by her cool manner. She didn't look me in the eye or shake my hand.

Ted squished in the back of the golf cart next to my things while I slipped into the passenger seat.

Marilyn handed me a kelly green knapsack with Lori K. written on it in bold black Sharpie.

"You'll need to carry this with you. Inside are two camp polos, baseball cap, first aid kit, and the orientation schedule. And most importantly a charger and your radio."

I looked inside the bag, pulling it out. "Radio? Like a walkie talkie?"

"Yes, we need to be able to contact you wherever you are, and the campus is enormous."

I looked over my shoulder at Ted. He leaned over, pointing to the radio clipped to his shorts. That was something I'd have to get used to.

Marilyn explained the living arrangements on the ride over. "The nonbunking female staff lives over the hill."

"Over the hill?" I asked. "Nonbunking?"

"As a division leader, that's DL, you're nonbunking, meaning you don't live with the campers. The counselors sleep in the cabins with the kids. You and the other DLs are over the hill."

"Oh, I get it. It's because we're old?"

Marilyn seemed confused and pointed beyond my shoulder, "No, it's over that hill."

Ted laughed along with me.

Marilyn pulled up to tiny cottages surrounding a gravel parking area. She stopped in front of a tilted, whitewashed wooden building that looked as if staples and duct tape might be holding it together. I was pretty sure that one good huff and one good puff would topple it. She picked up her clipboard and scrolled down with her finger until she reached my name.

"Here are the keys for room two." I must have looked concerned because Marilyn added, "It's my favorite room. I decorated it myself with furnishings from my grandmother's house."

I had my doubts.

"Later I'll show you the Cubs' bunk," Marilyn said.

"Cubs, like the baseball team?"

"No, like Woodlands' creatures. Your daughter Zelda's a Woodchuck and Hazel's a Chipmunk, and the youngest campers, the group you'll be taking care of, are the Cubs." Marilyn glanced at her watch. "I'll be back in half an hour to pick you up for your first meeting."

Ted threw the duffel over his shoulder and followed me up the three wooden steps. The screen door slammed behind us, rattling the building.

"Trust me, it won't be so bad," Ted said. "The only time you're in your room is to sleep. The firmness of the mattress will be the deciding factor."

I fumbled with the lock.

"Can you move a little faster? All kidding aside, your bag isn't getting any lighter."

I opened the door and Ted dropped my stuff at the foot of the double bed. He pressed his hand on the mattress. "This feels solid. You should be fine." He stepped into the doorframe. "Are you good for now?"

"I feel like I should tip you."

"The camp has a strict no tipping policy." He smiled. "I'll leave you to unpack. See you at the meeting."

After he left, I felt a wave of loneliness. The last time I'd felt this alone was when my parents drove off, leaving me in front of my college dorm, where I knew exactly nobody. I had put myself in a similar situation: no friends and a shared bathroom. What had I been thinking?

I took a deep breath and surveyed the room I'd be sleeping in for the next two months. The bed was two short steps from the door, a four-drawer dresser with a warped mirror hung over the bureau against the opposite wall, and a few misshapen hangers hung in a tiny closet in the corner. Surprisingly, the room didn't have that dank, musty smell I associated with cabins. Maybe because the room was filled with sun streaming through the catty-corner windows. In contrast to the basic items in the room, matching frilly lace curtains reminded me of my Grandma Mimi's. I bounced on the mattress and my butt dipped backwards into the middle where it sagged. I counted in my head the number of nights I would have to sleep here—sixty-two.

*I can do this. I must do this. I will do this.*

A stream of light fell across my face. I decided that was a good omen.

The bathroom was a decent-sized square with a window that looked out onto the woods behind the building. The sink had two separate spigots, hot and cold. The last time I'd seen plumbing that ancient was at least twenty-five years earlier at the bungalow colony I had stayed in with my brother and parents. You had to turn on both taps, cup your hands, and flip back and forth to get the right temperature to wash your face.

I was pretty sure showering would also be challenging. I pulled back the shower curtain to check out the fixtures and was relieved to find a shiny new showerhead poking out of the wall—there wasn't a hint of rust.

I had explained to Zelda and Hazel that my experience at their age was a day camp in upstate New York where you lived in a two-room cottage with your parents. They finally understood when I said it was like the movie *Dirty Dancing*.

The door across from mine opened and a well-coiffed petite blonde stepped into the hallway, wearing huge sapphire studs emphasizing her blue eyes, as well as several gold chains around her neck and a diamond tennis bracelet. She looked like she was ready to attend a gala. I felt underdressed. I had purposely left my engagement ring home. Why would I need to wear expensive jewelry at camp? I wasn't sure if I should've worn my gold wedding ring, but it was on my left ring finger where it'd been for the past fifteen years. I touched the gold filigree posts that were used to pierce my ears when I was sixteen.

"Hi, I'm Abby. Room one."

"Hi, Abby. Lori, room two."

Before we had a chance to talk, we heard a short, sharp toot. I peeked out the screen door and saw Marilyn sitting at the wheel of her golf cart.

As we stepped off the porch, she said, "I came to get you for the meeting, but I see you're not dressed."

Abby and I traded confused looks.

"What I mean is, you're still in your social clothes. That's camp-speak for your civies, what you wear when you're not at camp. You don't have to change your pants, just throw on the polo shirt that's in your knapsack. Camp rules, you know."

"Okay. Give us a second," Abby said.

We went into our rooms and changed into kelly green collared shirts with the camp logo stitched in white. I looked in the mirror with mixed emotions—it wasn't very glamorous, but on the other hand it was empowering. I was part of a team, and I had a job to do.

Abby and I came out in our matching shirts. Hers was way too large, almost reaching her knees. She looked at me, her arms stretched out. "This is ridiculous." I guessed she didn't find it empowering.

As we rode to the meeting, Marilyn's hair wafted in the wind, wiry gray strands threaded throughout. She was earthy, natural, without makeup, in contrast to the staged photos of her on the website. When she turned to me, her aviator sunglasses reflected my image. I looked pensive. *Mental note, remember to smile.*

Marilyn pointed out the sports fields and the dining hall as she drove and then swerved so sharply that I almost tumbled out as we passed the infirmary.

"It's good to know where the infirmary is, in case I ever fall out of a golf cart."

Abby giggled from the back seat. Marilyn gave me a puzzled look and continued driving as if nothing had happened.

A few minutes later, we arrived at our destination up a steep gravel road. Marilyn parked the golf cart next to three others.

The barn-shaped playhouse had a stage and high ceilings and was filled with at least a hundred young men and women sitting on rows of wooden benches.

Jack was leaning against the stage chatting when he saw us enter. I had met him in February when he came to the apartment to tell us about Woodlands. He greeted us, placing one arm around my shoulder and the other around Abby's as if we were his long-lost relatives. There was something smarmy about the way he introduced us. "Hey, everybody, this is Lori here on my right and Abby on my left." He squeezed us into his sweaty body. "They have joined our little family this summer."

Good thing I had plastered a smile on my face.

When Jack finally let go, I glanced around. A woman caught my eye and waved us over to her. She had a salt and pepper blunt haircut and a big friendly smile.

"I'm Gilda," she said. "My title is program director, but I do myriad odd jobs. Marilyn told me about you two. I'm looking forward to working with you this summer. Abby, I heard you're from Florida, I hope you're not one of those Boca bitches."

Abby seemed momentarily put off, but she smiled and said, "Would one of those so-called Boca *witches*—I don't curse—consider working at a sleepaway camp even for a second?"

"Well put. Let's sit down. Our lord and master is about to hold court," Gilda said.

I whispered into her ear, "Thanks for calling us away from him. I felt like part of his harem."

"Ha, I think you and I are going to get along great this summer."

# 3 Senior Staff

Jack and Marilyn asked for everyone's attention. Marilyn's demeanor had softened, and they both had ingratiating smiles.

"Welcome to Woodlands! I'm Jack, and this is my lovely wife and co-director Marilyn."

Marilyn waved.

"Take out the orientation schedules from your knapsacks. I would like you all to follow along as we go over this week's schedule. If you're a counselor, the cover sheet is green; if you are a specialist, the cover sheet is blue; and the senior staff's cover is orange."

I turned to Gilda, "Senior staff? Did Jack call us old?"

"At camp we're definitely the *alta kockers*," Gilda said.

Jack reached into a box on the stage and pulled out dark green T-shirts rolled up and tied with white ribbons. Marilyn began calling out names and Jack tossed the shirts.

Gilda leaned into me. "Each returning staff gets a loyalty T-shirt with a new slogan on it. This summer it's 'Back by Popular Demand.'"

Marilyn called Gilda's name. She popped up, smiling, caught the shirt and held it high above her head as if it was the championship boxing belt and turned so the entire room could see how proud she was. There was a smattering of applause and a few whoops.

I whispered in Abby's ear, "Do you think we'll be sitting here next summer having T-shirts thrown at us?"

"I can hardly believe I'm sitting here right now."

Marilyn talked about the importance of keeping proper tabs on the campers. "In the papers we gave you, there's a blank bunk report. Those need to be filled in daily. You are our eyes and ears. Jack and I need to know what happens during the day for all five hundred campers."

Then a man named Bob, head of Boys Camp, spoke about how everyone's time off worked. Then he introduced me. "Everyone, once again, this is Lori. She's going to be the DL for the Cubs this summer. Lori, please stand up."

"Do I get a T-shirt?" I said, laughing.

"We'll have to see if you're T-shirt worthy," Jack wisecracked.

"That felt a little harsh," I whispered to Gilda as I sat down.

"Yeah, when Jack's at camp, all the charm he laid on getting you to sign up gets flushed down the toilet. I always say it's one of the reasons for the sketchy plumbing."

"Next up is Abby, the DL for the Chipmunks," Bob said.

As Abby stood, I looked around the room and saw Ted leaning against the back wall. Between us were the fresh-faced young men and women, smiling and wearing the same shirt. A chill went through me causing me to shudder.

"Are you okay?" Gilda asked.

"It's weird, all of us dressed alike."

"Does it make you feel like you've been dropped into the middle of a cult?"

"Yeah, kind of." I let out a nervous giggle.

"And you haven't even drunk the Kool-Aid yet." Gilda laughed.

"If you're trying to make me feel better, it's not working."

"Why would you think I'm trying to make you feel better? I think summer camps are cultish. You either buy into it, or you don't. Let's talk at the end of the summer, and you can let me know your thoughts then."

I wanted to continue our conversation, but I heard Marilyn asking the female staff to head to the theater on the girls' side. Abby and I headed out together. We were halfway down the gravel path when Marilyn pulled up next to us with another woman riding shotgun and wearing expensive-looking sunglasses.

"Hop in," Marilyn said.

We climbed into the back of the cart.

"Hi, I'm Bethany, the head of Girls Camp."

Before we could reply, Bethany turned away and Marilyn jerked us forward. I held on tight, but Abby flew into me as we sped away. So far, the most important takeaway from the day was that golf carts didn't have seat belts.

Marilyn and Bethany were engrossed in conversation.

Abby had scribbled "Bosses?" on a notepad and nodded toward Marilyn and Bethany. I nodded yes.

Bethany's beautiful golden tresses shimmered in the sun. I caught hints of colored highlights, and I wondered what it would look like at the end of the summer after at least two missed salon appointments. Come to think of it, I'd miss my appointments with Zito. By the end of August, we'd all be washed out with our grays showing—the *senior* staff moniker would ultimately fit.

We came to an abrupt stop in front of the girls' theater.

Inside the theater was a sea of youth and beauty. I was used to being around large groups of awkward adolescents, but the last time I had been surrounded by so many striking young women must've been when I was one of them.

"I don't know about you, but I'm feeling ancient," I whispered to Abby.

"You got that right, girlfriend."

Gilda led an attractive, tall brunette with beautiful porcelain skin over to us. She couldn't have been more than twenty-five.

"This is Di. She lives in room three of your cabin."

We made our introductions and Abby asked, "Are you a division leader also?"

"No, I'm the head of sail," Di said with an Australian accent.

"What do you sell?" Abby asked.

"She said *sail* as in boats, right?" I asked.

Di had a cute giggle. "Yes, like boats. I take it you two aren't sailors."

"I'm a city girl. I get queasy watching a rubber duck in a bathtub," I said.

"So, I guess I won't see you on water skis?"

"You know, I've always wanted to try it."

"Well, you won't see me sailing, skiing, or whatever you do on a lake. I'm not a bathing-suit person," Abby said.

"What does that even mean?" I asked.

"Exactly what I said. I'm much happier swimming in this humongous shirt than in the water."

"It's a good thing you don't have my job because I have to wear bathers all day, every day," Di said.

Marilyn called for everyone's attention.

"I'm going to sit with my mates," Di said. "See you later."

"I would've thought they'd put someone more our age into the cabin with us," Abby said.

"Look around, how many people our age are in this room?" I asked.

The last person to speak was Dr. Jenny. She taught us how to identify tick bites and the inherent dangers if not properly and quickly diagnosed. Then she talked about the importance of sunscreen not only for ourselves but for the campers. She urged us to make sure each camper was sufficiently and repeatedly slathered.

Dr. Jenny stepped away from the microphone and leaned toward the audience. In a conspiratorial whisper she added, "I am available to talk privately if any personal matters, shall we say, pop up during the summer."

# 4
# Dirty-Water Coffee

Abby and I had some time to kill before our next meeting. She invited me to join her at the arts & crafts studio to meet her best friend, Maggie, who had been hired to run that program, and Maggie's husband Roger. In their *civilian* jobs, they all taught together at the same elementary school.

"Wait, your friend came here with her husband?" I asked.

"Yeah, they're one of those couples who does everything together." Abby gave the slightest eye roll.

"I guess that's nice and all, but there's no scenario where I could imagine my husband working here with me. Could you?" I asked.

"Barry? Are you kidding?" Abby said. "No way. It'll be a wonder if my house is still standing when I get home."

"Ronnie, my husband, would have no patience for other people's children."

"Trust me, I completely understand."

"Is Roger working with Maggie in arts & crafts?" I asked.

"Oh no, no, he's running the radio station."

Abby pushed the screen door open, and it slammed behind us. We had entered a vast wooden building with three ceiling fans whirring on ancient beams. The place smelled like turpentine, clay, and soapy water. But there was also a familiar comforting aroma—freshly brewed coffee.

Across the room stood a statuesque redheaded woman wearing an apron, bent over a slop sink, elbow-deep in suds and steam.

"Hey, Maggie, I want you to meet Lori. She's in the room across from mine."

Maggie turned off the faucet and rubbed the back of her hand across her forehead, wiping away the sweat before she dried it on the edge of her smock.

A large man sporting a goatee walked toward us. Everything about him was oversized including his resonant baritone. "Nice to meet another adult." It made perfect sense that Roger was the disc jockey.

"Wow, this is the second time today that my *advanced age* has been part of the conversation," I said.

"No disrespect intended. Maggie and I've noticed that we're old enough to be the parents of most of the counselors," Roger said.

"Of course, we would've had them when we were fifteen." Maggie smiled. "I just made a fresh pot of coffee. Can I pour you some?"

Maggie had set up a coffee station that included every type of sweetener and tiny containers of half and half like they had at diners.

I took a sip. "This is delicious."

"I know, right? Honestly, it's only Folgers, but I think it's the water from the slop sink that makes it so good," Maggie said.

We all looked at the filthy industrial-sized basin on the other side of the room. The spigot was covered in decades of dried clay and who knew what other kinds of toxic waste.

I looked inside the cup. "You mean I'm drinking dirty-water coffee?"

Maggie held hers up. "Yup."

There were four large wooden tables with benches, covered

in old paint, glue, and glitter stains. We sat down together at one of them. It brought back happy memories of making hand molds and popsicle stick boxes at the bungalow colony.

"So, tell us, what brought you to Woodlands?" Maggie asked.

"You mean instead of basking in the sun on a Greek Isle with my husband?"

"He was alright with you leaving him for the summer?" Abby asked.

"He's a trial attorney and preparing for a big case this summer." I shrugged. "With the three of us here there are no distractions, so he can mentally shelve us and work around the clock without any guilt."

I wasn't about to tell them how unhappy I was with my husband. Ronnie put his work ahead of his family. What really put me over the edge was when his colleagues took center stage in front of our marriage. It was all about what Ed, his managing partner, thought, and wore, and did. What I said didn't matter.

"Seems like a good solution," Roger said.

Even I bought it. "What about you guys? How did you all end up working here?"

"A friend sent her kids here last summer, and they had a blast," Abby said. "I looked into the camp, met with Jack, and told him that I'd only send my kids if I could go too. I waited a long time to have children, and there was no way I'd send them anywhere without me. If I can figure out a way, when the time comes, I'll go with them to college."

I laughed. "And your husband?"

"He wasn't at all happy about it, but I didn't give him a choice," Abby said.

I swirled the swizzle stick in my cup and thought about all the arguments Ronnie and I had about sending the girls to sleepaway camp. In the end I hadn't given him a choice either.

I looked up and asked, "What about you two? How'd you end up working at Woodlands, the sleepaway camp voted the best brother/sister camp on the Eastern Seaboard?"

Roger laughed. "When Abby said she was going to camp with her kids, we called Jack and asked if we could go with our son Tony. Jack wanted to meet us in person, so he invited us to his home on a Sunday morning."

Maggie said, "You're not gonna believe this. Roger, tell Lori about the first time we met Jack and Marilyn."

Roger shrugged. "It's early on a Sunday morning. We had to drag Tony out of bed, Sundays are his only day to sleep in. We knock, wait a bit, and finally a woman wearing a bathrobe, looking frazzled, answers the door. She just stares at us, twirling her hair."

"She doesn't ask who we are, why we're there, just stares blankly at us, obviously confused," Maggie said.

Roger continued, "I hear Jack call out, 'Marilyn, who is it?' And she says, 'I don't know.' Jack shows up in his bathrobe, and now we are all just staring at each other. I tell him who we are and that he asked us to come and meet him. Marilyn turns to Jack and growls, 'You didn't tell me we were expecting anybody.' She gives us a final once-over and turns away in a huff."

"Like we're the trash someone left on her porch," Maggie added.

"Jack's not embarrassed or apologetic," Roger went on. "He looks over his shoulder and says to Marilyn, 'I forgot we were having company.' He turns back to us and says, 'I'll call you tomorrow to make another appointment.' Then he notices Maggie's holding a cake box from the best bakery in Boca."

"He grabs the box from my hand, asking, 'Is this for me?' and then the door closes in our faces," Maggie said.

"I would have thought you were exaggerating, but Jack obviously has scheduling issues," I said. "When he came to visit us, he showed up three hours early! I hadn't even had the chance to tell my husband he was coming—talk about making things awkward."

"Awkward is being kind," Roger said.

"He's probably one of those guys, you know, because he's good looking, he thinks he can get away with being inconsiderate," I said.

"I wouldn't argue the point," Maggie said.

"Personally, I don't find Jack the least bit appealing," Abby said and took a sip of her coffee. "What nerve showing up early. How'd your husband react? If I surprised my Barry like that, he would've had a total conniption."

"Ronnie readied his arsenal of lawyering skills and peppered Jack with all kinds of questions. I was so embarrassed when he asked what if one of our daughters gets attacked by a bear."

The three of them nervously chuckled.

"Back to you guys. Why did you decide to work here after being treated so rudely?" I asked.

"Because Abby's kids, Cooper and Ashley, are besties with Tony, and they really wanted to go to camp together," Maggie said.

"I'd already signed on, and there was no way I was leaving them to swelter in the Florida humidity. I couldn't do this job without them, so now we all get to *schvitz* together in the mountains," Abby said.

"Also, our next meeting with Jack was perfectly normal. He drove to meet us at our home and was very convincing and nice," Roger said. "He never brought it up, so we didn't either. He acted like it was the first time he ever laid eyes on us. He even said, 'I can't wait for you to meet my wife, Marilyn.' I was tempted to ask him if he enjoyed the coffee cake."

"Your turn. How did you get suckered into working at Woodlands?" Roger asked.

Even though I could already tell these were my kind of people, I wasn't ready to share the intimate details of my life. "I'm not exactly sure how it happened, but my original summer plan was celebrating my fifteenth anniversary in Greece drinking their strong boiled espresso, and somehow ended up sitting here with you." I held up my cup. "Sipping dirty-water coffee."

Maggie raised her mug. "Let's drink to whatever circuitous route got us here and to new experiences." She looked at me. "And to new friends."

Maybe this could be a good summer.

# 5
# Sleeping Arrangements

Abby practically limped back to the cabin at the end of our first day of orientation.

"Lori, slow down. My legs are screaming. I can't remember ever walking this much in my life. I wish us schleppers got to ride around in a golf cart."

"I know how you feel, my flat feet are cramping from hiking up and down all the hills." I yawned. "I don't know about you, but I'm ready to pass out."

"Good luck with that," Abby said.

"What do you mean?"

"When was the last time you slept in a strange bed without your husband snoring next to you?" she asked.

I had an urge to spill my guts to Abby, telling her that not sleeping next to my husband was a goal of mine. Ronnie and I were using this time apart to decide whether we wanted to stay married, but since she and I had just met that morning, it might be a bit much. Instead, we stood facing each other in the narrow hallway, hands on our doorknobs, and I said, "Sort of feels like we're in college again."

"The next thing you know we'll get our periods at the same time and sit in bed gossiping, eating chocolate frosting right out of the container."

I smiled. "I think we're going to become fast friends."

"I feel the same way."

We opened our doors, looked over our shoulders, smiled, and entered our rooms.

I finally found a comfortable spot. My body sank like a brick, but my mind was looping, rehashing the events that had led me to this tiny room.

I might not be hearing Ronnie's snoring, but I could hear his voice in my head and the fight we had after Jack left the apartment.

We had just thanked Jack for stopping by to tell us about his camp. When the door closed, Ronnie said, "I can't believe you invited someone to my home without talking to me first. Let me make this perfectly clear, I see no reason why my kids need to attend sleepaway camp. They can go to the same day camp they went to last year."

"Since when can't I invite people to *our* home?" I took a calming breath. "If you're angry with me for not discussing it with you, that's fine, but don't take it out on Zelda and Hazel. Sleepaway camp will be a great opportunity for them."

"If they were away for the summer, what would *you* do?"

"What do you mean?"

"Your job is to take care of them. If they weren't here, what would you do every day?"

I took another deep breath and managed to put a pleasant look on my face before answering. "I thought you and I could go away to celebrate our fifteenth anniversary. You know how we've talked about going to Greece? Well, I thought this summer would be the perfect opportunity."

He didn't reply right away; I could almost hear the gears

turning in his brain. "Okay, let's figure out the cost. Two children in camp, ten days in Greece, and I suppose you'd still expect to go to the beach for a week at the end of August?"

"Ideally, yes. That's your special time with Zelda and Hazel."

"The cost for one summer would be staggering."

I pictured the beads of an abacus shifting in his head. "But isn't that part of the reason you work so hard, so we have money to play? The kids would have a wonderful experience, and we could relax and reconnect."

"And what would your contribution be to these plans?"

"Excuse me?"

"The way I see it, you reap all the benefits without doing any of the work."

It took all I had not to lose it. "What do you think I do? I'm the CHO—Chief Home Officer. All my time is invested in our family. I'm the person who takes care of Zelda and Hazel, this apartment, our lives. If I weren't here, our family would come apart. Should I start keeping track of my billable hours and hand you a timesheet at the end of each week, so you can calculate my worth?"

"You sound a bit defensive."

"It's hard not to be defensive when you're questioning the value of my existence."

"You're being overly sensitive."

"And you're being obtuse."

"I see no reason to send the girls to camp when it's your only job to take care of them."

I was determined not to turn this into a screaming match. "Well, *I* think it's important that they go to camp. They'll learn to be more independent and more resilient when things don't go their way. And I want them to start doing chores."

"Why can't *you* show them?"

"Because they expect me to do everything for them. The reasons I want them to attend sleepaway camp are the exact reasons that Jack just rattled off to us. The statistical stuff he was citing about how kids given the opportunity to go to camp are more likely to grow up to be successful adults with good decision-making skills, which I know you appreciate." I smiled but he didn't return one. "The part that stood out for me was that they would be better at advocating for themselves, and they would get to do it surrounded by fresh air and nature. Not stuck riding on a hot bus for over an hour twice a day like they did last year. Then, when they got back from camp, I'd give them tasks to do around the house."

"Like what?"

"Like making their beds, putting the dinner dishes away . . ."

"This argument has come full circle. Those are your responsibilities. I'll ask you again, what would you do to keep busy all day?"

"I get it. You've been harboring a grudge against me because I don't have a job outside this apartment. You think because I don't bring in an income, you have the right to make all the decisions, and I haven't *earned* a summer without the kids or a vacation. Well, screw you. I'm going to teach Zelda and Hazel that if you want something badly enough you find a way to make it happen. They will go to camp, and I will pay for it myself."

I was proud of myself for not backing down.

After I had racked my brain for a week trying to figure out how to muster up payment for two, I called Jack and asked if he had a job for me at the camp.

Fast forward four months, and here I was lying in bed after my first day of orientation. It wasn't only my thoughts keeping me up. The eerie silence was underscored by the ominous darkness. Falling asleep in Manhattan would probably be difficult for most people, but I was used to the constant noise of cars honking, sirens, and people shouting on the sidewalk below. The glimmers of light and shadows that crisscrossed my bedroom from the streetlamps and traffic lights were a comfort. Here in the mountains, the lack of noise kept me awake.

I must have finally fallen asleep only to hear birds tweeting before the sun was up.

# 6

# The Birds and the Bees

After breakfast Abby and I walked into arts & crafts. "You can barely smell the essence of mildew over the aroma of coffee," I said.

"Help yourself," Maggie said.

"Go figure, your dirty-water coffee is much better than the sludge in the dining hall," Abby said.

The orientation schedule lay open on the table. "So, what's up for today?" I asked.

Abby pointed to an item in bold. "10:15—Spend time getting to know your counselors."

My stomach flipped. "Are you as nervous about meeting the counselors as I am?"

"I hadn't really thought about it," Abby said.

"Really? What if we don't get along?"

"I used to get nervous meeting new students, but after twenty years, I don't even think about it anymore," Abby said.

"Lori, you're looking at it all wrong. You're in charge," Maggie said. "The counselors should be concerned about *you* not liking *them*. Trust me, if you go in with that attitude, everything will fall into place."

I glanced at my watch. "It shouldn't be a problem to change my entire outlook on life in, what, the next hour?"

"Come on, can you seriously be worried about what a bunch of teenagers think of you?" Maggie asked.

"It's more about, well, what if I suck at my job, and the counselors undermine me, and the campers take advantage of my lack of experience? Kids can smell fear, you know."

"You can handle this. Stop worrying," Abby said.

"Can I come to you for advice?"

"That's a given." Maggie smiled. "If I can't help, you can always go to Bethany, she's a lifer."

"What's a lifer?"

"Someone who went to camp here and never left."

Abby looked up from the schedule and said, "I'm surprised by how many adults can take off the entire summer to work at a sleepaway camp."

"Speaking about adults who work at camp, is it just me or are you guys having trouble keeping up with not only names but what each person does?" I asked.

"Yes, that's why Roger and I stayed up last night and made a flow chart listing names, titles, and who does what. Let me get it for you."

As she walked across the room I asked, "Am I the only one feeling overwhelmed?"

"And the campers aren't even here yet," Abby said.

Maggie placed the diagram in front of us. "We're smart. We'll figure it out together."

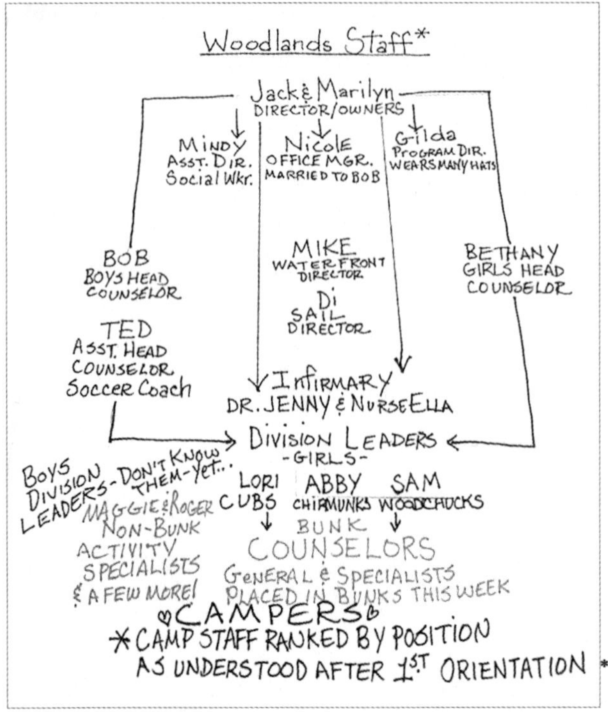

*

I ran my finger down her handiwork.

I laughed. "We're three rungs below Jack and Marilyn and only two rungs above the campers."

Maggie was looking over my shoulder. "Yup."

I went to the office to check for messages and smiled when I saw a bright blue envelope in my cubby—my first ever camp letter!

Leave it to Claire to think of sending me mail. She was one of those people who knew everything but wasn't a know-it-all—my go-to person when I needed guidance. I had called her to help me find a camp to send the girls to because she loved sleepaway camp. It was due to our research that I ended up at Woodlands.

* Woodlands chart by Linda Kunesh

We had met for lunch the day before I drove off to my summer adventure. She handed me a gift bag.

"I bought you something you might need while you're away."

"You didn't have to do that."

She smiled. "I thought it was one of those things that you may not have thought of and would be difficult to buy when you're stuck at camp."

I couldn't imagine what it was. As I unwrapped the tissue paper, I felt my cheeks blush and laughed. It was a vibrator.

"Take it out of the box," she said.

"Really?"

"Yeah."

I pulled it out and saw my name written on the shaft in purple block letters.

"I didn't want yours to get confused with anyone else's."

In my mail cubby, there was also a message from the mother of one of the Cubs.

At every meeting, it had been instilled in us that we provided a service, and a message from a parent needed to be answered ASAP. I dutifully took out the three-ring binder that contained the names of the counselors and campers, their photos, and information like allergies, parent names, and every possible number to reach them.

I sat down and opened the tab for cabin one. There was a photo of Chloe Martin. I dialed her mother.

"Hello, this is Lori Kramer from Camp Woodlands. I'll be Chloe's division leader this summer."

"Oh good. I accidentally forgot to tell you something important about my daughter. Since her father and I split, Chloe's been wetting her bed. When she's home with me, she's fine, but at her dad's, well, that's when it happens."

My first thought was, *Poor Chloe.* Then I wondered who was responsible for cleaning up after her. "Can you send her up with extra sheets in case she continues to wet her bed . . . and maybe some extra underwear?"

"Good idea. I'll throw in a mattress liner also. I know she's excited about camp, but she's probably nervous too. Hopefully, if she's happy and comfortable, she'll be able to control her bladder."

"Don't worry, we'll take good care of Chloe."

I made a few more calls to parents who had "accidentally" forgotten to tell me things about their kids. I hoped the counselors would be easier to deal with.

Walking through the gates of Girls Camp, I saw groups of young women sitting in front of the cabins they were assigned to. Thankfully, they had name badges. I put a smile on my face.

"Hey, Lori, come and join us."

I remembered Amber because of her elaborate braids. "Hi, I'm excited to work with you," I said, joining the group. I smiled at each expectant face and took a deep breath. "I thought the best way to get to know each other is to tell something interesting about ourselves. You know, something you wouldn't write on your résumé. I'll go first. My name is Lori and I've never been to sleepaway camp."

"How can you be a division leader if you've never been to camp?" Carrie asked.

Before I could answer, a girl with striking dimples jumped in. "Hi, I'm Genie and I was a camper here for six years and I can tell you from experience that there's nothing to it. If you have half a brain and can count, you can do this job."

I raised my hand. "I qualify. Genie, since you're a veteran, tell us about your experience at Woodlands."

"Sure. Like I said, I was a camper and one of my goals was to come back as a counselor and lose my virginity here. I mean,

I got my first period at camp, so I'm looking at it as, you know, another rite of passage."

Huh, interesting insight. "Okay, well, I did ask for something you wouldn't put on your résumé."

Nervous giggles led to everyone wanting to share their stories.

"I've lost my virginity twice," Jojo said.

"How can you lose it twice?" Genie asked.

"One time with a guy and then with a girl. I'm sticking with girls."

I hadn't thought about the night I lost mine in eons. "Well, I was eighteen . . ."

"What? Wait. Are you seriously going to tell us?" Genie asked.

"Isn't that what we're talking about?"

"Yeah, but you're like old enough to be our mother," Genie said.

I started laughing. "Let's switch to camp-regulated topics."

After the meeting, I fell into step with Genie. "I just wanted to say that if you need anything, I'm here for you."

"Like what?"

"An ear or a shoulder. I want to make sure you're okay. That you're safe. Do you have condoms?"

Genie rolled her eyes. "Thanks, but you're my boss, not my mother."

I stopped short and watched her walk off. She'd not only clarified her boundaries, but she had also made mine apparent. I was their supervisor. Not mother. Not friend. She also gave me a glimpse of what it would be like to have a teenager. I was clearly unprepared for either role. What made me think working at a sleepaway camp had been a good idea?

Bethany appeared at my side. "How'd your meeting go?"

"Okay, I guess. We somehow got on the subject of how they lost their virginity."

Bethany gave me a wry smile and flipped through her clipboard. "Nope, I don't see virginity listed as a recommended ice breaker."

"Well, it was more interesting than finding out what they'd bring on a picnic."

# 7
# Creatures of Habit

It seemed that the staff was expected to put on a talent show for the campers their first night. Luckily Genie was the head of the theater department and choreographed a short and easy song and dance routine for the DLs. Genie assured me no one cared that I couldn't carry a tune. After the first rehearsal, Mindy, the camp social worker and a lifer like Bethany, invited Abby and me to her room for a drink.

As Abby and I walked over together I said, "It feels like we've been invited to sit at the cool girls' table."

Abby said, "Yeah, like we've passed some kind of initiation."

I knocked, and Mindy shouted, "Shoes off. Close the door quickly. No insects allowed."

Abby and I heeled off our sneakers, adding them to the pile under the lone bulb circled by moths. As soon as we opened the door, we saw that Mindy's cabin was easily three times the size of ours. Abby tilted her head to the left subtly pointing out the private bathroom. Apparently, her pay grade and importance was way above ours.

Mindy held court in the swivel chair by her desk. Even though we all wore uniforms, Mindy wore hers with way more panache. Her red lipstick accentuated her jet-black hair. Her jewelry was more understated than Abby's, but I noticed a Rolex on her left wrist. Bethany was perched on the edge of Mindy's bed. Gilda rocked in an ancient upholstered chair. Bob and Ted sat on the floor with their backs against the wall, facing Mindy. Abby and I stood awkwardly in the middle of the room until Bethany slid over so we could join her on the bed.

Mindy poured what I thought was wine into plastic cups. I took a sip. It was refreshing, a little sweet and bubbly.

"What is this?" I asked.

"Prosecco," Bethany said.

"It's yummy." It went down smooth and fast. "Can I have a refill?"

"Help yourself," Mindy said.

It was late and I'd only had a salad for dinner—I was already tipsy from the first cup. Without warning, I let out a loud belch that stopped the conversation, and then I proceeded to giggle uncontrollably. Everyone laughed with me as tears streamed down my cheeks which, I was certain, turned bright red. "I sure know how to make an impression. I'll understand if you don't invite me back."

Mindy held up her cup and said, "To Lori, one happy drunk."

I wiped away a tear and asked, "Does anyone here smoke?" Maybe if I needed a smoke, there was someone I could commiserate with.

"Oh God, no, not since high school," Mindy said.

"I was a social smoker for years but gave it up when we were trying for kids," Bethany said.

"Are you asking about weed or tobacco?" Bob asked. "Cause it's yes to one and no to the other."

Ted said, "Never. I don't smoke. Why are you asking?"

"At the meeting, Jack listed it as one of the things we're not allowed to do here. He also said no alcohol and obviously no one listens to that." I held up my cup. "So, I wondered what other forms of contraband might be floating around." I pictured the Winstons hiding under the driver's manual in my Toyota.

I was buzzed when I left Mindy's room and craved a cigarette. There was something about drinking that always made me want to smoke. I sat on the edge of my bed, still wearing my sneakers, feeling antsy. All I wanted to do was light up. I wouldn't be able to fall asleep because all I could think about were the cigarettes stashed in the car. I rummaged through my bag for the keys, surrendering to my craving. I decided to take a walk to find a secluded place in the cool night air. I would enjoy the solitude and the endless stars I remembered from my summers in the mountains, while I clandestinely smoked.

I quietly closed the car door and took a deep breath. I knew that smell—tobacco. Had I conjured it? I turned toward the scent, and, like a cartoon character, I drifted toward the aroma. Peeking around the corner of the building, I saw a glow from the culprit down the path by the laundry shack. Without hesitation I walked directly toward it, like a moth to a flame.

"Hey, Ted, is that you? The man who said he never smoked," I whispered.

"Bloody hell. I feel as if I've been caught with my knickers down."

I laughed.

"When you brought up smoking, it felt like you read my mind because that was exactly what I was thinking. It's difficult to hide my bad habits. You're never alone at camp, but I thought the laundry shack at night was the one remote spot where I could find some peace and quiet. I've gotten away with it for decades, and now you show up and find me out before the campers even arrive." He held open an old-fashioned cigarette case that looked like something out of a black-and-white Bette Davis movie. "Care to join me?"

My fingers crinkled the cellophaned box in my hoodie pocket. I took it out. "I haven't smoked in fifteen years." I looked at the cigarettes in my hand. "On an impulse I bought these on my way to camp."

He arched his eyebrows. "Do you need a light?"

I hesitated. If I accepted his offer, fifteen years of not smoking would literally go up in flames. I knew I shouldn't, but at that moment I really wanted one. Ronnie's voice crept into my head, but I blocked it—I didn't want to hear his objections. Was it the uncertainty and long days of this job, was it the cravings, or was it because it was the wrong thing to do and I was tired of always being responsible?

I unwrapped the pack, took a deep inhale, and held up a cigarette. Ted awkwardly bent to give me a light.

I started to cough, damning myself for reigniting the addiction I had managed to control for so many years. When I caught my breath, I said, "Aren't you fancy with your swanky cigarette case. It seems out of place at a sleepaway camp."

He held it up as if surprised to find it in his hand. "It was a present from my grandmother to my grandfather, and it was left to my father, and now it's mine. We all have the same initials. I was named for them, Theodore Charles Mooney. My father went by Theo. I go by Ted. Made life easier when we were together. Anyway, I always have a memento of them with me."

"That's lovely." I paused for a moment. "So, the fact that you have it means they're no longer with us?"

He frowned. "Yes, they're both gone; Mum too."

"Same here. Both my parents died way too young and from smoking." I held up the cigarette, ashamed that it was glowing in my hand. "Yet here I am feeling like a teenager hiding and smoking once again."

He gave me a sideways glance, took a couple of drags, and looked up at the heavens. "No stars out tonight. I hope that doesn't mean rain tomorrow. I hate unloading duffel bags in the rain."

It was a good segue out of a sad conversation.

"Ted, tell me your story—you mentioned a son. Does your wife mind being alone in the summer?"

"Divorced. One son who spends the summers here with me."

"Don't tell me, his name is Theodore Charles Mooney the fourth?"

"No, she was having none of that. As *she* put it, she didn't want any of my family's rubbish on his tiny shoulders. Instead, *she* chose Max, just like every other boy in his class and his cabin. She thought she was being original, I guess the joke's on her." He took a drag. "What's your story?"

"Married my college sweetheart, had Zelda and Hazel, and became a full-time helicopter mom as you pointed out when we first met. Working at Woodlands is the first job I've had in ten years. Anyway, they're the reasons I'm here. What do you do in your real life?"

He let out a sardonic laugh. "When I'm not fighting over Max with her, I'm a soccer coach."

"I'm curious how you ended up spending your summers in another country taking care of other people's kids."

"Sometimes you need to escape from your everyday life, and sometimes that escape becomes part of your life. I'm happy when I'm at Woodlands."

That hit a nerve. There was something about Ted that made me feel I could trust him. "I've done the same thing. Escaped my real life."

A truth shiver ran the length of my body. That was the first time I had admitted out loud that I was happy to be on a break from my husband.

We stood quietly in each other's company until there was nothing left but the butts. I guessed Ted was now my smoking buddy.

# 8
# Campfire Karaoke

I awoke to the shrill beeping of my cheap alarm clock and turned it off immediately, aware of how thin the walls were.

I chose to get up almost an hour before the rest of my cabinmates so I'd have the bathroom to myself. I also had time for a brisk walk around the campus before meeting Abby, Maggie, and Roger for coffee.

The only activity in my day that didn't require me to think was getting dressed. I slid open a drawer, pulled out a white Hanes V-neck men's T-shirt and a pair of kelly green Soffe shorts. I grabbed a hoodie and laced up my sneakers in the hallway. I stood on the porch, took a deep breath, and was off. On the side of the road, I saw Abby talking on a cell phone in her car, in the only spot where she could get reception. I waved and picked up my pace.

It was 6:30, and a light mist blanketed the grass. I was trying to remember the last time I'd walked in the morning dew when I heard a motor. I moved to the side of the road thinking it was Abby, but it was Jack and Marilyn in a golf cart. They pulled up beside me.

"What're you doing up so early?" Jack asked.

"I like this time of the morning, it's peaceful, no one's up—well, aside from the two of you and Abby." I pointed toward the idling car.

"Yeah, this time of the morning is sacred for camp directors. Another successful day has passed, and a new one's beginning," Jack said. "Where're you off to?"

"For a walk down to the lake before breakfast."

"Where's your radio?" Jack asked.

"In my room. I didn't think I'd need it this early in the morning."

"You should always have it with you. You never know when you might need to contact someone. What if you needed help?"

It felt less like advice and more like a scolding. "I hadn't thought of that. I'll take it with me next time."

"Okay. If you're by the lake and need someone, Mike's down there in his trailer," Marilyn said as they drove off.

I wanted to believe the Bergers were looking out for my best interests. But instead, I thought, there goes my peaceful morning walk. It occurred to me that the Bergers pretty much owned me for the next eight weeks.

I cut across the girls' campus and ran down the hill to the path that led to the lake. Running always gave me a feeling of freedom, and I needed to feel that sensation. When I reached the water, I stopped at the edge, leaning forward with my hands on my thighs to catch my breath.

"What are you doing in my front yard?"

My racing heart jumped. "You just scared the crap out of me," I said, turning to face a man wearing a camp hoodie, unzipped, no shirt underneath, and green plaid pajama bottoms slung low on his hips. "You must be Mike."

He stood straight and saluted me. "At your service. Why're you alarmed? I live down here. I'm the one who should be surprised. You're Lori, right?" He gave me a once-over and smiled, and the hair on the back of my neck stood up. "I don't usually get early morning visitors. Join me for a cup of coffee, freshly brewed?" He ran his hand through his bedhead hair.

"Thanks for the offer, but I have a standing date for coffee," I said as I jogged off.

I entered the studio and the screen door slammed behind me, immediately getting everyone's attention.

"Hey, Lori, anything wrong?" Maggie asked.

"Are we on the clock 24/7? It hit me during my run that we're truly at the Bergers' beck and call for the next eight weeks."

"Seven days times eight weeks multiplied by twenty-four hours a day, that makes, let's see . . . 1,344 hours," Roger said.

"Are we talking consecutively?" Abby asked.

"Less our days off," Maggie said.

"Math aside, he knows when we're sleeping . . ." I said.

". . . he knows when we're awake," Abby added.

"And there are enough eyes and ears around here that he definitely knows if you've been bad or good," Maggie said. "I'll get you coffee while you fill us in."

"I met Mike down by the lake—the guy who lives in the trailer at the waterfront. There was something, I don't know, something salacious about him, you know, part sexy, part skanky."

"Salacious Mike. I love that. Can we start calling him that? At breakfast later I'm gonna say, 'Hey, Salacious Mike, can you please pass the salt?'" Maggie said.

"I don't think it's a good idea to make fun of a military man, especially a Navy SEAL. They can kill you with their bare hands," Roger said.

"What Lori says is true. We bartered our freedom in exchange for free camp for our kids," Abby said.

"That makes me feel dirty," I said.

"Your feelings match the coffee—both dirty." Maggie handed me a cup.

"What're we gonna do with this revelation?" I asked.

"We signed on to work here for the summer, so let's reframe it as a fun adventure we get to share with our kids."

"You know, Maggie, I find it irritating how you always see the big picture so clearly and put it into words so succinctly." Abby dunked a cookie into her coffee.

Maggie shrugged. "It's a gift."

"I guess I can get through anything as long as I can see the light at the end of the tunnel," I said. "At least we have each other for the next eight weeks. I'm happy we'll be sharing this experience together—otherwise I think I'd lose my mind."

"How bad can it be? Mindy and Bethany keep coming back year after year," Maggie said.

Abby and I trudged up another hill after having spent most of the day walking up and down the stairs of the four Cubs and four Chipmunks cabins.

We had decided to do the bunk assignments together. The cabins looked bleak with only the bare bunks lined up against the walls.

We sat opposite each other while I flipped pages to find the info on campers in cabin one. I read the special needs out loud.

"Let's see. Sarah is afraid of the dark."

"We should put her in the back because the bathroom light will be on all night," Abby said.

"Good idea." I wore a roll of masking tape like a bracelet and wrote Sarah's name in black sharpie on a strip that I stuck on the bunk where she would sleep.

We spent the rest of the day making beds and putting away clothes, toiletries, and sports gear sent ahead by parents. This way when the campers arrived they'd be greeted with familiar items from home.

In the last cabin, Abby started laughing. "Where should we put Samantha? She's afraid of sharks."

We just lost it, giggling uncontrollably. When we caught our breath, Abby said, "In all seriousness, it's important deciding where these girls sleep."

"Whad'ya mean?"

"Will she fight with the girl next to her? Will it be drafty sleeping under a window?"

"Or will they become BFFs and be the maid of honor at each other's weddings?"

"I wasn't thinking quite so long term, but yeah, that's what I mean," Abby said.

"If that's true, I hope we didn't screw this up because at the end of the day, every day, it'll be our headache."

"Or our joy." Abby smiled.

Whatever the outcome, it took the entire afternoon to decide the fate of ninety-six campers and twenty-four counselors.

The evening activity was Campfire Karaoke. When we arrived at the clearing, there was a fire blazing in the stone pit. The karaoke equipment was set up and people were milling about. Maggie and Roger waved us over to where they sat on benches facing the campfire.

Roger thumbed through a list of songs. When he found what he was looking for, he put in his request.

"Roger used to be the lead singer for a band when we were in college. I was his biggest groupie. Still am," Maggie said.

Jack picked up the microphone and welcomed everyone to the annual orientation, Campfire Karaoke.

"I like to start off each summer singing that funny camp song . . ."

I yelled out, "'Hello Muddah, Hello Fadduh'!"

"Yes! Come sing it with me."

Abby squeezed my arm. "Teacher's pet."

I needed to learn to keep my mouth shut. I turned to the other DLs, "Who's with me?"

Sam, who was half my age and would be Zelda's DL, said, "And commit social suicide?"

Jack spoke into the microphone. "Come on, Lori, can't keep our audience waiting."

I shrugged. "Time to face the music."

The song was cued. "'Don't leave me out in the forest where I might get eaten by a bear.'"

It was fine at first, but then Jack draped his arm around my shoulders, making me uncomfortable. When I maneuvered away, he grabbed my hand. His palms were sweaty, but I managed to keep a smile on my face the entire time.

"'Muddah, Fadduh, kindly disregard this letter.'"

I shook myself free and gave Jack a high five to avoid the possibility of a hug and quickly handed the microphone to Di, who was waiting with the next group up, the Aussie contingent who thundered to "Down Under."

Gilda patted me on the back. "You handled that like a pro."

A few songs later it was Roger's turn. It was incongruous to see this oversized man not only belt out "It's Not Unusual" in a deep, sexy Tom Jones voice, but he swiveled his large frame around like a professional dancer.

The entire staff were on their feet dancing, singing, and cheering Roger on. I was bopping between Maggie and Abby when Abby said, "Remember how women used to throw their undies at Tom Jones?"

I was caught up in the moment and without another thought, I reached under my T-shirt, unhooked my sports bra, pulled my arms through the straps, and tugged it out of my sleeve. I stood on the bleachers, swinging it above my head.

"'It's not unusual to find out I'm in love with you . . .'"

The crowd went into a frenzy when I tossed it, and it landed on Roger's belly. Astonished, he picked it up. The look on his face was priceless. He had a huge grin and he gamely twirled it above his head and flung it back into the crowd.

I surprised myself—I hadn't done anything that spontaneous and silly since I had taken my bra off while studying for finals in one of the carrels in the science library, and my roommate grabbed it and slingshot it over the cubicle.

Maggie and Abby had tears streaming down their faces from laughing so hard.

I watched the trajectory of the bra as it spiraled into the crowd. People were tripping over each other to catch it as if it were the home run–winning ball at a World Series. I couldn't tell who nabbed it and wondered if I'd ever see it again. At least it was clean.

Abby handed me her hoodie. "Here, put this on. It's apparent that you're cold."

Gilda found me once again. "I hate making a fool of myself even though I always manage to. But you, you don't seem to mind."

"Thanks. I think."

"What I mean is that you're good at it—you intentionally make people laugh."

I excused myself. I wanted to tell Roger how great he was, but then Ted appeared in front of me, my bra dangling from his finger. "I believe this belongs to you."

I took it, balling it in my fist. "Did you catch it?"

"No, but I made sure to retrieve it before it ended up flying from the flagpole tomorrow morning."

I hoped it was too dark for him to see me blush. "How very gallant of you."

He had a playful smile. "I'm glad you took my advice seriously."

"And that was?"

"Have fun and be campy."

# 9
# Rise and Shine

There was a buzz of anticipation in the dining hall. The campers were due to arrive in less than an hour and everyone was excited. Well, almost everyone. I couldn't wait to see Zelda and Hazel, but I wasn't convinced I was prepared to oversee forty-eight eight-year-olds. My stomach was in knots. I could barely swallow any food.

Jack spoke into the microphone, Marilyn at his side. "Marilyn and I want to thank you for your hard work this week preparing for the arrival of the campers. The buses left on time and should be arriving within the next thirty minutes."

The room erupted in cheers and applause. My mouth went dry, and my stomach somersaulted. I turned toward Abby, who looked panicked. I now knew what I must look like.

"Everyone needs to be wearing their Woodlands collared shirt, green shorts, sneakers, and your nametag. Absolutely no flip-flops. If you don't know where you're supposed to be for arrival, please see either Bethany or Bob. This summer is going to be the best summer ever!"

The room exploded once more.

Abby and I instinctively grabbed each other's hands. Both sets of fingers were ice cold.

"We can do this," I said, squeezing Abby's hand for reassurance.

"We have no other choice." Abby squeezed back.

"If you're finished with your breakfast, let's walk the bunks one last time," Bethany said as we swallowed our last sips of coffee.

I whispered in Abby's ear, "It's showtime."

The DLs followed Bethany and Marilyn to the brightly colored banners hanging over the porch railings of each cabin.

"Have we always had banners?" Marilyn's head was cocked to one side, her index finger twisting her hair.

"It was Maggie's idea," Abby said.

"I don't think she asked for my approval," Marilyn said.

Bethany saved the moment. "I think they look great, and I'm sure the girls will love seeing their names on the banners."

"Yeah, you're right. Okay, let's start with the Cubs," Marilyn said.

The counselors had done an impressive job decorating. A pink, yellow, green, or blue construction paper flower with a girl's name in the center hung over each bunk. The beds were made with the colorful linens and stuffed animals the parents had sent ahead. With a lot of work, the dreary cabins had been transformed into warm, cozy summer homes for the campers.

When my walk-through was done and had thankfully passed muster, I headed to the office to see if there were any last-minute phone calls from parents. Jack was walking out of the office, and our eyes met.

"Hey, Lori, I see you have your radio with you. Good girl," Jack said.

*Good girl?* What would he say if I called him a good boy?

"Yes, you've taught me to carry it with me wherever I go. But just so we understand each other." I probably should have shut up right then. "I will not be taking it with me in the shower."

I could tell he wasn't sure if I was serious or not.

"No one expects you to take the radio with you in the shower."

"That's a relief."

"You're funny. I'll have to remember that. Did you have your walk-through? I hope you're ready for the campers' arrival," Jack said.

"As ready as I'll ever be."

Frisbees were being thrown, footballs tossed, and Hula-Hoops whirled around limber bodies as I approached the soccer field. The nervous energy translated into laughing, hugging, and playing ball. And the kids weren't even here yet. The feeling of friendship and community was palpable. The past week had not only taught us what we needed to know about working with children—we had also become a team.

When the first buses arrived, the counselors went berserk, jumping, waving, and running alongside, trying to make out the campers' faces through the tinted windows. I smiled as the bus door opened and Di, who was volunteered to chaperone, climbed down the stairs.

"I have a busload of excited campers here from New York City!"

Girls started bounding out the door. Zelda and Hazel appeared in the doorway with their Woodlands knapsacks slung over their shoulders. They had spent the past week with Ronnie's parents. Their grandmother had probably been the one who pulled their hair into tight ponytails and put them on the bus. They wore the camp uniforms that I had painstakingly sewn their name tags into. They looked a little stunned, but otherwise they seemed to have managed fine being away from me. I hadn't realized how much I missed them until I saw them. Between my busy schedule, no cell service, and their running around with their grandparents, we only got to speak twice. I ran to them, needing a hug.

Hazel was visibly happy to see me and jumped into my outstretched arms. Zelda smiled at first but then became reserved—probably thinking, *I can't believe my mother is actually here*. Whatever was going through her mind, I didn't care. I squished her into me, telling her that I loved her.

Bethany broke up our reunion and handed Zelda and Hazel over to their respective counselors.

When they were out of earshot, Bethany told me, "Remember, at camp you're not their mother. You're Lori, the DL for the Cubs."

I couldn't argue with her. It had been made clear that my children were not supposed to receive extra attention from me because it would be unfair to the other campers.

"I know, but I couldn't help myself from getting a quick cuddle."

I suspected Abby would do the same with her kids.

After all the campers arrived, I walked under the Camp Woodlands sign and onto the path that led to the bunks. I took a deep breath before I walked up the six steps to the porch of the first cabin. I was exhilarated and exhausted; I had a sneaking suspicion that would be my state of consciousness for the next eight weeks. I was surprised how difficult it was to catch my breath when I reached the top of the steep wooden stairs. I didn't think I was in such bad shape until it dawned on me—I better watch it with the cigarettes.

I knocked on the door and was relieved to see smiling faces as I entered. There were girls sitting on their beds holding stuffed animals, girls going through their closets, girls hanging around the counselors. There were so many of them.

As soon as they understood that I was their camp mom, they all needed a piece of me and I was bombarded with questions.

After a full week of orientation, I still didn't have all the answers. I fudged my way through each cabin with a new catchphrase: "I can't wait until we learn about that together."

After tucking the campers in bed that night, I went to Mindy's room, our after-hours hangout. Drink in hand, Bethany congratulated me and Abby on our first ever tuck-in, saying, "Let's see how well you do when homesickness kicks in. Probably not tomorrow but by the third night, that's when the reality of being away from their parents sets in."

As I sipped my wine, a sense of relief washed over me—my first day with campers was over. I felt good but depleted. I left early and was tying my shoelaces when Bob and Ted walked up the stairs.

"Leaving already?" Ted asked.

"What can I say, I'm a lightweight."

"I hope your first day went well," he said.

I smiled. "It did, thanks for asking."

"Quick, close the door, no bugs," Mindy yelled when Bob opened it.

"You coming?" Bob asked Ted.

"In a sec." Ted turned to me and lowered his voice. "Let's meet up for a smoke tomorrow night. I'd like to hear how you're getting on."

I hesitated, thinking about being short of breath earlier, but said, "Tomorrow night it is."

Lying in bed I felt pleased with myself. My plan had come to fruition. I was with my daughters at camp. This could be a life-changing summer, the three of us making memories together.

I had a passing thought about how Ronnie must have felt when they left for camp, but it faded as I drifted off to sleep.

I awoke feeling refreshed. It was the first time in months that I'd slept well.

Abby had joined me for my morning walk before meeting up with Maggie and Roger for dirty-water coffee. Even though working at camp was part of the goal to overhaul my life, I hadn't figured on having to give up hazelnut coffee each morning.

"Are you guys ready for your first full day of activities?" Maggie asked.

"I can't believe we have to wake up the counselors as well as the campers. Our job should be to pop our heads in to say good morning," I said.

Maggie shrugged. "Children taking care of children."

Abby looked at her watch. "We better get a move on. If we're counting counselors, we each have sixty *children* to get ready for breakfast."

As we passed through the gates of Girls Camp I asked, "What do you think we'll find when we open the doors?"

"With any luck, everyone will have slept through the night and we'll actually have to wake them." We hesitated before entering the cabins. "Here goes nothing," Abby said.

I tapped lightly on the wood frame of the first Cubs cabin. The screen door screeched as I opened it. The room was quiet and dark with pinpoints of sun poking through the worn blinds. I sidestepped between bunks to pull up the shades, causing sleepy bodies to toss.

Each cabin was equipped with a radio tuned to the camp station. I turned the volume up just as Roger played "Reveille." That was met with grunts and whines.

"Good morning my little Cubs, rise and shine," I loudly sang out from the middle of the room.

I walked by each bed, pushing down on the mattress and addressing each girl by name and saying, "Wake up, sleepyhead," or "Today's the first day of camp." Slowly the cabin came to life. "Wear a hoodie to breakfast," I called out. "It's chilly this morning."

One camper, Leah, was whimpering. I didn't ask her how she was doing. I felt unprepared to deal with a crier at 7:30 a.m.

When I opened the door of the fourth cabin, most everyone was awake. I noticed that Jasmine, one of the counselors, was still in bed on a top bunk, her back to the center of the room. As I got closer, I heard snoring. I rubbed her arm and said, "Jasmine, it's time to get up."

She grumbled, shaking me off. I tried again and she inched closer to the wall. I looked at the other counselors, but they shrugged and continued helping the girls get ready. I wasn't sure what to do.

I whispered, "Jasmine, please get up. Don't make me do anything drastic."

She turned over, one eye opened and glared at me as she pulled the covers more tightly around herself. Was that a dare? I waited as the cabin emptied, then I opened my water bottle and dripped cold water on her head. She sprang up screaming, "What the fuck?!"

"As I said, it's time to get up." I looked at my watch. "See you in the dining hall in three minutes and watch your language."

I walked out, making sure the door slammed behind me.

At breakfast Bethany asked how our first morning went. I glanced over my shoulder and saw Jasmine, wet hair framing her sulking face as she shoveled cereal into her mouth.

"I was surprised that only one of my counselors, Amber, was awake and dressed, and at the other extreme, I couldn't get one counselor out of bed," I said.

"Yeah, there's usually one or two that give us a hard time."

I turned to see how my own kids were doing. Zelda was stabbing at a waffle and Hazel had a spoonful of cereal halfway to her mouth. They looked as though they'd made it through the night intact.

"Ready for Flagpole?" Bethany asked.

The silver flagpole stood tall and sturdy against the clear blue sky; powdered white lines fanned out down the slope of the hill from its base. The wet grass glistened, and the stripes shimmered under the rays of the morning sun.

Bethany arrived carrying the American flag on the clipboard held against her chest. The campers were in formation, lined up by division, one counselor at the front, the rear, and the middle. The DLs flanked Bethany, Mindy, and Marilyn at the top of the hill.

I stared into the smiling faces of two hundred and fifty mostly ponytailed girls, all wearing green.

"Good morning, Woodlands!" Bethany shouted.

They replied loudly and in unison, "Good morning, Bethany."

Bethany rattled off the daily announcements. "The Swans have their first social tonight with the boys at canteen."

Cheers came from the right flank.

"The Rabbits have canteen after lunch."

Squeals from the middle of the gathering.

"All campers in all divisions need to take their swim tests today."

A collective groan echoed down the hill.

"Linda Kunesh from the Otters, cabin three, has a birthday. Linda, please come up to raise the flag."

As she walked up the hill, her bunkmates sang, "Look at all the fun she's havin'/That's because she's in our cabin / Yay, Linda."

"How does everyone already know these songs?" I asked Bethany.

"Camp culture. Passed down by the older campers."

Bethany put a birthday tiara on Linda's head. She was all smiles as she pulled the cord, watching the flag catch the wind.

Most of the staff were not from the United States, and I wondered if they found this ritual odd. After the pledge was said and the formation broken, the girls headed to their bunks to start chores.

The first day of what would be the morning routine was set into motion. Aside from having to use a little water incentive on a counselor, everything was going well.

The activity after Flagpole was possibly the most important one of the day—cleaning the bunks. During orientation, Maggie made a prototype job wheel for the counselors to copy and decorate, listing the chores that each camper would do that day. It was hung at the front of the cabin and one girl was assigned a different task each day: broom, dustpan, clotheslines, porch, trash, washroom. The other girls got the day off. Then the DLs inspected the cabins, and one bunk each week would get the privilege of raising and lowering the flag together because they had the cleanest bunk.

Campers had to make their beds every day. As I watched the Cubs scurrying about, I smiled, thinking about how Zelda and Hazel were doing the same thing in their cabins. I would make sure that chores continued when we were home, and I'd add dishes and keeping their bathroom tidy. No day off.

# 10
# Learning Curve

We stood on the dock shivering—the sun was shining, but the morning chill hadn't burned off. I had passed my swim test during orientation, so I hadn't bothered to wear a suit—the water would be freezing.

Lifeguards were asking the campers questions and placing them in four different swimming lanes partitioned by green and white buoys. I stood at the far end of the dock so I could give the girls encouragement without getting splashed.

Mike suddenly appeared by my side while I was cheering them on. The only item of clothing he wore was a kelly green Speedo. He blew his whistle next to my ear to get everyone's attention. If his intention was to startle me, it worked.

"Okay Cubs, I know you're all here to pass your swim test. One of the rules at the waterfront is that you always need to be prepared, that means wearing your bathing suit, that means all campers, all counselors, including division leaders."

He turned toward me and put his hands on his hips, shaking his head in disgust that I'd broken his rule. Then he picked me up and threw me over his shoulder. I kicked and screamed but he held on tight.

"Watch what I do to people who come down to my waterfront unprepared."

He unceremoniously tossed me into the lake.

When I surfaced the campers were elated, jumping, cheering, and laughing. I'm sure he expected profanities to be flung at him, but I wouldn't give him the satisfaction. Instead, I swam to the dock and reached my hand up to Mike, hoping to pull him in.

"Really, Lori, I'm no sucker. The ladder's right there—help yourself."

I was wearing my sneakers and hoodie, which made it difficult to climb the steps. But when I managed to maneuver myself onto the dock, I raised my arms in the air like Rocky on the steps of the Philadelphia Museum of Art and jumped around in circles.

Everyone was entertained. I even got a smirk and nod from Mike. He had unintentionally given me a gift. I now shared an inside joke with the Cubs.

Later that day, the Cubs had arts & crafts, and I strolled through the rooms to see the projects that Maggie had set up for each bunk. There were six girls on potter's wheels perpendicular to a floor-to-ceiling chain-linked gate that surrounded the kiln. The rest of that bunk sat at a long table, hand-building pots while waiting their turn at the wheel.

The next room had buckets of beads. Jasmine, who was hired to work with Maggie in arts & crafts, was fully awake and snipping wire from a spool for each girl. Taped to the table in front of them was a diagram of how to bead the wire to spell out the word "Camp." I smiled at Jasmine, trying to convey a no-hard-feelings look, but she turned away.

A jewelry-making class occupied the coffee room, and campers in the fourth room painted with watercolors, using the tree outside the window as their model.

Maggie asked me to step outside. "Jasmine told me she was late this morning because you poured water over her head."

"I couldn't get her up." I shrugged. "But that's not a reason for her to be late."

"We need to keep an eye on her," Maggie said.

"I'll talk to her before things escalate."

"Good idea, I'll send her out."

Jasmine was not happy with me. Before I could say anything, she said, "You poured water on me, and that's not okay."

"You're right, and I'm sorry. But there are expectations that come with this job, and you were shirking them. You need to get out of bed and to arts & crafts on time. Everything here runs on a tight schedule."

"Great—now you and Maggie are ganging up on me."

"You're wrong. We want you to succeed—it makes everyone's life easier if you do."

I wasn't sure, but it seemed like Jasmine was about to cry. Then she threw her shoulders back and, with a defiant look on her face, said, "My parents told me that once I turned eighteen, I was on my own. I took this job because I needed a place to live until school starts."

I was stunned by her admission, but feeling sorry for her wasn't going to change the fact that she had to step it up. "Then let's work together to ensure that you keep the job."

I put my hand out to her. She looked at it for a moment, and then she took it.

"Truce?" I asked.

"I guess I have no choice," she said.

"That's one way to see it, but wouldn't it be better to look at this summer as a learning experience that could be fun for both of us?"

We stared at each other for a moment, until she finally said, "I'll try."

All the information thrown at me the prior week flew around my brain like a silver ball bouncing in a pinball machine, pinging all the things I was supposed to do every day. I was in a constant state of *tilt*.

One crucial thing I had to remember was the girl who needed a nightly growth hormone shot, Natalie in cabin three. When I entered the bunk, I was surrounded by twelve eager campers vying for my attention. But before they spoke, I said, “Hold up everyone, I’ll be back to answer your questions, but first I have to do something with Natalie.”

Natalie looked up questioningly and pointed to herself.

“Yes, put your sneakers on, throw your hoodie over your pajamas, and let’s take a walk together.”

I whispered into one of the counselor’s ears, “I’m taking her to the infirmary.”

When we arrived, Nurse Ella asked, “Who do we have here?”

“This is Natalie Goodman, here for her growth hormone shot.”

The nurse flipped the pages in front of her. “Ah, yes, here we are. Natalie Goodman, come with me, I’ll be administering your shot every evening.”

Natalie began crying.

“It’s okay, I promised your parents that we would take good care of you,” I said.

“My mother didn’t tell me I was going to get shots at camp.”

“If it’ll make you feel better, I’ll come with you and hold your hand,” I said.

Ella had the needle ready. “Where do you usually take your shot, in the arm or do you prefer the thigh?”

Natalie turned white and began shaking as she gripped my arm.

“I thought you needed a shot every day,” I said.

"My last name isn't Goodman, it's Grossman."

My stomach somersaulted. "Wait a second." I pulled out my clipboard and thumbed through the pages and, sure enough, Natalie Grossman was in bunk three. Natalie Goodman, bunk two. Oops.

"Natalie, I'm so sorry. My mistake."

Natalie was full-on sobbing, and Ella looked at me like I was a moron.

"I'll be right back with the correct girl."

Ella said, "Take my golf cart—it's getting late. Keys are in the ignition."

"Thanks."

I put my hand on Natalie's shoulder as we walked out. "Hop in. I was confused since we only met yesterday. I hope you'll forgive me."

She looked at me without saying anything.

"Could you imagine if you spent the summer getting growth hormones and when your parents picked you up, you were like six feet tall?"

She sort of grinned. That was a good sign.

"Hold on tight. I'm gonna floor it so we can end our little adventure with a fun ride."

When I made a sharp left turn onto the main road, she almost went flying out of the cart. I grabbed her just in time and jammed on the brakes.

"I guess this is a night you won't forget anytime soon," I said.

I considered asking her not to write home and tell her parents about my blunder, but I didn't want to put the idea into her head. I did some calculations; by the time she wrote and mailed it, at least five days would've passed. Hopefully by then I'd have my act together and everything would be running smoothly, and this night would only be a minor blip.

When I returned with the correct Natalie, Bethany was waiting for me.

Ella took Natalie to one of the examining rooms to give her the injection.

"I heard you brought the wrong girl to get a shot," Bethany said.

"News travels quickly here."

Bethany was not amused. "You know, this isn't a joking matter."

"I'm aware of that."

"Is that all you have to say for yourself?" she asked.

Feeling contrite I said, "I'm sorry it happened. I'll be more careful in the future."

"You must have really frightened Natalie Goodman. How's she doing?"

"Natalie Goodman is getting her shot right now, but Natalie Grossman is relieved and accepted my apology."

Bethany turned a deep shade of red. She looked at me and then down at her clipboard, flipping between the Cubs' bunks.

"Now you can understand my mix-up."

"Yes, I can see the problem. But please be more careful in the future."

"Not for nothing, but neither Natalie is particularly short."

The next night, I had my first crier, Leah from the other morning. The other girls ignored her, chatting or reading in their bunks.

"It's okay, Leah. Do you want to talk about it?"

She looked up at me, turned her freckled face into her pillow, and continued to sob.

I kneeled on the floor so that our faces would be at the same level. "Leah, please, you need to stop crying."

I picked her up and brought her outside. I guessed the shock of having me physically carry her surprised her because she stopped crying. She whimpered as we sat on the steps.

"Leah, I'm here to help you. Please tell me what you're feeling."

She hiccupped her response, "I miss, my, my, my mom."

To my great relief Bethany walked by.

"Hi there . . ." Bethany started.

"Leah," I said.

Bethany joined us on the stairs. "Of course, Leah. I saw you today on the tennis courts—you have a wicked serve. Maybe you and I can have a volley and you can give me some pointers. Would you like that?"

Leah nodded.

Part of me wanted to leave the two of them alone and tend to the other campers, making sure there weren't any other crises. But it made sense to stay and learn how a pro handled a homesick child.

Bethany put her arm around Leah to comfort her. "Can you show me your bunk? If you want, I can tuck you in and rub your back until you fall asleep."

Leah nodded yes.

After Bethany tucked Leah in, we walked to my next cabin.

"You're getting off to a rough start," she said. "Last night it was the Natalie mix-up, and tonight your first homesickness case."

"I'm trying, but there's a huge learning curve."

"I'm here to help," she said.

I understood that she needed me to succeed as much as I needed Jasmine to succeed.

# 11
# Gin & Tonic

I quickly learned that Sundays were the worst day of the week. The specialists were off so there were no watersports, no matter how hot the day was. Maggie and Roger were also off with Abby, who had finagled her time off to coincide with her friends' prior to signing a contract. That translated into no dirty-water coffee for me. Oh, and the dining hall staff was also off—Lazy Breakfast consisted of day-old bakery items and mini boxes of cereal served buffet style outside. The only redeeming thing about the situation was that sisters could hang out together.

I was standing next to Sam, Zelda's DL. "Does Zelda ignore Hazel when they see each other during the day?"

"Not that I've noticed. Did something happen?"

"I just saw Zelda shoo Hazel away when she went to sit with her, and it just about crushed my soul," I said.

"From what I can tell, you have two gorgeous daughters who love each other, and a mum who is foolish enough to follow them to camp."

I loved her Australian accent. "Foolish describes me perfectly."

Bethany joined us, holding an apple.

"Where did you find a piece of fruit?" Sam asked.

"It's not what you know but who you know." Bethany took a crunchy bite. "I saw what happened between your daughters and went to check on Hazel. She was in good spirits and excited about today's activities. Forget about what you saw earlier. Both of your girls have moved on, and so should you."

On Sunday night I sat with Bethany and Mindy drinking wine.

Bethany held up her cup. "Makes it all worthwhile, doesn't it?"

A knock interrupted our conversation.

Mindy yelled, "Come in, no bugs!"

A moth followed Ted and Bob inside.

Mindy jumped out of her chair. "You let Mothra in!" She threw a flip-flop-shaped fly swatter at Bob. "Squish it before I squash you."

"Alright, alright, calm down." Bob stepped onto Mindy's pristine white bed and expertly smashed it.

Mindy got up and smoothed out her duvet. "Now you can have a drink."

"We come bearing gifts." Ted pulled a bottle of Tanqueray, tonic, and a couple of limes from his knapsack. "We needed something a bit stronger than the spiked grape juice you serve."

"It's been a lifetime since I had a gin & tonic," I said.

"Allow me to make one for you," Ted said.

"Yes, please."

As he mixed me a drink he said, "In the summertime, my parents would sit out back with their friends smoking and drinking, and one night I nipped one when I thought no one was looking. Turns out my dad saw and boxed my ears." He had an impish grin as he handed it to me. "I promise no corporal punishment."

I found his wry British wit charming. "My dad moonlighted as a bartender. I would nip, as you say, from the apricot sours he made for my mother." After the first sip, I "ahh-ed," out loud. I'd forgotten how refreshing they were, especially after a long hot day in the sun. I held up my plastic cup and said, "This has officially become my drink of the summer."

He had a lovely smile. "Cheers!"

The next day, Abby and I spent the entirety of our morning walk complaining about Bethany.

"She's been hard on me," I said.

"If I'm telling one of my counselors what to do and Bethany overhears me, she'll say I'm wrong, and this is how I'm supposed to do it. She embarrasses me in front of the campers," Abby said.

"They can try to tell you what to expect, but when the campers showed up it was sink or swim. It'd be better if every scenario was approached with positivity. Instead, we're invariably made to feel like a fool," I said. "The only time I feel like I'm not being scrutinized by her is when we're all hanging out in Mindy's room."

"Why do you think she's nicer when she drinks?" Abby asked.

"I'd say it's because she's done for the day. The campers are sleeping, and she can relax a little," I said. "Or maybe it's because she's no longer the alpha girl. As you know, Mindy's the reigning *queen bee*. She has an edgy sense of humor, and she's hilarious—when you're not the target. Anyway, I think that's when Bethany becomes the intimida*tee* instead of the intimidator."

"We're hanging with a rough crowd," Abby said.

"Yeah, but I'd rather be in the room than have them poking fun at me behind my back."

"I'm wondering if it comes from the top down. Jack and Marilyn probably treat Bethany badly, so she passes it on to us," Abby said.

"All I know for sure is that I'm working my ass off, we both are," I said. "And I try to stay out of the way of the bosses."

I was still upset with myself for smoking again, but when I sniffed the sulfur, I felt like a hound tracking prey. I followed the scent toward the embers, careful not to trip on a tree root as I made my way to Ted and his lighter.

By the time I reached him, he'd already taken out a cigarette and lit it for me. "Lori, how nice of you to join me."

I took a drag, feeling the stress of the day melt as I exhaled. "Thank you, Teddy, I'm happy our covert operation is in full force tonight."

He froze, his cigarette glowing between his fingers in midair. "You called me Teddy."

"Oh, I'm sorry, is that not okay? You're Teddy in my mind, really, from the first time I met you. But if you don't like it . . ."

His mouth opened and closed. He took a drag. "No one has called me that in a very long time."

"Was it your ex?" I asked.

"No, *she* called me Theodore, I think mostly because it irked me so much. My nan called me Teddy. She was a special person in my life and the only one I'd allow to do it."

"Then I'll stop."

"No, don't, somehow it seems right when you say it, but only here, when we're alone."

"That's fair. I'd like to hear about your nan . . . Teddy."

"I haven't spoken about her in ages. I don't think I've ever told Max anything about her." He looked pensive, taking another drag. "She was the one person who loved me for me, a silly, hard-headed, gangly boy. I'd even say that I was her favorite." He smiled.

"Because you were named for her husband and son?"

"Maybe. I was always falling and knocking things over. I'd go through these spurts where my feet would grow before the rest of my body caught up, which put me off kilter. But it didn't matter to Nan. My parents would yell at me for being so clumsy. But she'd take me aside and sit me down and tell me stories about how the same thing happened to my father."

"That's so sweet."

"There were always my favorite biscuits and sugar milk with a little bit of tea that she made just for me."

"I know that feeling; it's a gift to have the pure love of a grandmother. Zelda's named for mine. She was my favorite person."

He had a faraway look in his eyes.

"Where are you right now?"

He smiled at me. "Sitting at the kitchen table with my nan. Thank you for bringing her back to me."

I hesitated, trying to think of something witty to say but what came out was, "You're welcome."

I squished the butt and tossed it into the sand bucket, under the fire extinguisher adjacent to the wooden laundry shack.

"It's getting late. Shall we meet again tomorrow?"

"I'd like that, Teddy," I said.

# 12
# Fireworks

"Roger and I are assigned to hang out with the kids who are afraid of fireworks," Maggie said.

"Yeah, we're going to watch a movie turned up extra loud and eat candy in the staff lounge. Happy Independence Day." Roger held up his dirty-water coffee.

As a Fourth of July activity, each cabin picked one counselor to dress up to compete for the title of Miss Ugly USA. Cubs cabin one was the winner—they had a secret weapon—Genie. Not only did she understand the assignment, she had an arsenal of makeup and costumes as the head of theater. The girls helped her dress. She had curlers rolled in her hair, her two front teeth blackened out, and a ragged blue dress with a red sash and her white bra on the outside. I was one proud momma bear when Genie's cabin won.

Later that night, the entirety of Woodlands sat around the baseball diamond, scattered between first, home, and third bases.

Girls Camp wore their red-white-and-blue finest, their hair tied with bandanas, a gift from Marilyn and Jack.

The local fire company and their families were invited—they brought a fire truck—a treat for the kids as well as a precaution. The pyrotechnics were set off in the outfield by Mike and Jack. We were directly under the rockets bursting in the air and in our eardrums. Watching the sparkly array of colors as they bloomed in the sky was thrilling. When the sky was lit, I glimpsed Zelda's and Hazel's awestruck faces.

The usual suspects were already in Mindy's room by the time I finished tucking in the campers. I handed the bunk reports to Bethany, then went to the minifridge and took out an ice tray and a lime.

"Gilda brought us a present—you've got to try this stuff. It has a real kick to it," Mindy said.

"What is it?" I asked.

"It's a combination of all the clear liquors—gin, vodka, tequila, and rum, with lemonade mixed in," Gilda said.

"Isn't that a Long Island Iced Tea?" I shook my head. "I don't have good memories of those."

Mindy held it up. "I thought that was made with Coke."

"And lemon juice. It's my husband's twist, no cola, only lemonade," Gilda said.

Gilda offered me a sip from her cup. I brought it to my nose and my stomach flipped. "No thanks, I'll stick to gin."

"What does your husband call this concoction?" Bethany asked.

Gilda shrugged. "I don't think he named it."

"I know, let's call it Jungle Juice," Mindy said. "Cheers to Gilda and the mixologist she married!"

There was a text message from Ronnie: *I have an appointment near Woodlands next week. Maybe we can meet. Call me.*

Hearing from him at all was surprising. The fact that he was making time for me was shocking. When I had driven out of NYC last month, we had barely been civil to each other. It wasn't only our arguments about camp, we had been fighting about anything and everything. I thought I had made it clear that I wasn't going to contact him, and he shouldn't call me. We had agreed that the next time we'd see each other would be Visiting Day at camp, two weeks away. I wondered if this was some kind of grand gesture, making me a priority, *or* if he wanted to start divorce proceedings. I used to know how he would react and how he felt about any situation, but over the past few years I had lost all insight into his inner thoughts.

I decided to call him from the privacy of Bethany's room.

"Lori, how are the girls?"

"*We're* all doing really well. I got to see Zelda and Hazel play softball, and Hazel is in the play. They both have good—"

"I don't have much time to talk right now. Let me tell you what I've planned. One of my clients is only about an hour away from the camp. So, I thought after my appointment we could meet for dinner and have the conversation I've been putting off."

"We've had so many unfinished conversations. I don't even know which one you're referring to."

"That's why I really want to sit down with you face-to-face before Visiting Day."

"Can you give me a clue?"

"Not now, I have my client waiting on the other line."

Seeing him probably wasn't a good idea, but my curiosity won out. "Okay, sure."

"Great, I'll send you the details. I gotta run. Love you."

Love you—did he mean it or was it just the perfunctory words you're required to say to your spouse, especially when you're in a bad place? Was it possible that since I'd been away, he realized how much he loved and missed me and wanted to fix things between us?

One of our open-ended conversations was about marriage counseling. He couldn't have been more inconsiderate when I suggested it.

"I barely have time to take a crap. I don't see how I can fit in a weekly meeting."

I was trying my best to keep our family together because Zelda and Hazel worshipped their dad.

Ronnie's next message said we had reservations at the fancy restaurant in town, and I should meet him at the bar at 8:00 p.m. I think the last time we'd met at a bar was before Zelda was born. He had liked pretending we were strangers, and he was picking me up. I showered and primped, tweezing and shaving for the first time since I got to camp. I didn't need any makeup because I was tan. I wore a sundress, which surprisingly hung loosely on my frame. It was a relief not having to spritz myself with bug spray after my shower. I put the key in the ignition and wanted to feel optimistic, but all I felt was trepidation.

At 7:45 p.m., I slid onto a stool in the middle of the empty, dimly lit bar and ordered a glass of Sancerre. The decor reminded me of a speakeasy, old and elegant, a relic from a different era. While I nursed my drink, I rehashed conversations we'd had as I heard the ticks from the gilded clock above the bar.

Ever since Ronnie had made partner, his priorities had shifted. He would try to be home to have dinner with us while we ate dessert, then as he took on bigger, more high-profile cases, we were lucky if he was home in time to tuck in the girls.

At first, I hadn't noticed the subtle changes. It was a new cologne a coworker turned him onto. Then it was his wardrobe. One day he came home wearing a cashmere sport jacket I'd never seen before.

"I usually have to coax you to go shopping, and now you went without me?"

"Yeah, Ed popped his head into my office and asked if I wanted to go with him to his tailor. When the managing partner asks you something like that, you say yes."

One of the last conversations we had before I left for the summer drove home how inconsequential I had become in his life.

"Lori, try to understand the pressure I'm under. If I win, I'll get a huge bonus and be the go-to person for these lucrative cases. I need to focus on my future right now."

"Don't you mean *our* future?"

He looked up from his work. "What? Oh, yes, sure, right, our future." And then turned right back to his notes.

At 8:45, my phone finally buzzed.

"Hi, Lori, please don't be upset, but I'm still with the client. He made dinner plans for me with a couple of his associates."

I gripped the fragile stem of the wine glass so tightly I was afraid it would snap. "Please tell me you're joking."

"I won't be able to meet you tonight. After the dinner I need to head straight to the office to pull an all-nighter to implement the issues we discussed."

"Can't one of your many lackies take care of it?"

"No, this is really important . . ."

"More important than me?"

"Lori, you're being unfair . . ."

"*I'm* being unfair?! You have no idea how difficult it was for me to get this time off. I always rearrange my life to accommodate you, and I always end up disappointed. You have absolutely no respect for me."

"Lori, I can't argue with you right now, I have people waiting for me and—"

I cut him off with a terse, "Goodbye, Ronald."

I shook with fury. I really wanted to tell him to go to hell—but—Zelda and Hazel.

I still had no idea why he'd even suggested our getting together. It would have been enlightening to find out which one of the many open-ended conversations he wanted to finish.

At least when I drove back to camp, there would be a gin & tonic and a much-needed smoke with Teddy.

Teddy lit our cigarettes. "I didn't think I'd see you tonight. Abby told me you had a date with your husband."

"Yeah, well, the evening didn't go as planned." I took a drag.

"You've been married for how long?"

"Fifteen years."

"Impressive. Me and the ex barely eked out five."

"Well, right now you wouldn't consider ours a marriage goals situation. If you like a good pun—here's one—the trial *attorney* is on a trial *separation* from his wife. When he made plans to meet me, well, I stupidly thought things would be different." I turned to wipe the tears welling up.

We stood side by side, quietly smoking, caught up in our own thoughts. Teddy looked up and blew a smoke ring. "A separation, a break, like from that American sitcom, *Friends*?"

I scoffed. "I hadn't thought about that, but sure, like Ross and Rachel but with two children and a mortgage."

"If you don't mind me asking, who initiated the estrangement?"

I didn't answer right away. I took another drag of the cigarette and watched as the smoke dissipated into the night. "I'm tired of constantly being disappointed by him. So, yeah, it was me."

"If it helps, me and the ex were always at odds. Sadly, it became the usual state of our marriage. For what it's worth, I understand your frustration. Did you at least take yourself out for dinner?" he asked.

"I ended up sitting at the bar drinking and eating peanuts by myself."

Teddy smiled. "Did anyone offer to buy you a drink? Because if I saw a beautiful woman like you, I would absolutely buy her a drink."

Was he flirting with me? "Okay, let's hear it, your best pickup line."

"I find when I'm in your country all I have to say is hello. Women here seem to find my accent alluring."

I burst out laughing.

"Laugh all you want, but it works."

"Then tell me what you say when you're home, just another Brit on the prowl."

"If it were you, I'd probably ask if it was true what they say about redheads."

There was that roguish grin.

"If nothing else, it made you smile. I'd take that as a sign to keep going." He took a drag. "You should've called me. I would've gladly kept you company."

I looked up at the stars, then I smiled at him.

Teddy returned my smile and said, "For what it's worth, I'm sorry your night didn't work out as planned. But I'm happy you're here with me sharing a smoke."

# 13
# OD—On Duty

"Lori, how's it going?"

I was reading the schedule on my way to meet the campers and was surprised to hear my name. Jack was straddling his bicycle directly in my path. I'd learned to avoid him—each encounter was awkward. He saw me before I saw him.

"Good." I smiled, hoping it looked sincere.

"Marilyn and Bethany have been telling me that you're doing a good job, the campers and counselors like you, that you're a team player."

I felt a legitimate grin form on my face. Complimented out of the blue. Too bad my husband wasn't around to hear it.

"Thanks. Good to know."

"Do you intentionally avoid me?" Jack asked.

The smile fell from my face, "I'm not sure what you're asking me."

"I've noticed that whenever I'm near, you abruptly turn away."

I stood on the edge of a wide-open field but felt unable to move. I hadn't thought Jack noticed me at all, and here he was calling me out. "If that's happening, I'm sure it's coincidental."

"Just so you know, I'm watching. I'm always watching."

We sipped our morning coffee, gossiping and reviewing the day's schedule.

"What the hell does this mean, I'm scheduled for OD tonight?" I asked.

"Didn't Bethany mention something during one of those endless orientation meetings about having to sit a couple of nights on OD? I remember thinking, what does OD stand for, but then the subject changed, and I forgot about it," Abby said.

"You, my dear friend, have the attention span of a gnat," Maggie said.

Abby waved her hand as if shooing away a swarm.

"So, what does OD stand for?" I asked.

Roger had just walked in from the radio station. "On Duty. I have it tonight too. Basically, you stay up until the counselors have signed in from their night off."

"You mean I get to work my ass off all day in the hot sun, taking care of forty-eight eight-year-olds, and then stay up past midnight to make sure a bunch of drunk twenty-somethings sign in after a night off?"

"Well put," Roger said.

"I guess it won't be awful if we do it together."

"That would be great, but I'll be across campus on the boys' side."

"The two of us stuck in the same hole, yet alone. Here's a thought—doesn't anyone worry about us walking around like zombies from lack of sleep?" I asked.

"But aren't you guys up late drinking with the Bergers' minions every night?" Maggie asked.

Maggie had declined Mindy's invitation. She told us, "I

don't want to hang out with the ladies. After all, I brought my husband here with me."

"But I'm in bed by eleven," I said. "I need at least seven hours of sleep in order to function. Having a cocktail before bedtime helps me unwind and fall asleep, just like having coffee with you in the morning helps me start my day. Tonight, I won't be under my covers until almost 1:00 a.m., and that gives me only five hours, and that's if I fall asleep right away."

I tucked in the last of the Cub bunks and looked at my watch. It was 9:00 p.m.—cocktail time. I could almost feel the bubbles from the tonic tickling my nose and my lips puckering from the lime. I swear I was salivating, just thinking of the gin & tonic I wouldn't be having. Camp had turned me into a lush.

I climbed the creaky wooden stairs to my OD post, a musty two-room shack. Each room was lit with a single bulb hanging by a thin wire, and ominous shadows appeared on the walls. A small wooden table in the middle of the main room had been carved with initials; a heart with STEVE & AMY '84 caught my eye. I wondered if their love had prevailed.

I decided to do something that reminded me of my summers in the bungalow colony, when my girlfriends and I would trade stationery and then write letters together. I pulled out the flashlight I'd bought from the camp website and placed it in the middle of the table—instant lamp. Then I unwrapped the fanciful paper and a pack of colored gel pens. I was going to write letters to Zelda and Hazel. All the other campers got letters from their mothers, and I wanted my kids to get one too. I hoped they were getting mail from their dad.

The notecards had dragonflies across the top and bottom, but the best part was that the envelopes had one flying across the front. I had a thing for dragonflies. I started my letter to Zelda with a bright blue gel pen, her favorite color.

Later, I walked the perimeter of Girls Camp, beaming the flashlight in front of me. There was a porch light outside the OD shack and a spotlight emanating from the roof of the middle cabin; otherwise, it was completely dark and silent. I stopped to look up at the glittering stars.

Inhaling the sweet smell of the summer night, I shivered. There was a clean, fresh chill in the air. I went back inside, put on my hoodie, and started Hazel's letter with a purple pen.

As I addressed the envelopes, I heard laughing. It was midnight. Yawning, I peeked out the window to see a stream of raucous drunken women leaning into each other, staggering toward me. On the porch, I said in a stage whisper, "Keep the noise down, the campers are sleeping."

"Oh good, Lori's on tonight," a tipsy counselor said as she hurried past me and lunged for the bathroom door. "Some of you can be real bitches."

Who were the bitches, and what bitchy things did they do?

A line formed to sign the clipboard acknowledging their return. The stench of sweat, weed, and alcohol was pervasive. I took a step toward the open screened window.

"I hope everyone had a good time," I said.

"It sucks for you that you have to wait up for us," Genie said.

"It does. I'm missing out on sleep without any of the fun."

By the time I noticed that two signatures were missing, the counselors were gone. It was 12:15 a.m., they were due back by midnight, and I just wanted to go to bed. But I waited another fifteen minutes in case they showed up. I hated to get anyone in trouble. I appreciated how hard the counselors worked—they needed to let off a little steam. While waiting, I wondered who the bitch was. It couldn't be Abby or Maggie; they hadn't sat OD yet.

It dawned on me that no one had mentioned what the protocol was if a counselor didn't sign in. Should I notify Bethany, the Bergers, or call the police? At 12:30 a.m., I packed up my stuff, turned off the light, walked to the office, and slid the roster through the mail slot. I decided the prudent thing to do was knock on the Bergers' door to let them know that two counselors hadn't signed in. If something happened to the women, the faster it was reported, the better the chances of finding them.

I heard a car behind me. I turned to see it pull up in front of the office, and the two missing counselors got out. Seeing me, they ran over.

"Lori, can we sign in?"

"Sorry, I waited until 12:30 for you. I don't have the sign-in sheet anymore. But you saved me from waking up the Bergers to let them know you weren't accounted for."

"Wake up the Bergers? What in the hell for?"

"I didn't know where you were, if you were in danger . . ."

"I can't believe you were going to get us in trouble for being a few minutes late. You're such a bitch."

I laughed, shaking my head, turned, and walked away into the darkness. Bitchiness eventually rises to the surface.

# 14
# Bears and Worms and Mike

I woke to the sound of rain pattering against the window. I rolled over, thinking it was a perfect day to sleep in. By the time I reset my alarm, fluffed my pillow, and drew the covers back up, I was fully awake. Damn. I dressed and was ready to go walking. I put my ear to Abby's door and heard her rhythmic breathing—she was sleeping in.

I wore my bright green rain poncho over green sweats and a camp hoodie. I didn't own rain boots, and even if I did I wouldn't wear them for a power walk. However, I'd brought water sneakers with me for swimming in the lake. The thought of touching the muck at the bottom made my skin crawl. I slipped them on before stepping out into the rain.

The steady drizzle made the lush campus look dreary. The only sounds were the squishing of my shoes on the wet ground and the slow drips of raindrops from the trees. I turned my radio volume up, so I'd hear it through my hoodie. Hopefully, the rain would break the suffocating humidity of the past few days.

Mindy's and Bethany's rooms were dark, as was the office. Seemed that everyone but me had made the sensible decision to stay in bed. Even the gnats that usually greeted me each morning had decided it was too miserable to bother. Jack would probably radio the DLs calling for a rainy-day schedule, which meant a later breakfast. I knew the campers, and especially the counselors, could use the extra sleep. Having nonstop fun each day was exhausting.

Passing the baseball diamond, I thought I saw something move, deep in the outfield. The fog was thick, and even when I squinted, I couldn't tell if I imagined it.

I reached the steep paved path that led down to the lake. Taking it, I picked up my pace. The smell in the air changed—familiar, like damp metal. I remembered it from my childhood summers in the Catskills. I looked down and sure enough, wiggling worms covered the trail. I was covered in goose flesh—I abhorred worms and snakes, anything that slithered gave me the willies. I slowed my pace to avoid squashing them.

A thick mist covered the lake. If I hadn't kayaked in its brisk waters yesterday, I'd swear it didn't exist. I decided not to do my usual trek, it was damp and gloomy. The thought of a hot cup of coffee in arts & crafts seemed much more enticing than this desolate walk.

My hood did little to keep my hair dry and water kept dripping into my eyes. I reached into my pocket for a tissue. Instead, I found the lighter Teddy had given me, but I didn't have a cigarette. I flipped the lighter around in my hand when I remembered a conversation we'd had—he mentioned he hid a pack of cigarettes at the beginning of each summer, just in case. I'd asked, "In case of what?"

He'd just smiled, taken a drag of his Winston, and told me where. At the time I thought the idea was completely nonsensical, but if he were standing in front of me right now, I'd kiss him.

It was under a boulder behind the boys' swim shack. The rock was heavy and needed to be pushed with both hands. I shuddered when I saw more squiggly worms, but they weren't enough of a deterrent. Once I had it in my mind that I was going to smoke, my entire body craved nicotine. I needed something to clear away the worms. *The radio.* It had a long, thick antenna. I pulled up my slicker, unclipped it from the elastic waistband, and gingerly moved the worms away, but I didn't see the red packaging. Using the antennae as a hoe, I moved the soil around a bit until I saw the tip of a plastic bag poking out of the ground.

Bingo!

There was a green director's chair with the word LIFEGUARD in large white letters under the eaves of the swim shack. Sitting down, looking around, I didn't see another breathing soul. I lit the cigarette, inhaled, and closed my eyes, savoring the taste, the peace, and the solitude. When I finished my smoke, I was ready for a cup of coffee. I sighed. The simple pleasures of life. I crushed the butt into the muddied sand, picked it up and tossed it into some bushes, then popped a piece of Trident in my mouth and looked up the hill. At the top of the path, a bear was staring at me.

It was massive, standing still on its hind legs. I was frozen in place, mouth dry, heart pounding, and I could feel the color drain from my face. The bear yawned and stretched, making it clear that I was no threat. I was dumbfounded by how wide and long its jaw was when it opened its mouth—my head could easily fit inside. I walked that hill every morning, and though it seemed as long as a football field when I hiked it, the distance between us now felt sickeningly short.

The bear went down on all fours and shook its body—splattering raindrops like a harmless puppy. We locked eyes as it started walking leisurely down the hill toward me. I couldn't breathe.

Through the gloom and over the pounding of my heart, Jack's booming voice echoed from the radio. "Attention, attention all division leaders. There has been a bear sighting."

No shit.

"Keep all campers inside until further notice. Repeat. Keep all campers in their bunks until you get an all clear from me."

The bear's back seemed as wide and as long as a picnic table, and the distance separating us was quickly disappearing. Think. What did I know about bears? Don't run because they'd chase you. Well, that wasn't going to happen because I was paralyzed with fear. I had to move—had to do something to protect myself.

My radio. I can call for help. Pulling up my poncho I went to unhook it—gone. Crap. I'd brought it with me. Where was it? I must have left it by the boulder. Smoking was indeed going to kill me. If I moved quickly, I could run around the shack, grab the radio, and barricade myself inside the wooden building. Could a bear blow down the shack? No, that was a wolf, but I was pretty sure he could ram it to the ground.

I had no one to blame for my predicament. Ronnie was right, I'd no business taking a job that placed me in the middle of the wilderness when my natural habitat was Bloomingdale's. I had to think of something, or the bear would make my kids motherless. Ronnie would remarry and my children would be raised by a wicked stepmother, just like the ones in the Disney movies that played on a never-ending loop in my apartment.

Idiot, why didn't I stay in bed? Idiot, why didn't I stay in New York City?

The bear padded downhill, the gap between us becoming smaller by the second. Everything seemed to be happening in slow motion, but my senses were in overdrive. I smelled its pungent scent mixed with dampness and my own sweat. The bear's pace picked up. I willed myself to move, cautiously stepping backward toward the shack. It didn't have a door, but hopefully I could defend myself with a paddle. If I were attacked, I'd be damned if I'd go down without a fight. The tough Brooklyn girl in me always came out when cornered.

I took off toward the rock and grabbed for the radio but fumbled it, startled by a loud noise coming from behind me. There was a Jeep zigzagging toward the bear while blaring the horn. The bear reared on his hind legs, again showing its full height. The Jeep sped forward, lights flashing and horn honking, aiming straight for the bear. The bear dropped to all fours, scowled, and then turned around and bounded back up the hill, disappearing into the dense bushes.

The car stopped. Mike was at the wheel and a woman holding onto the crossbar pulled herself up from the passenger seat. She had long platinum blonde hair, dimples, and a panicked look on her pretty face. I knew her: Anya, who ran the camp's website.

"Lori, quick, jump in."

I climbed into the back seat and proceeded to shake.

"What the hell are you doing down here when there was a bear sighting, and why didn't you come to the Airstream? How many times have I invited you over?" Mike said.

Anya noticeably tensed.

"I, I, didn't think about you." My teeth were chattering. "I, I, was enjoying the solitude, I thought I was safe."

Anya grinned. "Mike, despite your massive ego, you're not the first person people think about. Not everyone's in love with you."

Mike placed his hand on Anya's thigh. "I never said anything about love, I said that most ladies *lust* after me." He turned and winked at me.

"I'm thinking that Lori's not one of them," Anya said.

I was nearly attacked by a bear, and they were flirting. Could it be? Anya was a good ten years younger than me, and I was at least ten years younger than Mike.

"But seriously, why were you out for a walk when there was

a bear sighting?" Mike asked. "You're either really brave or really stupid."

I took a deep breath, trying to control my chattering. "I was out before the sighting." I sat on my hands to keep them from shaking.

"Lori, were you really scared? It was only a cub, a baby. It was just looking for someone to play with," Mike said.

"Mike, stop teasing. That bear was at least as big as you. Of course she was frightened, just like you would've been if you were standing face to face with it." Anya turned and patted my knee. "Lori, you may not know this, but Mike was a Navy SEAL so he's very brave and strong," Anya gushed.

"And loyal and true?" I asked.

"Yup, and because of that he thinks he needs to save everyone and be the hero of the day."

Anya had it bad. She looked at him, starry-eyed.

"Today, Mike, you are my hero," I said.

"If I hadn't seen the light from the tip of your cigarette, I'd have left you down here to fend for yourself." Mike looked at me from the rearview mirror, winking again.

"The fog must be playing tricks on your eyes," I said.

"Don't worry, your secret's safe with us, as long as our secret is safe with you," Anya said.

I sighed. "Today would have been a good day to stay in bed."

There were now at least three people who knew my secret. I had to remember, you were never truly alone in this place. There was always someone or something lurking around every bush.

"What happens now?" I asked.

"What, with the bear? I'll swing by and pick up Jack and we'll look for the clan," Mike said.

"Then what?" Anya asked.

"Don't you worry your pretty little heads. Jack and I will take care of it," Mike said.

I was waiting for one of his winks, but none came.

"Mike, it's amazing how quickly you went from hero to zero," I said.

"What, why?" He seemed completely baffled.

"Can you drop us *little* ladies off at arts & crafts while you big strong guys save us from the scary beasts?" I asked.

Anya looked at Mike and burst out laughing.

Mike wasn't happy with either of us when he dropped us off. Anya had her arm around me as we walked into the arts & crafts studio. Abby and Maggie jumped up to greet us.

Maggie gave me a hug. "Abs said you must have gone for a walk and then we didn't hear you on the radio. We were so scared."

I was still shaken but felt better sitting with my friends. Maggie handed me a steaming cup of coffee, and I held it for warmth and then took a sip to calm myself.

"You alright?" Roger asked.

"What the hell was I thinking? Me, a girl from Brooklyn, pretending to like the great outdoors and other people's children and wild animals. I was supposed to be on a Greek Island this summer, drinking ouzo on a balcony overlooking the Mediterranean."

"If I'd been with you, I think I would've peed myself—or outright fainted," Abby said.

"You know what they say: You don't need to run faster than the bear, you only need to run faster than your friend," Roger said.

"Roger!" Maggie elbowed him.

Roger chuckled. "What? Too soon?"

"I'm just so happy to have you sitting here with us right now. Could you imagine the call Jack would've had to make to

Ronnie? 'Hey, Ronnie, so, your kids are fine but your wife, well, she was eaten by a bear.'" Maggie hugged herself.

"'Now that your wife's incapacitated, I'll send you a bill for what you owe.'" Roger was on a roll.

"You know what keeps running through my mind? Remember how pissed I was when Jack told me I always had to carry my radio with me, even on my morning walks? Even though I ended up not using it to call for help, I was glad I had it with me."

I needed to change out of my wet clothes and wash the stink of fear from my body before waking my bunks for breakfast. Abby walked back to the cabin with me.

"I guess it makes sense that Jack told us not to mention the bear sighting to the counselors, and especially not to the campers. No need to alarm anyone," I said.

"You know, Lori, you are so naive," Abby said.

"What do you mean?"

"His real motive is to avoid campers writing home about it. Could you imagine dealing with all the parents calling to make sure their kid wasn't attacked by a bear?" Abby said.

"I hadn't thought about it like that."

Di was still in pajamas when we walked into our cabin. "Do you guys ever sleep?" She looked me over. "Are you sick? You look a little pale."

"I met up with a bear on my morning walk."

"You can't be serious," Di said.

Before I could comment, the radios gave off an awful squeal before Jack started talking. "All's clear. Repeat, all is clear. Please start moving your campers to breakfast."

# 15
# Decisions

I saw Jack outside the office, and instead of avoiding him I went to speak to him.

"Jack, thank you for telling me to carry my radio with me on my walks. I was happy to have it this morning."

"You know, Lori, in the short time you've worked here, you've become the biggest pain in my ass."

I thought he must be teasing me, so I laughed.

"Everything's a joke with you. Do you ever take anything seriously?" Jack's voice was getting louder.

"What are you talking about?" I stood there, completely confounded.

"I know that you rearrange the schedules, my schedules, that I work on all winter to guarantee everyone has fun. Who do you think you are, that you can change things without asking me first?"

I had no idea what he was talking about until I remembered how last week two of the Cubs bunks had been scheduled for gymnastics and the other two for softball. But everyone wanted gymnastics and I had cleared it with the head of gymnastics so all four bunks could do it—but I'd forgotten to inform the softball counselors. It wouldn't have been a big deal, but the two women had gone to ask Gilda, as head of programming, why the Cubs hadn't shown up, and Jack had happened to be with her.

He had immediately radioed me. "Lori, why aren't Cubs one and two at softball right now?"

"Oh!" I began, "All the girls wanted to do gymnastics . . ."

Jack cut me off and barked back, "I don't care what they want!" His voice had boomed and echoed in the gymnastics shed, stopping all activity.

I ran outside so no one would hear the rest of his rant.

"I make the schedules because I know what works."

Obviously, he didn't know squat about eight-year-old girls. Even though I knew I had made the right decision for the campers, I radioed back, "Understood."

And now, Jack's sneer made it clear that he enjoyed my discomfort. He continued his tirade, "No one has ever questioned me about my schedules because this is *my camp*, I make the rules, not *you*!"

I stood frozen while Jack pointed his finger in my face and kept yelling at me.

"Now I have to worry about you being attacked by a bear. Nothing like this happens to anyone else. Only you. Why must you walk around the camp by yourself? What is it about you that you're either creating your own drama or you're always in the middle of some kind of trouble?"

I tried to stay calm, but my heart thumped hard in my chest. "I take my job very seriously. My campers are happy and well cared for . . ."

"Your campers? Did you just say *your* campers? *All campers* are mine. You've no idea how hard I worked getting them signed up."

But I did know. Jack had been charming and persuasive when he came to tell us about *his* camp. Then the follow-up emails, only two beds left for my daughters, so, yes, I did have an inkling of how hard he pushed to sell Woodlands.

"This camp was falling to pieces before I bought it. I made it successful. *Me*. I keep the campers happy. I keep them well cared for. Me. Not you."

I could see the vein in his temple pulsing, and the hand not pointing in my face was clenched into a fist.

"Do you hear what I'm saying to you?"

"It's hard not to, since you're screaming in my face." I took a step back. If he planned on striking me, I wasn't going to make it easy for him.

He stopped for a moment. He was perspiring profusely, and a band of sweat formed on his upper lip. He was practically panting with rage.

In a place where it was virtually impossible to be alone, I stood face-to-face with a madman. I was sure people were witnessing his diatribe, but no one was willing to challenge Jack and come to my defense.

"Give me one good reason why I shouldn't fire you right here, right now."

No matter what I did or said, this wasn't going to end well. But I'd been married to and arguing with a lawyer for the past fifteen years, and I knew how to win an argument. "Do you really want to fire me? The campers like me. I didn't ask for the bear to appear. Go ahead and fire me and wait for the harassment papers to show up on your desk. If you want to take me down, I'm more than happy to bring you along for the ride."

Both of Jack's hands were now clenched. I thought for sure he was going to pummel me. His already loud voice went up a few more decibels. "How dare you threaten me? Who the hell do you think you are?"

It seemed like the angrier he got, the calmer I became. "If you lay a hand on me, I will have this camp closed within twenty-four hours."

Jack started shaking from the effort of keeping his anger in check. He unclenched his fists, snarled at me, and abruptly walked away, slapping his hands onto his legs.

I took a deep breath, shivered, and turned toward my cabin. I was proud of not breaking down. I went to my room where I felt safe, locked the door, threw myself onto my bed, and began to sob. I didn't know what to do—I didn't understand what had just transpired. When I calmed down, I decided I needed to speak with someone. Mindy, the camp's social worker, seemed the best choice. I needed clarity and she knew Jack well. She'd be able to explain and untangle what just happened.

I picked up my radio. "Mindy, please come in for Lori."

"Mindy is with *me*. She works for *me*. Not you!"

I dropped the radio, unnerved when Jack's voice invaded the sanctuary of my room. How stupid of me. Of course Jack heard all and knew all—he had just screamed that in my face. I sat on my bed feeling confused and isolated. I obviously couldn't get back on the radio again, and if I could, who would I call, Bethany? Abby? Maybe Gilda?

I held my pillow against my stomach, recalling the phone conversation I'd had with Jack back in February. I had been trying to figure out a way to pay for camp when I surprised myself by impulsively calling him and asking for a job.

The conversation came back to me as if it were yesterday.

"The timing of this call seems opportune. Marilyn is sitting next to me. Do you mind if I put you on speaker?" He didn't wait for my reply. "Marilyn, Lori just asked me if we had a job for her."

Marilyn had replied, "We're in the midst of staffing and one of the more challenging positions to fill is division leader. Jack's sitting next to me smiling and nodding."

Jack had continued, "After I met you, I could tell you were *swimming* in leadership skills—can't resist a camp pun—and thought you'd be perfect in the role of division leader."

"What makes you think I'd make a good one?"

As soon as I'd asked the question, I felt stupid. If they were willing to hire me, I should have shut up and listened.

"Your energy. You seem to have common sense, but the real tip-off was hearing you say, 'I wish I could go to camp.'" They both chuckled.

"Doesn't every parent say that?"

"Are you kidding? Most parents want to hand over their kids as soon as we've met," Jack said.

Marilyn had added, "It takes a certain personality and a lot of spunk to work with kids. Jack said he had seen those qualities in you."

I distinctly remembered rolling the word "spunk" over in my mind and thinking that was the trait TV boss Lou Grant hated when he used it to describe Mary Richards, the star.

My *spunk* might be my downfall.

I certainly wasn't in any shape to be with the campers. I wasn't sure how long I sat on my bed, agonizing over what to do, when I heard a squeak from the screen door. My heart jumped. Jack wouldn't dare come into my room, would he?

"Lori, are you in here?"

I was relieved to hear Abby's voice.

"I've been looking for you. It's not like you to leave your counselors without direction. My goodness, your eyes are all red and swollen. Then I heard Jack on the radio, so I thought, *uh oh, I'd better find her*. What the heck is going on?"

I felt tears welling up and fought them back. "Isn't camp supposed to be a happy place?"

"You'd think so. Tell me what happened."

Before I could answer, our radios let out a high-pitched screech and we heard Bethany announce, "All DLs, please meet me at the OD shack. All DLs meet me at the OD shack. Please copy."

"Abby and Lori copy," Abby said into her hip. "Go wash your face. We can talk on the way over." Abby suggested that we take the long way around to avoid passing the office. "I'm sure you want to avoid Jack."

"If I never see him again for as long as I live, I'll die a happy woman. You know what? I *don't* plan on seeing him ever again."

"It's gonna be difficult to avoid him," Abby said.

"Not if I drive out of here this afternoon."

"Really? You would do that? What about Zelda and Hazel?"

"I can't leave them here with that jackass in charge. I'm going to pack them up right now. Tell Bethany that I will not be at her meeting today, or ever."

Abby stopped. "Hold up a second, you're really gonna leave me all alone here?"

I hugged her. "It was great meeting you, and I've enjoyed working with you, but I will not allow anyone to humiliate me, especially not Jack."

Zelda's empty cabin felt like a steam room, hot and muggy, which perfectly matched my temperament. Methodically, I stripped the bed and threw all her neatly folded clothes on top of the sheets. I stood on the bunk, searching for her trunk in the rafters when the screen door slammed.

Zelda ran over. "Mom, what're you doing?"

She was with Hazel, and Bethany was behind them.

"Before you make any rash decisions, I thought you should have a conversation with your daughters," Bethany said. "I'll leave you alone. Come find me when you're done."

"Why is all my stuff on my bunk?" Zelda asked.

"Because I need to leave, and I don't want you staying here without me."

The duffel was on the floor, and I began tossing in sneakers, cleats, and rollerblades.

Zelda placed herself in front of me and grabbed my arms. "Stop packing and tell me what's going on."

Hazel's eyes were brimming with tears while Zelda's looked panicked. In my anger I hadn't given any thought to how my kids would react.

"I had a huge fight with Jack, and I don't want to work for him anymore."

"Who's Jack?" Hazel asked.

"The camp director."

They both had blank looks.

"I don't know him," Hazel said.

It was absurd how he was always up my ass but had no connection with my kids, the campers he supposedly kept so happy. Come to think of it, I'd never seen him or Marilyn at any activities.

Hazel broke the silence. "But I don't want to go home." She could barely get the words out.

"Neither do I. You can go. You said camp was where we'd learn independence. We don't need you here," Zelda said.

Depleted, I sat on the unmade bed. It was true, I wanted my children to become self-reliant, but her words stung.

Hazel threw her arms around me, nuzzling my neck. "I don't

want to go home, and I like having you here. Please don't go and please let us stay."

I could tell by Zelda's out-of-focus expression that she was building her case. Not only did her facial features resemble her father's, she thought and acted like him as well. I missed the days when my children had hung on my every word.

Zelda stood with her hands on her hips, ready to lecture me exactly like her father would. A ray of sunshine fell across her face, accentuating her freckles. Her hair was tied in a ponytail, frizzy strands forming a halo. Even though she looked angelic, I braced myself for the tirade that was about to begin.

"I don't understand. First you gave a big speech about how you wanted to send me and Hazel to camp to become confident and responsible—your words. And then you change your mind and tell us that if you don't go to camp, then me and Hazel can't go to camp. So here we are, together at camp, and now, right in the middle of the best summer ever, you want us to leave just because you don't like this Jack guy? It makes no sense."

Hazel looked upset. "Why do you always have to yell at Mom? Can't we talk about this calmly?" Hazel turned toward me. "Mom, I want you to stay but if you can't, why do *we* have to leave? I love it here," Hazel said.

I hadn't thought this through. As campers they got to play with their friends all day without a care in the world while I dealt with the behind-the-scenes bullshit. From the campers' point of view, Woodlands was a fabulous place.

"But we need to support each other." As soon as I said that, I could hear how absurd I sounded.

Zelda crossed her arms. "If you want to leave, I absolutely support that. I don't need you here."

I winced.

"Zelda," Hazel said, "that was just plain mean. I think what Zelda was trying to say was that the only time we even see each other is across the field at Flagpole. Zelda and I don't spend any time together either. She even pretends not to know me when I wave to her."

"Why do you snub your sister?"

"I don't want to be the kid who gets treated differently because my mother works here or because everyone thinks my little sister's cute."

"Do I embarrass you?" I asked.

"Well, yeah, sorta."

"First you tell me you don't need me. On top of that, I embarrass you. Just when I thought my day couldn't possibly get any worse."

Hazel sat down next to me and put her hand on my thigh. "Mom, I love you, and I love that everyone knows you're my mother, and you never embarrass me. But it's impossible for me to leave right now."

"Please tell me why it's impossible to leave right now. I need a good reason to leave you here without me."

"I have a singing part in the play, and I'm the only girl from my division who has one, and you've taught me that if I joined a team or a play, I have to see it through to the end. You said it's inconsiderate and rude to let the other kids down."

"I'm so close to getting my junior lifesaving certificate," Zelda added. "I only need to dive to the bottom of the lake and retrieve a weight, and I'm learning how to sail and water ski. When I'm old enough, I want to come back and be a lifeguard at the waterfront."

"Also, I made you a present in arts & crafts, and Maggie said she wasn't going to fire the kiln until right before Visiting Day," Hazel said.

"And I don't want to miss color war and that's at the very end of camp." Zelda, hands on her hips, glared at me defiantly. "I'm not leaving until the very last day."

We silently stared at each other. My children had made compelling arguments. At least they'd been listening. If I took them out of camp today, I would lose all credibility, and they'd never listen to me again.

I sighed. "Okay, you win. You can stay."

They both looked astonished.

"Really?" Hazel asked.

"I asked you to convince me and you did."

"Thanks, Mom," Zelda said.

"Wait a second, what about you, are you staying?" Hazel asked.

I couldn't walk out of camp and leave my children behind, with Jack in charge. "I'm not sure."

Hazel sat on my lap, gave me a hug, and whispered in my ear, "I love you no matter what you decide."

Zelda shrugged and said, "I hope you don't expect me to put all that stuff away."

It occurred to me while showering that I'd be sitting across the table from Marilyn at dinner. That would be awkward. Attending meals was mandatory, but even if I could skip it, I wouldn't—I was starving. I wasn't about to say anything to her about her husband. I'd wait to see if she brought up our encounter. I doubted she would, but you never knew.

Dinner wasn't appealing—it was always some form of fried chicken and spaghetti—so I ate another boring salad. Marilyn barely looked at me, but to be honest, she rarely did.

That evening's activity was Campfire. Thankfully, it required minimal assistance from me. I just had to make sure that the Cubs showed up wearing straw campfire hats and insect repellant.

The sun hadn't set but you could already see the moon. The Swans stood at the entrance to the campfire, singing a welcoming song and ushering the girls to the benches facing the fire. Quite a few hats sported multicolored feathers that stuck out at odd angles. I took inventory, counting forty-eight Cubs for at least the twentieth time that day. Then I searched out Zelda and Hazel. It was difficult finding them under the straw-brimmed hats.

The Swans began teaching camp songs with hand motions while the rest of us followed along.

Everyone was smiling and singing loudly. Correction: everyone but me. This was my kind of activity, being with your girlfriends, sharing joy and camaraderie through song. I felt cheated that I couldn't get into the spirit.

After the songs, the Swans explained what each feather represented. One by one, each Swan stood and told the group what she had done to earn her colors: taking part in a tournament, scoring a bullseye, being in the play, and numerous other accomplishments.

I noticed only a few hats had an oversized white feather with a bright green tip.

Mindy explained, "Ah, yes, the elusive green tip. It's given to the camper of the week. There are only eight of those given each summer."

"Did you ever get one?"

Mindy laughed. "I was way too naughty."

Marilyn handed the DLs a bag of green feathers to distribute to their bunks.

"You literally get a feather in your cap just for showing up. Which is mandatory." Mindy laughed and took my hat, ripping the rim so it would fray. "So, tell me, what're you thinking?"

"How happy Zelda and Hazel are and wondering if I left them here, would they still be happy?"

"Probably, but I'm sure they have some comfort knowing that you're here."

She rolled the short sleeves of my white polo and turned my collar up in the same camp chic style she wore hers. She put her hands on her hips, appraising me. "*Now* you look like you belong here."

"I wish I felt that way. If it weren't for my kids, I would've left hours ago."

"If it weren't for them, you wouldn't have been here in the first place."

Sitting on a bunk in the middle of the cabin, I was surrounded by mosquito-bitten children.

"Everyone told me they had bug spray on—what happened?" I asked.

"I guess I missed my ankles."

"My daddy says I'm so sweet that the bugs bite me anyway."

"I don't like the smell."

I administered Afterbite to pretty much all the campers and a few counselors.

When I finally got all four cabins into pajamas and lights out, I headed straight to Mindy's room feeling slap happy, my mind going over the day's events. I knew who was behind the door by their shoes: Timberlands, Sperrys, Nikes, and Adidas. I also knew that the two guys weren't there, no Tevas or Converse. Kicking off my Pumas I entered quickly, making sure not to let any pesky bugs in. Mindy sat at her desk, a glass of iced red wine in her hand. Bethany teetered on the edge of the bed sipping a Prosecco. Gilda sat opposite her, rocking in the shabby overstuffed chair, twirling her finger in her ice-filled plastic cup of jungle juice while Abby sat on the Ikea rug nibbling from a bowl of Chex Mix.

"Good evening, ladies," I said as I handed Bethany my bunk reports.

"What took you so long?" she asked.

"Playing nurse to itchy girls takes time. I'm pretty sure some of them pretended to have mosquito bites. I finally get it, they're in need of a mother's attention."

Bethany gave me a knowing smile. "I told you it would start to make sense."

"What can I pour for you?" Mindy asked.

"I got her covered." Gilda was already at the mini fridge pulling out the ice tray and tonic.

"We were talking about your crazy day today. I don't know which part was worse, the bear or our ignoramus of a boss," Mindy said.

"I would definitely say Jack. With a bear you pretty much know where you stand, while Jack's—what's the word I'm looking for—erratic," Gilda said.

"That's the perfect segue to ask all of you why you keep coming back, and why should I stay?" I plopped myself on the floor next to Abby.

"Well, for starters, there's this," Bethany said, waving her arms around the room. "The camaraderie, the sisterhood, the teamwork."

"No offense, but I'm not lacking for friends. I mean, you've been wonderful to me, and I enjoy hanging out with you, especially in the evenings, but that is not enough of a reason for me to stay."

"I love the break from my life. No cooking, no cleaning, no

husband, and if you think about it, you don't even have kids. At least as program director, I don't have one-on-one camper responsibilities," Gilda said.

"The reason I put up with all the bad behavior is that Jack pays me a boatload of money," Mindy said. "The more of an ass he is, the more cash he throws at me to cover his rudeness and the blunders he makes when speaking with a parent."

Bethany placed a friendly hand on my shoulder and said, "I loved camp as a kid, and I love it even more as an adult. I think you should stay. Work through one whole season. Every summer has its highs and lows. I'm sure there's lots of fun in store for you over the next few weeks." She became my boss again when she added, "And after all, you did sign a contract."

"Which he broke this afternoon. I'd have been mortified if my daughters had seen me getting reamed."

"For what it's worth, I admired how well you handled the situation. You didn't back down, you didn't cry. I would've crumbled and gone straight to see Mindy," Bethany said.

"We all heard how trying to go to Mindy didn't work out so well for Lori," Abby said.

I glanced at my watch. "I would've been home in my comfortable air-conditioned apartment by now, if Bethany hadn't thwarted my plans by bringing my kids while I packed."

Bethany shrugged. "There've been plenty of times that I wanted to walk out, but I never considered taking my children because they love it here. So as a working parent at Woodlands with a lot of experience, I thought you should take into consideration that Zelda and Hazel are having a great time. I didn't want them to miss out on the rest of their summer."

Gilda asked, "So why didn't you leave? I mean, we would've understood if you did."

I took a deep breath and, feeling vulnerable, I said, "I don't feel safe here anymore, so how can I leave my children with a *jackass* in charge?"

"Don't you think you're exaggerating? Do you really not feel safe?" Bethany asked.

"I swear to you, Jack was this close to punching me, so no, I don't."

There was a knock at the door. Mindy looked around the room as if she were counting heads. The usual people were already drinking so she asked, "Who's there?"

"It's Marilyn. May I come in? I brought treats."

Everyone looked around, stunned.

Marilyn walked in, carrying a plateful of brownies. "I figured Lori was here, and I wanted to bring her a peace offering from me and Jack. They're hot out of the oven."

My stomach somersaulted from the aroma. I couldn't remember the last time I'd indulged in a brownie. I hadn't eaten much at dinner and was ravenous. That was my constant condition since I got here, hungry and exhausted.

Marilyn bent down to offer me the plate.

I was tempted to take one, but instead I said, "It's going to take a lot more than baked goods to make peace."

"I know, but I thought it would be a good start. I wish I were here to say that everything will be alright and that I can protect you from Jack, but I'm so busy trying to avoid a confrontation myself that I can't help you. I came by to say that I hope you'll stay till the end of the summer."

"We've been trying to convince Lori to stay," Bethany said.

"Will you stay?" Marilyn asked.

"Marilyn, I'm pretty sure you saw Jack verbally abusing me smack in the middle of camp. You watched and let it happen."

Marilyn turned pale. I looked her in the eyes, watching her

squirm, struggling to find words. "Lori, I don't know what to say. You're doing a good job. Today had nothing to do with your capabilities, and yes, I should've done something, but I was . . . I was paralyzed."

She erupted into tears. The rest of us looked at each other, surprised. Bethany stood and awkwardly put her arms around Marilyn, leading her to sit, where she continued crying into Bethany's shoulder. There was another uncomfortable silence. When she finally contained herself, she said, "I'm married to a bully. It's always his way, even if I find a better way. I'm never right. Everything has to be his idea. He gets his way by intimidation, and he can be so nasty. You saw it firsthand this afternoon. The truth? I was afraid to step up and protect you."

I felt a sudden sympathy for her. My relationship with Ronnie might be in trouble, but at least I wasn't afraid of him. And I refused to be intimidated by Jack.

Marilyn changed the subject. "Jack wanted me to ask you if you're planning to shut down the camp."

"What're you talking about?" Gilda asked.

"I threatened to have the camp closed within twenty-four hours because of harassment."

"I wish I had your chutzpah," Bethany said.

"To answer the question, I haven't made any phone calls . . . yet."

"Please don't. I don't know what he'd do if you shut the camp down. I don't know what he's capable of, and I'd hate to see him put to the test," Marilyn said.

I stared at her in disbelief. Jack probably had no idea that Marilyn had come to see me with a peace offering. She was trying to pacify us both.

"I think Jack ought to apologize directly to Lori. It was nice of you to come by with the brownies, but if he has the balls to scream at her, then he should have the balls to apologize," Mindy said.

"That's exactly what I'm thinking," I said.

Marilyn shrugged and without another word, left, looking dejected. Bethany stood. "I'm going to make sure she's okay." She followed Marilyn out the door.

Mindy shrugged as the door closed. "That was enlightening and unexpected." She held up her wine glass. "I think the worst offense of the day was Marilyn interrupting our detox time. Cheers!"

# 16
# Curtains

It was raining when Abby and I left Mindy's room. As we reached the road, a lightning bolt so immense that Zeus himself must have thrown it illuminated our path. Abby's blonde hair stood up on end, and we jumped into each other's arms. The sky was mesmerizing; staring up, we watched the light fade against the clouds. Then a Thor-sized clap of thunder made us run. This wasn't how I'd pictured spending my summer: chased by a bear, screamed at by my boss, and almost getting electrocuted. The raindrops started bouncing around our feet as we ran to our porch with our knapsacks over our heads.

Everything was soaked. I kicked off my sneakers and left them in the hallway. "G'night!" I called to Abby. I undressed and threw my clothes into the laundry bag. I sat on my bed rehashing my day and realized that even though part of me was ready to drive out, I couldn't. Not just because of the girls; I wouldn't give Ronnie the satisfaction of being right. When I told him I was working at the camp, he'd been quick to criticize me. *"Come on, Lori, you know just as well as I do that you wouldn't last a day in the middle of the woods—no air-conditioning, but plenty of mosquitoes, spiders, and snakes."*

Today I'd taken on a bear—well, sort of. And I stood up to my boss.

My cigarette pack had fallen on the floor. I stared at it. I should've done the smart thing and gone straight to sleep. Weakness won, and my resolve was broken.

I went to the closet and pulled Teddy's lighter from the pocket of my rain slicker. There was no smoking allowed at camp and specifically not in the wood buildings, but at that moment, I didn't care. I turned off the light, pulled the blinds, and closed the curtains. I lit a cigarette, took a long drag, and proceeded to cough uncontrollably through my tears as I watched the tip turn to ash.

I opened the window to flick the ashes outside. A gust of wind blew in, ruffling the frilly curtains, and my cigarette touched the hem, which immediately started to burn. I had to douse the fire and do it fast. I jumped on my bed, unhooked the curtain rod, and pushed it out the window. I felt resistance. I gave it a hard shove, and the screen fell out, followed by the rod and the smoldering curtain. Thank goodness for the rain beating on the roof, hiding the commotion I was making. The fire quickly fizzled, but it smelled like a burning tire had run over rotten eggs.

I sprayed Febreze Meadows of Rain, not missing the irony. That was a close call—I could've burned the entire cottage down. I felt sick to my stomach thinking what might've happened if the fire had spread. I was ready to climb into bed when it struck me that the screen, burnt curtain, and the rod were sitting on the ground outside of my room. I needed to remove the evidence; otherwise, I'd have to make up a lie about why all the debris was on the wet ground outside my window. I rushed out the door trying not to make a sound and picked up the screen and rod and what remained of my singed drapes. While the hardware seemed undamaged, the drapes that were once sheer, white, and frilly, were now wet, muddied, and charred. I took the tattered, bedraggled mess inside to hide it until I could figure out what to do. I wrapped it in a beach towel and shoved it under my bed.

I turned on the lamp, sat on the bed, and waited for my heart to stop racing. This was exactly the way I'd felt in high school, trying to sneak stuff past my parents, but they always found out. It occurred to me that smoking had gotten me in trouble both at the beginning and end of this nightmare of a day. I threw myself back on my bed with my hands covering my face in shame and disgust.

In the morning, I saw that my tiny room was in shambles. Wet leaves and mud were caked on the carpet, my clothes were covered in crud, and my hands and face were dirty. I threw the clothes I'd slept in on the floor to cover the mess; I'd deal with that later. I needed to shower before I walked the bunks to wake the campers.

Feeling lucky I hadn't caused too much damage, I made a promise that I'd never again smoke in my room. But I still had to figure out how to dispose of the evidence.

The day was clear and sunny with no humidity—a relief after yesterday's rain. I was walking with my group to the tennis courts when I saw Lars, the laundry guy, driving by in his pickup truck.

"Hi, Lars," I called, waving him down. "Sorry to bother you, but I have some personal laundry that needs to be done. Would it be possible for you to squeeze my stuff in before the end of the day?"

Lars was from Poland and somehow managed to take time off from his civilian job to work at Woodlands every summer, always accompanied by gorgeous, svelte, leggy women eager for an adventure in America. Along for the ride, they spent the summer cleaning up after the privileged scions of the middle class so they could then spend another three months traveling across the country. Lars, an affable guy, was popular with the senior staff ladies. For a modest tip, he serviced our personal needs.

"For you, Lori, anything. Hop in and I'll drive you to your cabin."

As he drove, Jack's voice interrupted our conversation. "Lars, come in for Jack."

"Lars here." His smile disappeared.

"You are needed immediately at boys' field hockey. Did you hear me? ASAP!"

Lars looked annoyed. "Got it, on my way."

"It's reassuring to know that he treats all of us equally," I said.

"My English is not perfect but is reassuring the correct word?"

We both snickered.

I quickly threw my laundry together not wanting Lars to get yelled at for tardiness. I ran out, tossing the bag into the back of the pickup truck, and waved him off.

Crossing the road and heading to the tennis courts, I was relieved that I'd taken care of one mess.

# 17

# Whistle Blower

The Cubs had arts & crafts. One of the projects was tiling trivets. Last night, I could've used one of the tiled ashtrays I made when I was a camper.

After walking the rooms, making sure the Cubs were engaged, I sat with Maggie and was soon elbow-deep in beads, rummaging for the perfect color to add to the necklace I was stringing.

"You know what the Swans call those bracelets they all wear?" Maggie asked.

"No, what?"

"Camp bling."

"I love that."

"As the Aussies say, it's brilliant," Maggie said.

Anya joined us. "Lori, you're just the person I'm looking for. Can you come outside with me?"

I looked into Anya's big light-blue eyes. "What's up?"

"Mike has a surprise for you."

I wondered what it could be. I followed her to where Mike was leaning against a tree. He had a playful glint in his eyes. He pulled a small square box out of the front pocket of his tight jeans and handed it to me. "Open it."

I looked at Anya and she nodded and winked at me, exactly like Mike. Who knew a wink could be contagious?

I smiled as I pulled out a silver whistle attached to a green and white diamond-stitched lanyard.

"I want you to wear this at all times in case I'm not available. If you, I mean *when* you, need to be rescued again." Mike smiled.

I was touched by his thoughtfulness. Mike was being chivalrous and playful, and he had literally saved my ass yesterday. "Thank you for rescuing me and for this whistle. May I give you a *bear hug*?"

Instead of a hug, Mike became military on me; he saluted and said, "Yes ma'am, happy to help." Then marched off.

"See, he's really a good guy," Anya said.

"Thanks." The whistle was already around my neck. "I'm sure it was your idea."

"No, it was Mike's. He bought it after relocating the bear clan in the woods. Although, I did make the lanyard."

"I can't believe you actually met up with a bear," Teddy said later that night.

"I was on my morning walk when I decided I wanted a cigarette. I was digging up the pack you hid down by the lake when I saw it."

"You mean it was my fault you almost got mauled?"

I took a drag and smiled. "I'm just saying."

"I feel awful. I wish I'd been the one to save you."

He looked so sincere that I had to smile. "Thank you, I appreciate that. It was a good thing Mike showed up when he did."

Teddy pointed to the whistle hanging around my neck. "Where'd you get that?"

"Mike gave it to me."

"Why?"

"So I can use it if I ever come face to face with a bear and he's not around to save me."

"I didn't know you and Mike were such good chums."

"I wouldn't say that, but I'm at the waterfront at least twice a day."

Teddy took a drag. "Has he come on to you?"

"Yes. Pretty much every time I see him, he says something lecherous to me, and as far as I know, to every other woman that crosses his path. But we all have his number—as a matter of fact, we refer to him as Salacious Mike."

He snorted. "But you accepted a gift from him."

I tugged at the lanyard. "Yes, I thought he was being gracious and funny. You wear a whistle for work, and now I'll wear one too."

He looked at me for a moment and blew a smoke ring.

"It almost sounds like you're jealous that Mike saved me from the bear?" I smiled at him.

"As I said, I wish I'd been the one to rescue you. Mike and I will never see eye to eye, but if you want to hang out with him, I'd understand."

"If I wanted to hang out with Mike, I'd be hard pressed to find time to do it. Plus, he thinks he's God's gift to women. As if. Anyway, I prefer your company."

He didn't say anything.

"Are we good?" I asked.

"I suppose."

18

# The Boy Scout Handbook

"Hey, Lori, I heard we have the same day off. Do you want to go on a road trip with me?" Gilda asked.

I had been wondering what I'd do on my day off since I certainly didn't want to go home. "That sounds great."

We decided to skip the camp breakfast and be decadent, eating all three meals in restaurants with clean utensils and table service. The idea of no buffet line made me giddy.

The town diner was retro with red and white checkered tablecloths, silver swivel stools with red vinyl covers, and glass domed plates filled with doughnuts and pies along the counter. We sat down and hot coffee magically appeared, poured into big clean white mugs by a woman wearing a crisp white apron, a teased bleached-blonde bouffant, and a big friendly smile. "I'll give you gals a minute."

I inspected the spoon before using it to swirl the cream in my coffee.

"What're you doing?" Gilda asked.

"The cleanliness of the utensils in the dining hall are sketchy. I wipe them down before I eat because I'm convinced I'm going to get lockjaw."

She smiled. "I know for a fact that your tetanus shot is up to date so you're safe."

"How do you know that?"

"One of my many jobs is making sure all senior staff medicals are filled out and filed."

Sipping the piping hot coffee, I sighed. It wasn't made from dirty water, but it was freshly brewed and delicious. My stomach grumbled while reading the two-column list of items I could add to my eggs—feta cheese, spinach, and tomatoes with a side of crispy bacon. It was heavenly sitting in that kitschy diner before I even took a bite.

As we ate, Gilda showed me an itinerary she got from a TV show about hidden gems in New England. I loved walking through quaint towns, so I was game. We mapped out our trip as we ate. Gilda suggested dinner at the fancy restaurant directly across the street where I'd sat waiting for Ronnie while nursing a drink. At least now I'd get to try the food.

As we paid the check, I noticed the sheer, frilly curtains on the windows. They looked like the ones in my room. Maybe I'd find some at a yard sale during our adventures.

Gilda's itinerary included an antique toy store and a small shop known for its Madagascar vanilla beans. We walked around a bit and then drove to a bakery owned and operated by ex-convicts. We bought onion and olive rolls, sharing them for lunch.

We leisurely drove to the next destination where we cruised the local shops before stopping for homemade ice cream. Without my usual hesitation, I ordered a double-scoop cone with cherry vanilla and triple chocolate—I deserved a treat. The daily fruit, yogurt, and salads always left me wanting, and I refused to eat the greasy, carb-heavy dinners.

I licked the cone. "This is completely decadent."

"I'm so happy you joined me. I've been wanting to do this drive forever."

We sat on a bench under a tree enjoying our treats. Gilda dug into an ice cream sundae that had a mound of whipped cream and a maraschino cherry on top.

When we were done, we crossed the street to a store called Secondhand Rose that had a big red flower painted on the window.

There were racks of clothes, shelves filled with knick-knacks, dishes, and tchotchkes of all shapes and sizes. Gilda was picking through books, and next to her I saw a copy of *We're Going on a Bear Hunt*. It was one of my kids' favorites.

I wandered off to a back room that was set up like the kitchen in the bungalow colony. A faux green marble-top table with chrome edging stood in the middle of the linoleum floor surrounded by matching chairs. The windows were covered in a white cotton eyelet.

I asked the shopkeeper, "Do you have any other curtains?"

"In that box over there, in the corner."

I rummaged through the pile, sneezing from the dust mites and musty smell, but I kept going—I was on a mission. I found something that came close. They were sheer and frilly but had embroidered yellow daisies on the trim.

They were five dollars, so I decided to buy them, despite the daisies. I was walking to the front to pay when another book caught my eye, *The Boy Scout Handbook.* I randomly thumbed the book open and found myself looking at a chapter on how to build a campfire.

"I think I'm going to buy this," I said.

"Why?" Gilda asked.

"The last time I tried to build a fire was at a condo we rented last winter in Vermont. I didn't know that you had to open the flue. Hell, I didn't even know what a flue was, so I ended up setting off fire alarms as the entire apartment filled with smoke."

"Where was your husband?"

"Out skiing with the girls. When they got back, they made me feel like I was completely useless. It was not one of my finest moments."

"Yeah, I hate when my family gangs up on me. I always remind my girls that I wiped their asses, and they need to treat me with a little more respect."

Thinking about lack of respect, my mind drifted to the earlier part of the smoke-filled condo day. Ronnie, Zelda, and Hazel had been getting ready to ski. I hadn't meant to eavesdrop. I wanted to tell them that I loved them and to have a great day, but instead I overheard a conversation. I held my breath as I listened.

"Why doesn't Mom ski with us anymore?" Hazel asked.

"I used to carry her skis, and then when you two came along she had to carry them herself," Ronnie said.

"But we carry our own stuff," Zelda said.

"True, but it took a few years before that happened."

"We always had to wait for her at the bottom of the hill," Hazel said.

"When you two became better skiers than Mom, she gave up for good."

"We get in so many more runs now," Zelda said.

"But there's no hot chocolate breaks without Mom," Hazel said.

"You can have hot chocolate at lunch. We're here to ski. Besides, it's more fun skiing with just Dad anyway," Zelda said.

"Won't Mom be bored by herself all day?" Hazel asked.

"Nah, you know how she always complains that she never has time for herself," Zelda said.

"But isn't she alone all day when we're at school?" Hazel asked.

"Your mom manages to keep herself busy—she does yoga, meets friends for lunch, orders in dinner . . ."

Ronnie had made me sound as if I did nothing. But the worst part was that he allowed the girls to giggle at my expense.

Whenever Ronnie disappointed us by not showing up for dinner or recitals or sporting events, I had made a point of not saying anything derogatory about him.

I could see Ronnie on his knee, buckling his boots. He stood up and said, "If you're ready, I'll race you to the lift."

I clearly remembered now that when I finally exhaled, it had come out as a sob. "I'm okay with good-natured, clever teasing," I said, turning to Gilda, "but it hurts when I overhear my daughters making fun of me, and my husband not only doesn't stick up for me, he eggs them on."

Gilda had entertained me with camp stories all day. My favorite one was when the Swans snatched the sneakers off the porches of the younger girls and swapped them with the older girls' shoes. Gilda went on, "It caused mass confusion, but I thought it was so simple yet ingenious. When Marilyn got wind of it, she ranted on about calling parents and punishing the girls. Mindy finally got her to calm down and had to explain to her that pranks are what camp is all about."

As we were seated in the dining room of the restaurant, I thought when it was first decorated, it would've been considered classy. Now it just reminded me of an aging lady in need of a facelift.

"I had a great time today, I haven't laughed so much since I got to camp," Gilda said, holding up her wine glass. "Cheers."

I had been able to let go and relax on our excursion. No campers, no bosses, no wild animals, and no husband. We'd both spent the day giggling—from trying on silly hats at the secondhand store to sharing stories about our daughters to commiserating about our husbands—both attorneys.

We clinked glasses. "You're fabulous company," I said.

"You're much more fun than those alpha chicks, Bethany and Mindy," Gilda said.

Gilda wasn't wrong in her description of them. They were the women I looked to for advice and I wanted to impress during the day and make laugh in the evenings. I said, "Mindy's always helpful, insightful, and even-tempered, which I appreciate. Bethany says she has my back, but I'm never exactly sure where I stand with her."

"What do you mean?"

"When I'm at activities with the campers, it seems like she goes out of her way to find something to criticize me about." I took a sip of wine.

"Give me an example."

"Yesterday one of the Cubs was sitting under a tree reading a book during volleyball. Bethany marches toward me and starts scolding me for not forcing her to play. Meanwhile I had a long conversation with the mother during orientation that volleyball is the one sport she can't play because her finger is still healing from a volleyball injury."

"She's learned that technique from Jack. Always approach a situation ready to criticize instead of assuming you have your reasons and giving you a chance to explain."

"We're all adults here. We all have children. Give us some credit for common sense. But after the kids are tucked in and we meet up in Mindy's cabin, it's like we've been the best of pals since the beginning of time."

"You know, if we were in high school, they'd be the mean girls. But since we're all adults here, and it's camp, we have to get along—kumbaya and all that."

"I enjoy relaxing with a gin & tonic. It's a great way to unwind and laugh about how ridiculous our days are, but the best part is when we tear into Jack. It makes me feel like I'm not alone, you know—he's a schmuck to everyone, not just me," I said.

"Yup, he's an equal opportunity schmuck."

# 19

# Ninety-Nine Bottles of Beer on the Wall

The two aspirins I popped before I went to sleep didn't help the next morning. My head throbbed as I wobbled down the hall to the bathroom, only to discover that I had my period. Ugh! It was trip day, and I would spend it at a water park with menstrual cramps when all I wanted was to crawl back in my bed and lie there in the fetal position for the next twenty-four hours, blinds drawn, oscillating fan on full blast. Instead, I'd be in a damp bathing suit, trying not to heave while taking care of other people's children.

I heard a light tap on the door.

"Come in, I'm up."

"You're not dressed yet. Wait, you don't look so good," Abby said.

"I just got my period, and I'm moving kind of slow. Give me a couple of minutes."

"That's bad timing. I'll go hang out with Maggie until you're ready. We can skip our morning walk. We'll do plenty of walking around the amusement park," Abby said.

"Wow, Abs wasn't exaggerating—you do look like crap," Maggie said as I walked into arts & crafts.

"All I can say is, I'm not a happy camper. Do you think I can call in sick today?"

They both stared at me and then cracked up.

Maggie mimed a phone. "I'm sorry Mrs. Schapiro, we lost your daughter at the water park. Yes, her DL wasn't feeling so well today, so there was no one covering her . . . I knew you'd understand."

"I should've asked how many sick days we get before I signed my contract. Maybe I can snooze on the bus. I think it's a two-hour drive."

"As if," Abby said.

"What do you mean?" I asked.

"Don't you remember being on bus rides as a kid, all the screaming and singing and giggling?"

"You know, 'Ninety-Nine Bottles of Beer on the Wall,'" Maggie said.

I put my aching head in my hands and rubbed my temples. "It's going to be a rough day."

"Do you need a Midol?" Abby asked.

"I already took, waiting for them to kick in."

The three of us left the studio together and saw Mike, in tight denim shorts, waving flags semaphore-style as a convoy of yellow school buses arrived to take the campers to the amusement park.

"Hey, Mike, seriously, is there anything here that you don't do?" Maggie yelled to him from across the road.

"I haven't done any of you lovely ladies." He winked at us.

"And you never will," Abby yelled back. "Lori, you're right, lascivious is the perfect word to describe him."

"I said salacious, but lascivious works just as well."

I sat down in the back of the bus with forty-eight excited campers and twelve happy counselors. We hadn't yet left the camp property when the singing began—nonstop, continuous, repetitive singing. Thank goodness I had taken those Midols.

"Hey, Lori," the girls sang in unison.

I had to reply because eight-year-olds are relentless. "Someone calling my name?"

"Hey, Lori."

"Wait, I hear it again."

"You're wanted on the telephone."

"Well, if it isn't Sarah, I'm not home."

I chose Sarah because she was having trouble making connections with the other girls. She seemed delighted.

While the singing continued, I sat with my shins up against the seat in front of me and my head resting on my knees.

The DLs and the nurse parked themselves by the splash pools, so we were easily found in case of an emergency. I must've dozed off on the chaise lounge facing the wave pool because a familiar voice calling, "Mom," startled me awake.

Zelda was standing in front of me wearing a bikini that accentuated her slim hips, long torso, and stretched-out pony legs with knobby kneecaps. Her extremities were growing faster than the rest of her. Zelda's skin was so pale that you could see every vein in her prominent rib cage.

"What's up?" I asked.

"I need you. Can you come with me?" She was paler than usual.

I looked to Bethany who gave me a nod. "Of course."

Zelda's camp BFF, Tara, and their counselor, Rosie, were with her. "We're going to go on the Lazy River while we wait for Zelda. Can we leave our stuff here?"

"Of course." I turned to Zelda. "Do you need to see the nurse?"

"No, I need you in the bathroom."

My fierce, independent daughter looked so needy and fragile. I grabbed my knapsack and Zelda allowed me to take her hand, making me think she really must not be feeling well.

We slipped into a stall together. Zelda had dropped her bikini bottoms to the floor and was sitting on the toilet whimpering. I saw the red stain that clashed with the orange polka dots on her suit. *Oh.* I knelt in front of her, took her face into my hands, kissed her on her forehead and said, "Congratulations."

"I can't believe this is happening when we're at a water park."

"Well, you're in luck because I also got my period today and I'm fully equipped to help you."

"Do I have to wear a tampon?" she asked.

"Only if you want to go swimming. It's up to you."

"Will it hurt?"

"It mostly feels uncomfortable the first few times, and then you forget you're wearing one. Let me show you how to use it."

"I think I know how. Allie explained it to me at her pajama party."

"Would you like my help?"

"Eww, no."

I picked up her bikini bottom and washed it in the sink while my baby took her first step into the sisterhood.

"How're you doing in there?" I bent down, handing her the rinsed bathing suit bottom under the door.

"Mom, go away."

Even though Zelda shooed me, I was grateful she'd found me and that I hadn't missed this moment. When I was twelve, I'd been the first to get my period, so I couldn't rely on my friends. I had a vivid memory of my mother, who'd never used a tampon, trying unsuccessfully to teach me; it made me wince, then smile.

A few minutes later Zelda walked out of the stall, and I hugged her before she pushed me away.

"Let's go find Tara."

By the time I got back to the lounge chair, it was surrounded by heaps of green Woodlands knapsacks. My foot got caught in a strap, and I fell onto a seat.

"How's Zelda feeling?" Abby asked.

"She got her first period today," I said.

Abby laughed. "Like mother, like daughter. How old were you when you got yours?"

"Just about the same age as Zelda."

"It's a rite of passage, getting your period at sleepaway camp. Zelda was lucky that you were here with her," Bethany said.

I felt tears well up and tried to hold them back but couldn't.

"What's wrong?" Abby asked.

I couldn't catch my breath. I tugged at the Hello Kitty towel I was sitting on to wipe my face, but the tears were unrelenting. "I have no one to call."

"What does that mean?" Bethany asked.

"Oh, I know. You can't call your mother," Abby said.

I nodded. "My mother left me sitting on the toilet moaning to call my grandmother. There's no one for me to call."

"I didn't even tell my mother—my sister helped me," Bethany said. "I remember one day about a year later my mother told me she was taking me to the doctor because I hadn't gotten my period yet. She was so angry when I told her I had."

"It was like a coming out party in my house," Abby said. "My grandmother, mother, aunt, and sister were all there. My aunt went and bought a cake from Carvel to celebrate. Because, you know, nothing says 'welcome to monthly cramps' like Fudgie the Whale."

I smiled, listening to their anecdotes as the tears continued streaming down my face.

"Why do you think it's hitting you so hard?" Abby asked.

I took a deep breath. "Zelda getting her period made me realize how much I miss my mother. Today was the first time in ages that I wanted her, and well, the reality of not being able to share this moment . . ."

"I understand. I'd give anything to share a bran muffin and a cup of coffee with my mom so I could catch her up on my life," Abby said.

"You guys are making me miss mine, even though we argued all the time. It'd be wonderful to hear her hollering at me once more," Bethany said.

"I'm sorry. I don't want to bring you all down with me. I feel like I'm crying more now than when my mom died." I wiped my eyes with the back of my hand. "When she was diagnosed with lung cancer, I was pregnant with Hazel, and Zelda was only two. Hazel was born less than a month after Mom died. I was juggling so much, I guess I didn't have the time to properly grieve, and now look at me."

"Go figure, all of us lost our mothers when we were young. Do you think that's why we followed our kids to camp?" Abby asked as she leaned over and hugged me.

The four of us sat together on cheap plastic lounge chairs, surrounded by knapsacks, on a sweltering Monday afternoon in July, at a waterpark, as sisters.

Abby and I waited outside the dining pavilion. Sitting in the hot sun the entire day was both relaxing and exhausting, and I still wasn't feeling well. We'd decided to hold onto the meal tickets instead of handing them out to the counselors. If they lost the tickets, there'd be no dinner for them at the park *or* at camp.

Slowly, all of Woodlands made their way to the pavilion in various stages of disarray. Some were sopping wet from the splashdown ride, others carried seedy-looking stuffed animals. Hair was flat against heads, and everyone dragged their feet.

Hazel approached, smiling and walking arm in arm with her camp BFF, Jenna.

"How was your day?" I asked.

"Great, we went on every roller coaster twice!" She grinned from ear to ear.

"What made your mouth blue?"

Hazel stuck her tongue out. "Dippin' Dots."

I counted off each meal ticket as my groups slowly trickled in. Jasmine, my least reliable counselor, showed up with three campers.

"Who are you missing?" I asked.

"What do you mean?"

"You had four campers at the start of the day." When she looked at me blankly, my voice became shrill. "Who are you missing?"

Alexis, one of the campers, said, "I haven't seen Kaylee since we went on the Loop-de-Loop."

"Jasmine, where's Kaylee?" I tried not to sound panicked.

"I don't know." She didn't seem concerned at all.

"What do you mean, you don't know? You've lost Kaylee? You had four girls with you at the start of the day, and you didn't notice that one was missing?" I tried to keep my voice level as my stomach twisted.

"She's probably with her brother." Jasmine shrugged as if it was no big deal.

"Right, she has a twin brother." I asked Abby, "Who's the DL for the eight-year-old boys?"

She flipped through her paperwork. "That would be Jeremy."

I unclipped the radio from my shorts pocket. "Jeremy, come in for Lori. Jeremy, please come in for Lori."

"Hey, Lori, Jeremy here."

"Do you know where Kyle Bloom's group is?"

"Yep, I'm walking with them to dinner right now."

"Is Kaylee with them?"

"She sure is."

"Thank you." I turned to Jasmine. "You and I will have a conversation later when we're back at camp."

"It's no big deal. She was with her brother."

I took a deep breath to calm myself. I was about to tell Jasmine to stand off to the side and wait for Kaylee, when I saw her walking up the hill, happily chatting with Kyle. I wasn't angry with Kaylee; after all, she was only missing her twin. But I wished I had the authority to fire Jasmine on the spot. What I could do was add her name to the Do Not Resuscitate list so she wouldn't be asked back.

Zelda tapped me on the shoulder as I counted out five tickets for Genie and her campers.

"Mom, can you come with me to the bathroom?"

"Sure, give me a sec." I handed the rest of the tickets to Abby, asking her to cover for me. "How're you feeling? Did you have a fun day?"

"Okay. You told me I had to change the tampon every three hours."

Walking with Zelda to the bathroom reminded me to put my grievances in perspective. No one was hurt. Everyone was where they were supposed to be, and I was grateful to be with my daughter on the day she got her period.

I'd deal with Jasmine back at camp.

When the buses pulled up in front of the gate leading to Girls Camp, I was relieved to be back home. Home. I was surprised that after only a few short weeks, I considered Woodlands home.

The cramps had subsided, but there was still a dull ache in my head that wasn't helped by the endless singing and chatting on the bus. I couldn't wait to take a hot shower and crawl into bed.

Marilyn was there greeting everyone asking, "Did you have fun?"

I counted heads for the umpteenth time that day as the girls tumbled off the bus. It reminded me of arrival day, watching a stream of girls descend the stairs. I was proud of how far I'd come and confident that I knew what I was doing.

I pulled Jasmine aside before she walked up the steps to her cabin.

"You had one job to do today, take care of four campers, and you managed to screw it up. I wouldn't be as angry as I am right now if you at least owned up to it, but the fact is that you were unconcerned about a missing child."

She blankly stared back at me.

"Do you have anything to say for yourself?" I couldn't believe how much I sounded like my father, or worse, Jack.

"You're overreacting. Everything turned out fine."

"I just gave you an opportunity to take responsibility, and you didn't. I have no choice but to write you up."

She crossed her arms. "What do you think Bethany and Marilyn will say when they find out one of *your* campers was lost?"

She was calling my bluff—I'd underestimated her.

I stared directly into her eyes and abruptly turned away, nearly bumping into Marilyn, who said, "Lori, can you meet me in the lounge after you tuck in your bunks?"

Was I in trouble? Had Marilyn overheard my conversation with Jasmine? "Sure." I caught up with Bethany. "Marilyn asked me to meet her later in the lounge. Do you know why?"

"Huh, me too. I wonder what that's about."

"I was afraid that maybe I did something wrong," I said.

"Are you kidding? You've been busting your ass ever since you got here. We all have," Bethany said.

I paused for a second. "Thanks."

Marilyn and Jack stood at the back of the staff lounge facing the group with big smiles on their faces. It looked like all the DLs from both Boys and Girls Camp were already there as well as Bob, Teddy, Mindy, and Gilda—the senior staff.

When Abby and I walked in together, Jack said, "Our outstanding lower camp DLs have arrived. What can I get you ladies to drink? We have sodas, iced tea, and juices."

I whispered into Abby's ear, "We're outstanding while everyone else is inside sitting."

"Come on in, we have plenty of food for you," Marilyn said.

I stood next to Mindy and said softly, "I don't want a stinking 7UP. What I need is a gin & tonic."

"Once the Bergers leave," she said under her breath.

Laid out on the kitchen counter were several pizzas and an assortment of sushi. I was a bit of a sushi snob. In my real life I'd never consider eating a tuna roll from Costco, but right then it looked extremely appetizing.

Once everyone had food and drinks in their hands, Jack stood in the middle of the room and said, "I want to thank everyone for their hard work these past couple of weeks. I know I don't always say the right things."

There were some snickers coming from the crowd. Mindy whispered in my ear, "You think?"

It was difficult keeping a straight face.

"I admit I have trouble expressing myself, but Marilyn and I want you to know how much we appreciate you keeping the campers safe and happy."

Those were the first kind words I'd heard from Jack since I'd gotten to camp. I whispered in Mindy's ear, "Did you tell them to act civilized?"

She mimed zipping her lips.

Jack and Marilyn walked through the room, personally thanking everyone.

"Lori, we think you're doing a fantastic job. My instincts were right on target when we met. You're a great addition to Woodlands," Jack pumped my hand as he spoke.

I wanted to point out how disrespectful he had been the other day, but frankly, sometimes it was smarter to keep my mouth shut. "I appreciate the compliment." I held up my plate. "And the sushi."

When the Bergers left, Bob stood by the window watching them walk to their house. "They've closed the cottage door. We can relax."

There was a collective exhalation and nervous giggles. The atmosphere in the room instantly felt lighter, the chatter grew louder, and people began laughing.

Teddy strode toward the door.

"Where're you going?" I asked.

"I'll be back in a jiffy."

Bethany and Mindy were right behind him.

Teddy returned, balancing a case of Heineken on his shoulder. He stopped at my side and whispered, "Meet me tonight?"

"I'm not feeling well. Can we meet tomorrow?"

I was surprised by how disappointed he looked. "Sorry you're ill. Is there something I can do?"

"Nothing a good night's sleep won't cure."

"Tomorrow it is."

Bethany carried a shopping bag full of jungle juice and gin. Within minutes everyone had a beer or cocktail in hand.

Abby whispered, "I've had enough fun for one day. I'm going to bed."

"Okay, I'm going to have one drink and call it a night."

I joined Teddy and Bob.

"How are things going for you guys?" I asked.

"I don't know about Bob, but trip day always leaves me knackered. It's nice to be here with everybody knocking down a few beers," Teddy said.

"Trip day being over is huge. We successfully made it past the first big milestone of the season," Bob said.

"I don't understand," I said.

"A third of camp is over."

I laughed.

"What's so funny?" he asked.

"I thought only my homesick campers counted down the days, and it turns out the head of Boys Camp, a self-proclaimed lifelong camper, is doing the same thing."

"It's not about drawing an X on the calendar. For me, it puts into perspective how much time I have left to achieve the goals I've set for myself this summer," Bob said.

"If you don't mind me asking, what're your goals?"

"There are the corny ones, you know, like personal growth. But the others are all camper related. Mostly I want to encourage campers to come back to work when they're eighteen."

"Self-actualization—that's a very evolved ambition for a grown man who wears shorts and Tevas for a living," I said.

Bob's eyebrows arched. "I give you an honest answer and you mock me."

"Actually, I'm really impressed. You're making me feel a bit shallow. I have only one goal, and that's to make it out of here alive," I said.

"Aren't you being a bit melodramatic? I've been here for two decades and Bob for over ten years, and we've never come close to any life-or-death experiences," Teddy said.

"Well, I've been here for a little over three weeks, and I've already come face-to-face with a bear and an irate camp director, so you gentlemen are not reassuring me," I said.

"Touché," Teddy said.

Mindy joined us and handed me another cocktail. I was buzzed, and for the first time all day, I felt no pain.

"I'm so jealous that you had the entire day to yourself. What did you end up doing?" I asked her.

"Forget about my day—I heard Zelda got her period today. Mazel Tov!"

Teddy and Bob backed away from our conversation.

I felt the tears welling up in my eyes once again. "I know it's silly, but I can't seem to stop crying."

"For what it's worth, I think that's a natural reaction. The end of your daughter's childhood and all of that. I think it's really sweet."

"Thanks, I appreciate that. I'm going to head out before I become a blubbering mess again."

In bed I took a deep breath and felt a little bit better, acknowledging and understanding why I cried so much, mourning the loss of the two women whom I had loved most in the world, my mother and my grandmother. I hoped that this would be a transforming summer for my daughters, molding them into the strong, smart, resourceful women they were named for. I thought my mother and grandmother would be pleased to know that they were my role models.

# 20

# Reading by Flashlight

I saw Mindy getting ready for our afternoon kayaking. She was zipping up a life vest when Mike, under the pretense of assisting her, trapped her against a tree. I called out to him the way you would to distract a dog.

"Hey, Mike, over here, you're just the person I was looking for."

He spun around and gave me a lewd smile.

"What did you have in mind?" His arms were akimbo—his Speedo was camouflage—making sure I got a full-frontal view of his *charms.*

I obviously hadn't thought this through. Mike would probably misinterpret the gift I bought him and double down on his flirtations. I hesitated for a moment but decided to give it to him anyway. "I brought you a present."

I handed him the bag.

"Such a tiny bag. Lori, did you buy me a Speedo?" He winked.

I didn't want to laugh, but I couldn't help myself. "No, seems you have an endless supply. This is something I'm pretty sure you don't have."

He pulled out *We're Going on a Bear Hunt.*

"I was scared but you weren't, and I will always be grateful for that."

It took a second, but then he smiled, an honest, sincere smile. "Thank you. It's nice to be appreciated."

The moment was awkward, but before I could back away, he pulled me in for a bear hug, which under the circumstances seemed appropriate.

Teddy bent to light my cigarette with the precision of an athlete.

"I hope you're feeling better," he said.

I had a split-second debate in my head and said, "Yeah, I had horrible cramps and a headache for most of trip day."

I watched Teddy's face to see if he understood. "Oh, yes, your menses."

I laughed. "Yes, my menses. My father used to ask me if I was 'unwell.' I told him I was perfectly well, but I had my period, although yesterday I was indeed unwell."

Teddy blew three perfect smoke rings toward the twinkling stars. "I'm happy you're feeling better. I missed your company last night."

I took a drag and smiled at him. He held my gaze.

"Lori, I'm not very good at making friends. You know, not just a sports buddy. Someone I can talk to about things, real things. I consider you a friend."

His vulnerability pierced my heart. The night was clear, and the moon was shining on his face. How'd I miss those striking green eyes? He was so easy to talk to, and I trusted him. "Yes, I also consider you a friend."

He continued, "Maybe we can meet more often. I like telling you about my day and was disappointed I wouldn't hear about yours. I was hoping you felt the same way."

In a short time, Teddy had become more than a work colleague; he was my confidant. He always gave helpful advice, and

I enjoyed his company. Plus, his voice and his accent were music to my ears. "Yes, I'd like that."

I was having trouble falling asleep, so I opened *The Boy Scout Handbook* and started to read by flashlight. I even pulled the covers over my head for authenticity. For my own personal satisfaction, I learned in detail how to build a fire in the wilderness where there were no flues to be found.

The next day started with choice period, which meant that the campers were scattered throughout the campus. I spent as much time as I could at the *Grease* rehearsal because Hazel was cast as Frenchie, the beauty school dropout.

The campers seemed oblivious to the fact that they were performing in a sauna, their hair matted down, T-shirts sticking to their backs. Despite it all they were smiling and singing their hearts out. I, on the other hand, was sweltering by the back door, hoping for a breeze. Sliding over the wooden bench to move closer to an open window, I felt a sharp pain in my leg.

"Ouch!"

A piece of wood lodged in the back of my thigh.

Maggie was across the field outside of arts & crafts demonstrating how to twist embroidery floss into friendship bracelets. Limping over, I showed her the injury.

"I could probably get that out for you, but it would be smarter if you went to the infirmary so they can pull it with sterile tweezers and bandage you up with Bacitracin," Maggie said.

"Do you really think that's necessary?"

"As the self-appointed guardian for you this summer, absolutely."

I hugged her. "Thanks, Mom. While I'm there, maybe I can score us ice pops."

"You know they only hand out ices to patients if they don't cry," Maggie said.

"I will do my best to be stoic."

"In that case get me cherry."

As I passed the theater, the ensemble was attempting, "We Go Together." Humming along, I limped my way to the infirmary, swatting away the ever-present gnats and *schvitz*-ing with the effort. It had to be over a hundred degrees in the shade.

"Hi, Lori, what brings you here?" Nurse Ella asked.

"There's a piece of the theater embedded in my leg." I turned around, showing her my right thigh.

"Sit down, take a load off. I'll get the tweezers."

My shirt was drenched under the knapsack. I slipped it off my shoulders and untied the bandana I kept on the bag. "Can I get some ice from your freezer?" I placed one cube in the kerchief and tied it around my neck; another cube nestled in my cleavage, kept in place by my sports bra.

"That's a brilliant idea, sticking an ice cube down your shirt. I'll have to recommend that to the counselors," Ella said. "But what will we suggest to the guys, stick it in their jockstrap? Which reminds me . . ." She knocked on the bathroom door. "Is everything okay in there?"

We heard a muffled grunt and then, "Yeah, almost done."

"I wonder what could be taking him so long," Ella said.

Connor, the guy Genie planned on losing her virginity with, emerged seconds later, proudly holding his specimen cup—it was filled with a gooey substance. Ella and I looked at each other. It took us a second to realize what was in the cup before we began laughing.

Connor, who seemed so proud of filling the cup, looked baffled. "I don't get what's so funny. You asked me to fill this cup, and I did."

"You're right, I'm so sorry. I'm acting extremely unprofessionally, and I apologize. We're laughing because I needed your urine, not your sperm."

"Well, why didn't you say that in the first place?"

"My fault, I should have been clearer. Again, so sorry," Ella said.

Connor walked outside to the water cooler.

"How often does a mix-up like that happen?" I had to tell Teddy about this. He'd find it hilarious.

Ella shrugged. "First time for everything. Come with me—I'll operate on you."

"Is my injury serious? Are you going to have to send me home?"

"Not to worry, I expect you to make it. The only thing that can save you from camp is the calendar, and you still have more than half the summer left." Ella pointed to the bulletin board. There was a big red X for each day that had passed.

"Ow!"

"All kidding aside, look at this, it's huge."

It was the size and shape of a darning needle. My throat went dry, and the room started spinning . . .

I came to on the examination table. There was a cold compress on my head, and my feet were elevated on a pillow. Ella was standing over me with a cup in her hand.

"How're you feeling? You fainted. Here, drink some water—you're dehydrated. The heat and the humidity are hard on the campers but even harder on us adults. We're so busy running around taking care of the kids, we don't drink enough water."

I tried sitting up and plopped back down.

"Here, let me help you. Hold onto my arm."

Ella pulled me up with one hand and deftly placed a pillow behind me so I could rest against the wall. I drank the water and immediately began feeling better.

Ella gave me an ice pop, and I tore off the wrapper. "So, you have to faint to get one of these?"

"Or you can masturbate." She smiled.

I nearly snorted the cherry ice through my nose.

"Come on, I had to give him one, I mean we were laughing at him." She added, "We can't let that piece of information leak—we wouldn't be able to keep up with the demand."

"I had a confrontation with Jack today," I told Teddy that night.

"Lucky you, what happened?"

"It was choice period and he wanted to know why one of the Cubs, Jamie, wasn't rollerblading. He said her mother was adamant about Jamie learning to skate, so she could work on her balance. Jamie had no interest in skating. She just wanted to sit at the potter's wheel."

"And?"

"Let me ask you this, if you wanted your child to skate, wouldn't you send rollerblades with her?"

"Ideally."

"I grabbed skates from the closet of a bunkmate. Jamie immediately fell on her butt and could barely make it from one side of the enclosure to the other. After about ten minutes, she asked if she could stop. I knew that Jack was listening, so I told Jamie, 'There's only ten more minutes left till lunch. Why don't you try going back and forth a couple more times?' She reluctantly rolled away by pulling herself along the gate. Then Jack said, 'Good girl.' I decided to give him an out, and I said, 'Yes, Jamie is certainly trying as hard as she can.' He doubles down with, 'I wasn't talking about Jamie. I said you're a good girl.'"

Teddy had a huge grin on his face. "I can't wait to hear what you said to him."

"I told him, 'The last person to call me a good girl was my father when I was about ten. I would prefer it if you don't treat me like a child.'"

Teddy said, "Good for you."

"I was glad I called him out just to see the look of surprise on his face. Then his lips curled into a sinister smile. He looked me in the eye and said, 'No one here has ever spoken to me that way.'"

"I love that you didn't back down."

"I said, 'In what way, honestly and truthfully? Because that's all you're ever going to get from me.' Then he said, 'No one challenges me. It might be interesting to have someone question my authority. Just don't do it in front of any of the staff.'"

Teddy clapped. "Well played, Kramer. Well played."

"Now I have to remember not to call you Teddy or question Jack's authority in front of anyone." I held up my cigarette. "And of course we don't smoke together every night behind the laundry shack." I took a drag. "That's a lot of pressure. Anyway, I don't know what to do about Jamie. She hates skating."

"Take a photo of Jamie at the skatepark, ask Anya to load it on the website, and like magic"—he snapped his fingers—"Jamie's a skater."

It was refreshing to have someone actually listen to what I said and offer useful advice. "Thanks." The slight breeze picked up the scent of detergent through the open window of the laundry shack mixing with cigarette smoke. "The smell of doing the wash. I don't miss that. One of the benefits of working at camp—no chores." I took another drag. "Another thing I like is that each day is different here. Keeps me on my toes, or should I say skates—having to be prepared for the unexpected."

"Woodlands has always been my sanctuary, especially since my marriage fell apart. And as you said, you never know who or what will change your life on any given day." He smiled at me.

"My home life has become so predictable, eating the same thing for dinner every Thursday night. This job is the most exciting thing that's happened to me in years. I guess that's what happens after fifteen years of marriage. Everything becomes routine, even sex." Until I said that out loud, I hadn't realized it bothered me.

"Sex is easy. It's the love part that's difficult. With my ex, we couldn't get either right."

We smoked in silence.

"What about here at camp? You must be popular with the counselors," I said.

He smiled. "Of course, when I was in my twenties and early thirties, I had a great time."

"I bet. A different woman every night?"

"No, I'm not like that. I'd take my time to find someone I connected with, you know, a person you could have a conversation with after shagging."

I laughed. "The only time I've ever heard someone use the word shagging was in an *Austin Powers* movie."

Teddy arched an eyebrow.

"So, who's the lucky woman this summer?" I asked.

He looked me in the eye, turned away, and took a long drag. "Here's the conundrum, I'm old enough to be the father of every counselor here."

"True, but I'm sure there's someone who appreciates a mature man."

He snickered. "The age-appropriate women, like you, are married."

I couldn't help thinking, *If I weren't married.* And I couldn't remember a time when I'd felt as comfortable and free talking with Ronnie as I did with Teddy. Ronnie's and my conversations were about the girls, schedules, and logistics. Every utterance seemed to be dissected by him as if I were his opposing counsel. Yet another example of how I felt his disdain. I was happy not to be in touch with him. Teddy was watching me, and I came up with something to say. "Making it harder to find a summer dalliance?"

"That's hardly the reason I come back every year, although it was a nice perk while it lasted." He smiled. "I'm not looking for a relationship. Life is easier here—no dealing with the ex. I get to hang out with Bob, my best mate. And most importantly, Max is happy here, no bouncing between me and his mother. He can enjoy himself with no outside pressures."

"What about maybe falling in love again? Finding the right woman? Having more children?"

"I always pictured more children, but there's never a woman. I've resigned myself to just me and Max."

"I guess it makes sense that you work at a camp where you're surrounded by children and no romance," I said.

"I hadn't thought about it that way, but here I am."

"What happens when Max goes off to college?" I asked.

"You ask a lot of questions." He blew a smoke ring.

"Sorry. I'm trying to figure this out. You're tall, handsome, athletic, and easy to talk to."

Teddy was gazing up at the stars. When he did that, he was ready to say goodnight or change the subject. He surprised me when he took out two more cigarettes, lit them, and handed me one.

"Did any of your summer romances make it past the last day of camp?" I asked.

"There was one woman, but in the end, she was more interested in someone else—Mike."

His eyes glazed over.

"She picked Mike over you? There's no accounting for taste."

Teddy shrugged.

"I guess she's the reason for the animosity between the two of you."

I could tell this wasn't a subject he wanted to talk about. And there I was, teasing him.

"Was she the one who got away?" I asked.

"No . . . yes . . . maybe. That was a lifetime ago."

"You're the whole package. Some lucky woman is going to snap you up."

"Who knows?" He took another drag, stubbed out his cigarette, and flicked it into the fire bucket. "In the meantime, I'm here, enjoying your company." He paused for a second as if he wanted to say more but held back. "Shall we call it a night?"

# 21

# The Pizza Joint

The next day, Mindy informed me that our nighttime meetup was being moved into town. I jumped at the chance to get off campus.

I was surprised to see Bob behind the bar when I walked into the Pizza Joint.

"Moonlighting?" I asked.

"A couple of times a summer they let me tend bar—it's like a dream come true."

"Well then, I'll have . . ."

"You'll have the usual Tanqueray and tonic with a twist of lime." Before I could say anything, Bob said, "Yeah, I know, no diet crap."

"You're *my* dream come true, a bartender who knows my name and my drink order."

Bob grinned and winked. "Look at us, satisfying each other . . ."

"And to think, a few weeks ago we didn't even know each other's name." I took a sip and gagged. "Are you trying to kill me? There's way too much gin in here."

"Please, I've seen how hard you work. If you can handle the campers, you can handle a little extra gin."

I was wondering how much of a tip to leave when Mindy grabbed my hand and waved her credit card. "Drinks are on me tonight." Bob looked across the room to the table where Bethany and Gilda were sitting, waving at him.

We clinked glasses. "To letting loose," Mindy toasted.

I had heard that Wednesdays were notorious for the mischievous events that always seemed to happen when the specialists went out, and everyone else who had off eventually made their way to the Pizza Joint by the end of the evening. It had been a Wednesday when I stayed up late signing counselors in from their night out and was called a bitch. Well, this bitch was excited to be partaking in the legendary Wednesday night antics.

I'd heard that several summers ago, a group of lifeguards tore a toilet from one of the local dive bars and threw it out the window, and the owner had immediately banned all camp staff from his establishment. A bill for the damages was sent to Jack.

We joined Bethany and Gilda at their high-top table, perfect for people watching, particularly the body language of the flirtatious counselors.

"Look at Genie, she looks so happy chatting up Connor. He's the lifeguard she's been talking about," I said.

"All the girls are talking about him," Bethany said.

"Genie said she planned on losing her virginity to him," I said.

"If I was picking a guy to lose my virginity to, he would be in the top ten." Bethany eyed him up and down. "Make that top five."

"Well, that ship has long sailed for all us broads," Gilda said.

"The fantasies never stop," Bethany said. "I'm spending my summer marooned on a mountain surrounded by beautiful, young, chiseled bodies, and I don't have my man here to satisfy me." Bethany sighed.

Gilda grimaced. "Personally, I have no problem taking the summer off from my husband. I don't have to feed him or clean up after him or kiss him for that matter. At camp I have people cooking and cleaning for me."

"Anyone here you're looking to kiss?" Bethany asked Gilda.

"Don't be ridiculous. I've already got one guy I avoid."

"Whether or not we're having sex, I'm pretty sure that there's lots of sex happening right under our noses. Just look around this room," Mindy said.

I caught Genie's eye, and she waved at me. I smiled and winked. She blushed.

We were gossiping about who we thought was hooking up with whom when Nicole stopped by our table. I had barely seen her since my first day when she signed me in and handed me off to "Sir Theodore."

"Ladies, look how handsome my man looks behind the bar." Bob winked at her, and she grinned like the Cheshire Cat. "He's so stoked when he gets to do that."

"Nicole's gonna get her kicks tonight," Bethany sang.

Nicole turned a deep red. "Am I that obvious?"

"Hey, you're lucky to have your husband here. We got bupkes. It's your duty to enjoy yourself. Someone should be having fun, and since it's not gonna be one of us, it may as well be you," Bethany said.

The gin went straight to my head while my stomach was running on empty. I got up to get some popcorn from the old-fashioned popper at the other end of the room. The bar was packed, and the musky scent of pheromones was pervasive. Sex was literally in the air. I bumped and squished my way through the crowd, stopped several times by counselors who seemed surprised that I was drinking in the same establishment as they were.

"Lori, it's so weird that you're here. It's like I'm partying with my mother," Jasmine said.

"Well, the good news is that I'm not gonna rat you out to your father, but the bad news is I'm not paying for your drinks."

That got a laugh from the cute tennis coach whose arm was around her shoulder. I kept moving until I was stopped by my cabinmate, Di.

"Look at you, Lori, all hot in that tight white jean skirt and slinky purple tank top. I like this look on you," she said. "I'm gonna have to raid your closet."

"It looks better than boxy gym shorts and T-shirts, that's for sure—although I gotta say that stuff is much more comfortable." I tugged at my skirt, noticing my muffin top had disappeared. "Where's that tall, handsome baseball coach you've been seeing?"

"He's over there, talking with some of his mates."

Four attractive guys were huddled together, swigging beers. It looked like they were wearing their social uniforms: polos in various loud colors; collars up with a pony, lizard, or penguin logo; and jeans slung so low that their boxers were sticking out.

I continued my push through the masses when Genie grabbed my arm and pulled me close. "Isn't Connor the most gorgeous guy you've ever laid eyes on?"

"I must admit you have very good taste in men. Has it happened yet?" I asked.

"I'm hoping tonight." She was all dimples. She smiled and winked, and I blushed.

I was scooping popcorn into a red and white striped carton when Teddy tapped me on the shoulder.

"Hey, come join us in the back," I said, nodding to our table.

"As soon as I get Bob to mix me a drink."

I carried popcorn in each hand, making it difficult to navigate my way back through the thickening crowd. Both cartons were half empty by the time I reached my destination.

"How come you didn't fill them up?" Gilda asked, taking a handful.

"Between spilling some and people helping themselves as I passed by, this is all that's left. Are any of you sweating? My drink went straight to my head, and it's so hot in here." I fanned myself with a menu, but that wasn't enough, so I fished an ice cube out of my glass and wedged it into my bra.

Teddy sauntered over to our table holding two tall glasses with lime slices hugging the rims and placed one in front of me. "Cheers."

"Of all the gin joints near all the sleepaway camps in all the world, I'm glad you walked into mine," I said. "Thanks for the drink, but I think I've had enough."

"Nonsense. Bob made it specially for you."

"Where's my special drink?" Gilda asked.

"Why it's right over there behind the bar." Teddy pointed at Bob.

"You smartass Brit, you think you're so clever," Gilda said. "Ladies, I'm going to get us some special drinks from behind the bar."

Teddy slipped onto Gilda's seat. We were trying to chat, but it was hard to hear over the din of the crowd and the music from the jukebox.

Teddy emptied his glass, banged it on the table, and whispered in my ear, "I'm going outside for some fresh air, care to join me?"

I knew he was going for a smoke. I slithered off my stool and offered it to Gilda, who had returned, impressively carrying three sweaty glasses.

"Where are you guys going?" Gilda asked, placing the drinks on the table.

"To get some fresh air," Teddy answered.

As I stepped down, I heard Bethany say, "I've known Ted for years, and he's never asked me to get some fresh air."

We walked out the side door, and I took a deep breath. Inhaling the cool summer breeze, I immediately felt better. It was a clear, cloudless night with endless twinkling stars. I followed Teddy through the parking lot, away from the glare of the streetlights and into the darkness. Once my eyes adjusted, I saw movement in the shadows.

Genie was pressed up against Connor, whose hands were exploring her body. Hers were resting comfortably on his ass. I was worried that she would see me, but she was totally engrossed. We passed no less than six other couples in varying stages of intimacy.

"There are too many eyes here," Teddy said.

"Yeah, but they're all closed."

"Nonetheless, let's go out to the street where only the townies will see us."

We were in the alleyway alongside the diner when he lit us up.

I wavered for a second but decided to tell Teddy how close I came to almost burning down my cabin. I spilled the details in what seemed like one endless breath of confession.

"Wow, all of that really happened, and no one knows about it?"

"I feel a huge sense of relief telling you."

"What are you going to do about it?"

"Funny you should ask. Come with me." I led him to the front of the diner that was closed for the night. "Those curtains in the window are exactly like the ones in my room."

"I can practically see your brain pulsing through your skull. What are you thinking?"

"I haven't quite figured out the details." I walked over to a window to see if it was locked. Then walked to the side of the building.

"What're you doing?"

"I'm checking to see if any of these windows are open."

"I'm afraid to ask why."

"Isn't it obvious? I'm going to climb in and steal the curtains."

"Exactly how much did you have to drink?"

"Enough to make me think this is a really good idea. Are you with me?"

Before he answered, I found what I was looking for in the rear of the building. "Look at that window up there—it's only got a screen. I can easily knock it out. I'm good at that—I've had practice."

"Lori, this is a really dumb idea. Come on, let's go back to the bar."

"You go ahead. I should be able to climb on that dumpster and jump down into the kitchen."

"How will you get back out?"

"I don't know, but I'm sure I'll figure something out."

He looked at me for a second and said, "Okay, come on, let's do this."

"You're in?

"I'm not sure why, but yes, I'm in."

"Okay, then I need you to boost me up so I can reach the window."

I kicked off my black kitten-heeled mules and stepped onto Teddy's cradled hands. I braced one hand on his head, the other on his shoulder. He lifted me and I was able to push the screen into the diner. I heard a dull thud.

"Can you climb in?" Teddy asked.

"I'm not strong enough to pull myself up. Move closer to the wall so I can step onto your shoulders."

As Teddy maneuvered us, my skirt hiked up over my hips. "I'm not properly dressed for burglarizing."

"Clearly this break-in was not premeditated. You can use that in your defense if we get caught."

I'd already committed the breaking and was about to do the entering. I managed to heave my butt onto the windowsill and from there I threw my legs over and into the diner's kitchen. Easing myself onto the butcher-block table below the window, I jumped down onto the floor, pushed through the kitchen door, and stood in the middle of the diner. There was light streaming in from the lamppost in front of the restaurant.

I stepped onto the red vinyl seat of the booth I'd shared with Gilda. My heart was racing and my hands were shaking, but I managed to detach the rod from the hooks and slide the curtains off. I ran across the room and did the same thing in the opposite booth. For some reason it made sense to keep the diner aesthetically balanced. With both sets of curtains rolled up under my arm, I calmly walked back through the double doors into the kitchen and sat on the butcher-block table. I called out as I stood up, "Teddy, are you still out there?"

"Of course, I am. Did you think I was going to leave you stranded inside?"

I couldn't lift myself up high enough from the table. I looked around the kitchen and found a box of potatoes. I heaved it onto the counter and was able to climb back out by stepping onto Teddy's shoulders and shimmied my way down so that he was carrying me piggyback. He walked over to a car and sat on the trunk so that I could easily slide off him.

"Oh my God, I can't believe what I did. Stealing curtains because I almost burned down a building." I nervously giggled. "What has my life come to?"

"Well, I don't know about that, but I haven't gotten into this kind of mischief in forever. I feel like one of those twenty-somethings I reprimand for doing stupid things like breaking into diners. Let's head back before people start wondering where we are. Where's your car so we can stash the evidence?"

I looked around, trying to get my bearings. "It's over there."

I unlocked my trunk and Teddy tossed the curtains in. Out of the corner of my eye I noticed a shiny white bag with a red rose on it. I picked it up, looked inside and said, "I have another idea. I'll need your help again."

"Now what?"

"Come back with me to the diner. I want to hang these curtains."

"Why?"

"I'll sleep better knowing that I made a trade instead of outright stealing."

"That's ridiculous."

"Is it? Cause it makes perfect sense to me. Are you with me once more? Please."

He looked at me and then the bag in my hand. "As my dad always said, 'In for a penny, in for a pound.'"

"You're the best accomplice."

I stood in the middle of the diner admiring my handiwork and wondered if anyone would notice.

All that climbing made me hungry, so I walked over to the counter, lifted one of the glass domes, and helped myself to two doughnuts. I grabbed napkins and wrapped the contraband in them.

I stood on the potato box and stuck my head out of the window. "Teddy, here, take these."

"Your rap sheet is getting longer and longer." Teddy caught me again, but this time he held me in his arms like I was his bride. "But we do make a great team." He grinned.

"I agree. What will our next caper involve? I know, let's have breakfast tomorrow at the diner."

"Cheeky."

Teddy and I walked back through the parking lot, munching on doughnuts and licking our fingers.

"It seems like there are more people snogging out here than drinking inside," Teddy said.

I noticed JoJo's iridescent long blonde hair under the streetlamps. She was wrapped around Julia, the survival counselor.

I heard lots of heavy breathing and some moaning.

"It's been a very long time since I made out with anyone in a corner," I said.

"Personally, I think that some things should be done privately in a *room*." Teddy shouted the last word.

There was laughter and then from somewhere to our left we heard, "Hey, Mooney, piss off and mind your own bloody business."

"I'm telling you, Lori, kids today have absolutely no respect for their elders."

"Lori, is that you?" Gilda yelled from across the parking lot. "Hey, where have you two been?"

Teddy whispered, "Don't feel like you owe anyone an explanation. It's better to keep people guessing."

"Are you two fooling around?" Gilda asked. Before I could respond, she said, "Lori, you're all disheveled, what's that white stuff on your shirt and, wait a second, your leg is bleeding."

Teddy's black polo shirt was speckled with sugar, and I looked down to see that my purple top had white flecks down the center. I tried to dust away the evidence with the napkin, but it only smeared the powder. I looked down and indeed my right shin was trickling blood.

"What happened?" Gilda asked.

I fumbled for a second before I said, "It was dark, and I walked into some bushes. I didn't notice I'd cut myself. Do you want to go back to camp? I think I'm done for the night."

"Can you drive?" Gilda asked.

I was insulted by her question until I realized that there was no way I could drive a straight line, let alone a winding uphill road in the pitch black. I was tipsy from the gin, my hands were shaking from the robbery, and I'd been wounded during the evening's escapades. I was a hot mess. "No, I don't think so." My reply came out somewhere between a giggle and a sob.

"Okay, hand over your keys," Gilda said.

I put my hand in my left front pocket where I'd kept my keys ever since I'd learned to drive back in high school. They weren't there. I panicked. I hoped I hadn't dropped them in the diner because I didn't have the energy to break in a third time.

"I seem to have misplaced my keys," I said.

"I have them. Here you go." Teddy tossed them to Gilda.

"Ted, do you need a ride, or have you already had one?" Gilda asked him but looked at me. She probably thought we were doing drugs and having sex in the back seat of my Camry.

"No, I'll wait till Bob leaves and catch a ride with him. Can you tuck our friend in when you get back? She's had a difficult evening."

Gilda smirked. "I'll bet she has."

Nothing was said as Gilda pulled out of the parking lot. I was relieved when we passed the restaurant and saw no police. All I wanted to do was close my eyes.

"Are you gonna tell me what's going on between you and Ted?

"We just went out to get some fresh air," I said.

"That's all? Nothing else?" She gave me a sideways glance.

I took Teddy's advice. "Yup, that's all, nothing else."

Yawning, I shut my eyes. We drove on in silence for a bit, and then Gilda said, "You know, if anyone finds out that you were doing coke, you'll be fired."

I burst out laughing.

"What's so funny? Do you think I'm stupid? You leave the bar with Ted, you come back disheveled with white stuff all over you . . ."

"I'm sorry I laughed, but what you said was so ridiculous I couldn't help myself."

"So, are you going to tell me what happened?"

"Nah, I don't think so. Your imagination is much better than the truth."

Gilda harrumphed and concentrated on the road.

When we pulled into camp, Gilda asked, "Do you want me to drop you off at the infirmary?"

"Why?"

"Cause you're bleeding."

"No, I have a first aid kit in my room. Thanks for driving."

"No problem. If you ever want to talk, I'm here for you."

"Thanks, I appreciate that."

I gave Gilda a hug, walked into my little room, looked at the naked windows, and smiled.

## 22

# Bad Decision

"Lori, come in for Bethany. Lori, come in for Bethany."

I jumped when I heard the radio crackling my name. When I grabbed for it, clipped to the pocket of my shorts, I nearly burnt my leg with a cigarette. I tossed it into the fire bucket.

"Lori here."

"Your location? I know you're not with the Cubs."

I grimaced at Lars, who was standing with me and three other women who were taking a smoking break from laundry duty.

Ten minutes ago, I had been on my way to the gymnastics shed when Lars pulled up next to me in his truck. Stepping up and leaning into the open window on the passenger side, I'd spotted a pack of cigarettes on the seat.

"I've never tried a foreign cigarette."

He grinned. "Lori, you smoke? Shame on you!"

"Only when I'm frazzled and exhausted, you know, Woodlands."

"Hop in. I'm on my way to the laundry shack. Join me, and you can try one."

Down the hill, the Cubs had been removing their sneakers and getting ready to tumble. Three gymnastic coaches and four Cub counselors were with them, so I got in.

Now I had to think fast.

"Cubs one and three are at gymnastics, and the others at tennis." I coughed. "I'm indisposed in my cabin."

I figured using the code for I'm on the toilet was the best excuse.

There was a terse, "Meet me at the infirmary. I'll explain when you get there."

Lars offered to drive me, but I was already running, my heart pounding. I got to the infirmary in record time. I pushed open the screen door. Bethany was standing next to Erica, the head of gymnastics, who was profusely sweating as she spoke on the phone explaining what happened, I assumed to a parent.

"Becky fell off the balance beam and broke her arm."

My throat went dry. I was barely able to ask, "Can I see her?"

Bethany ignored my question. "Where were you?"

I walked toward the exam rooms and said over my shoulder, "In my cabin."

Becky, ashen, was sitting on the examination table. Nurse Ella was putting her arm in a sling. I sat down next to her.

"May I hug you?"

Becky immediately started crying. I held onto her and rubbed her back, letting her get it out. I felt incredibly guilty. What if Zelda and Hazel were hurt, and their DL wasn't with them? I should've been at the gymnastics shed, but, no, instead I was off smoking a cigarette. Not only bad for my health but against camp policy. This was the third time smoking had gotten me into trouble: the bear, nearly burning down my cabin, and now this. Tonight, I would have to tell Teddy I couldn't smoke with him anymore.

Nurse Ella said, "We're taking our very brave Becky to the hospital for X-rays and a cast. I've already contacted her family."

Bethany walked in and placed her hand on Becky's knee.

"Don't worry, we're going to take good care of you." She gave me a stern look. "Can I talk to you for a second?"

I whispered into Becky's ear, "I'll be right back."

She was trying to hold back tears. "Will you come with me to the hospital?"

"Absolutely. I'll hold your hand the entire time."

She had the saddest expression as she nodded her head.

Bethany was in the room across the hall. "Were you smoking?"

"What?"

She sniffed my hair. "I can smell it on you. I don't really care if you were or not, but not when you're supposed to be with the campers. I'll have to report this to Jack, and he'll want to fire you on the spot."

I didn't want to admit to smoking so instead I said, "I will make sure to follow all of Woodland's policies closely." I wanted to add except for the drinking one, but now was not the time to call Bethany out about breaking rules.

Bethany looked me in the eye, and I could tell she was trying to figure out what to do. "Okay, we'll stick to the story that you were indisposed."

23

# A Moment of Truth

I heard Teddy whistling, his signal letting me know he was on his way to our rendezvous spot. If I told him I was going to quit smoking, there would be no reason for us to meet each night, and I very much enjoyed being in his company.

"I can't believe half the summer has flown by," I said.

"Time is different at camp—a day feels like a week, but the nights, the nights disappear in seconds," Teddy said.

"You mean our time together?"

"Yes, that's exactly what I mean. This, what—hour or so—is what gets me through the days, knowing that I'll have you to myself."

An unexpected shiver ran down my spine. "I also enjoy our time together."

We both took a drag and Teddy looked at me. "You got me talking," he said. "I never had that with anyone."

"Not your ex-wife?"

"Especially not her."

"You're going to meet my husband on Sunday."

"I'm well aware of that." He watched the smoke he exhaled swirl upward toward the iridescent moon.

"I'm nervous about you meeting him. He can't know about this." I held up my cigarette. "Or about us."

"What's there to hide? Two friends hanging out, enjoying each other's company?" Teddy asked.

"I do feel very connected to you." I reached out my hand, and he took it.

"Not as connected as I would like us to be." He brushed his lips across my knuckles.

An electric current pulsated through my body, and the way he looked at me made my knees weak. It scared me. If I didn't leave right then, I might do something I'd regret.

I eased my hand away, tossing my cigarette into the sand bucket. "It's late. I'm gonna call it a night."

I was lying in bed, thinking about Teddy and how he'd just kissed my hand. No one had done that before. I rubbed my knuckles under my nose. My body flushed. I reached into the end table drawer and pulled out the vibrator, smiling at my name written in purple on the shaft.

I began fantasizing about Teddy holding me, kissing me, making love to me, and treated myself to an exquisitely explosive orgasm.

I pulled out the bright green bathing suit that I bought on sale at the end of last season. Green was one of my favorite colors to wear because it enhanced the green in my hazel eyes, but now that every piece of clothing I wore was green, it was less appealing. The halter top plunged a little too deeply to wear at camp, but it was the least revealing of all my bathing suits. I hadn't thought to purchase something more modest.

There was no rush to meet up with the Cubs. By the time they meandered through the reeds, dropped their stuff in the corral, and checked in with the lifeguards, a good fifteen minutes would've passed. It was a gorgeous day with a slight breeze. I decided to take the longer picturesque route, walking on the road and down the hill from the boys' side of camp. The vista was magnificent, a wide-open field surrounding the glistening lake where the blue horizon seemed to go on forever. My yoga instructor talked about finding a moment of zen in your busy daily life. My plan was to stand at the top of the hill and do just that.

Off to my right I heard a sharp whistle. I turned to find Teddy and a group of young boys playing on the soccer field. The boys looked like miniature professional athletes decked out in their Woodlands soccer shirts, cleats, and shin guards. It was unusual for me to see him during the day or, for that matter, to see anyone from Boys Camp. Our schedules were different. When Girls Camp was scheduled to be down at the lake, the boys were up the hill, playing sports. Any mixing of sexes was prescheduled, predetermined, and highly supervised.

I stopped and waved. He gave me a subtle once-over, nodded, and smiled. I hoped he couldn't see me blushing like a teenager. I started to walk when I saw two boys running toward each other at full speed. The collision happened with less of a boom and more of a moan. Both boys fell backwards, and one immediately began crying. The other boy must have heard him and decided he could cry as well.

I was about to run over to help, but Teddy was already on the ground comforting them. I was too far away to hear what was said, but they quickly got up on their feet and gave Teddy high fives, ready to resume the game.

When I reached the top of the hill I stopped, took a deep breath, closed my eyes, and tried to empty my brain of all thoughts, but it was impossible. All I could picture was the sweat glistening on Teddy's face.

When I opened my eyes, the lake was buzzing with activity. Girls were swimming and shrieking as they flew down the slide while others jumped off the docks holding hands. I couldn't tell if any of the laughing girls were Zelda or Hazel. The Cubs were assigned to sailing and water skiing. I stopped at the check-in board, slipped my card into the active swimmer side, and went to put on a life jacket.

Mike was standing on the sand in a *Baywatch* red Speedo, or, as Gilda referred to it, his banana hammock, silver whistle shining from the middle of his broad chest. He grinned as he checked me out.

"Hey, Lori, that suit suits you."

Ignoring him I clipped on a purple life vest, picked up a paddle, and walked toward the Funyaks—amateur kayaks made from heavy duty plastic that sat on top of the water and needed no special skills to navigate.

I paddled to the middle of the lake and spotted Mindy; her Bain de Soleil tan shimmered under the direct rays of the sun. Even in the humidity, every hair on her head was perfectly in place and her lips had a fresh coat of her trademark red lipstick.

"Come here often?" I asked.

"Yes, especially on sweltering summer afternoons."

We stopped, oars across our laps, enjoying the peacefulness.

"I swear each summer goes by faster and faster. Tomorrow's Visiting Day, so we're at the halfway point. How's the summer been going for you? Do you think you'll be back next year?" Mindy asked.

"I don't see a placard on your kayak saying 'psychiatrist is in,'" I said.

"I'm here for you whether we're on the lake holding paddles or in my room holding a glass of wine. If you want to talk, you have my full attention."

I felt close to Mindy—she'd been incredibly supportive from the beginning with advice about dealing with the campers, Bethany, and the Bergers. Looking around I saw that we were in that sweet spot where it was too far for the swimmers and too reedy for the boats.

"I never envisioned myself working at a sleepaway camp. I have to say there were some rough patches in the beginning, but it's been fun being with the campers, meeting you and the other women. Plus, Zelda and Hazel love it here. If Jack wasn't running the camp, I think this could be an idyllic place."

"What do you mean?"

"The Bergers are lousy bosses. They don't inspire or encourage us. On the contrary, they do their best to point out our faults."

We floated aimlessly for a bit and then Mindy said, "Thanks for telling me that. I hadn't looked at things through your eyes. I'm always getting feedback from Bethany, Bob, and the Bergers, so it's interesting to see things from your point of view."

"And?"

"I can see the dysfunction. Perhaps I can find a way to work with Jack and Marilyn to fix it before next summer."

"It won't matter for me 'cause I'm sure there's no way the Bergers will ask me back, and between you and me, that's a good thing. I'll just have to figure out something else for my kids to do next summer."

"Don't be so quick to decide. A lot happens over the course of a year. People change, your needs change, we all change for whatever reason. I mean, look at me. If you told me I'd end up spending more than half my life here, I would've had you committed, but now it's part of who I am."

Not for a second did I think that Woodlands could become a permanent part of my life. We floated in silence before I voiced the question that was really on my mind. "You've known Teddy for a long time, right?" I asked.

"Who?"

"Ted. I mean Ted."

I was flustered for a second. Saying Teddy aloud felt as if I'd revealed my private thoughts about him.

"I've known him for well over ten years and he's always been Ted, just plain, dependable Ted. Does he know you call him Teddy, and he lets you get away with that?" Mindy asked.

"He was surprised at first, but yeah, he's okay with it."

"The best way to describe him is that he's an enigma. He said he was married, though I never met her or saw a photo, but there is a kid. He doesn't gossip, complain, or flirt. I know he does a good job and gets on well with his campers and counselors. He's been sitting on my floor for years and every so often you get a snarky comment from him. But I can't say I really know him."

Yesterday I would've said Mindy's estimation of Teddy was spot on, but now I wasn't so sure—the way he kissed my hand last night and how he'd just looked at me.

"Sometimes he's quite charming," I said.

"You only think that because he has a British accent."

I laughed. "You're probably right."

A flotilla of sailboats filled with squealing Cubs drifted toward us.

"Lori, look at me, I'm a sailor!"

"You certainly are!"

They were excited to see me in the water with them and started waving and vying for my attention.

"I'll make sure the bosses know how well you interact with the campers," Mindy said.

I smiled and was about to say something when one of the girls tried to get my attention by standing and was smacked by the boom, which sent her flying overboard. The other three girls tried to help her and ended up capsizing their Sunfish. Trying to quickly maneuver myself out of the kayak, I ended up tumbling into the lake and swimming the short distance to where they were bobbing in the water. Thank goodness for life vests. Brittany was rubbing the back of her head where the aluminum had hit her.

"Are you okay?" I asked.

She looked at me, and I could tell she couldn't decide whether to cry or not. Her dunked shipmates were giggling so she opted to join them. That was a relief, but I would still have to call her parents that evening to let them know what happened.

Carrie, one of the Cub counselors, and a sail lifeguard swam over to instruct the girls on how to right the craft and get back in. After several attempts they were safely back in the boat.

As we treaded water, Carrie asked, "Do you think I'm not capable of doing my job?"

"What? Yes, I mean no, wait. I think you're doing a great job. Why?"

"I saw what happened, and I was all over it. You didn't have to jump in, especially when the head of sail was watching." She looked over her shoulder in the direction of Di on the sail dock.

I waved to Di and shouted, "Carrie's doing a great job!" I egg-beated my legs as firmly as possible to push my torso up and gave her two thumbs up. To Carrie, I said, "My jumping in was in no way a negative assessment of your abilities—it was my maternal reflexes. You're doing a great job in the bunk and here."

I always looked over my shoulder, worrying about what the Bergers thought about everything I did. I should've realized that their abysmal management style trickled down to the waterfront.

Carrie looked askance when she said, "A bunch of the Cub counselors and I were talking about how you think we're all useless."

I gasped. "I think you all have the hardest jobs, working around the clock with no rest and having to sleep with the campers. Counselors are underappreciated and underpaid. I am truly sorry if I made you feel disrespected in any way. I am figuratively," I panted, "and literally treading water to keep myself afloat. Please accept my apology if I haven't let you know how much I appreciate all that you do for campers and for me."

I reached out to hug her, and she hesitated for a second but then she let me.

"We good?" I asked.

"Yeah."

As I swam toward Mindy, I was thinking that I'd need to make sure to meet with each counselor one-on-one to tell them how much I appreciated how hard they worked—even Jasmine.

Mindy held the Funyak for me, and after two failed attempts, I managed to clumsily squirm into its well.

Mindy looked horrified. "Oh crap, you jumped in with your radio."

I looked down and sure enough the radio was clipped onto the vest, where I'd been instructed to attach it at the beginning of the summer, so that I could be reached on the lake. "Why do you look so distraught—because I fried it?" Jack would probably misconstrue my waterlogging his radio as yet another screw up. "They must have backups."

"It's one of Jack's pet peeves. He goes bonkers when someone breaks one of them."

"Even when the person went diving into the lake to fish out one of his *paying* customers?"

That night I sat on my bed thinking about Teddy. I heard three low whistles. Outside I followed the smell of tobacco and the faint glow from his cigarette. As I rounded the corner, I saw Teddy leaning against the laundry shack.

"Let me get that for you." He lit my Winston with precision.

After a couple of drags, I said, "I enjoyed watching you coach the boys this afternoon."

"I was surprised to see you, especially out of uniform. You looked like a mirage in the middle of a hot, sweaty afternoon."

"You were so good with them. I admired how quickly you got those boys up off the ground and playing. I could use some tips on how to motivate my campers. Sometimes I think they pretend to be injured just so they can sit in the shade."

"I find it hard to believe that you have trouble doing anything you set your mind to. From my vantage point, you're smart, competent, and resourceful."

Over the weeks I'd come to appreciate Teddy's perspective. He always managed to turn my negatives into positives. Ronnie enjoyed throwing my shortcomings in my face.

"Thanks, that means a lot coming from a veteran." I took a drag. "You know soccer wasn't invented when I was growing up."

"That's ridiculous, people have been playing for centuries. Where I grew up, you could kick a soccer ball before you walked," he said.

"I was fairly adept at stoop ball and hand-clapping games," I said. "In my neighborhood it was all about Spaldings."

"Those pink rubber balls?"

"Just so you know, you use your hands, not your feet. You'd be surprised how much coordination you need to toss the ball, clap in front and in back, and then catch it."

"You'll have to teach me."

We were both quiet, enjoying the cool night air. I looked up at the heavens; the glittering stars were mesmerizing. When I looked down, Teddy was smiling at me, his eyes sparkling as brightly as the stars.

"What's that grin all about?"

"I can't stop thinking about seeing you in that revealing bathing suit . . . and," he took a deep breath, "fantasizing about what's underneath."

I felt my cheeks blush as he stepped closer, taking the cigarette from my hand and tossing it into the bucket. He looked into my eyes as he pulled me into him, firmly placing one hand on the small of my back and the other across my shoulders. He kissed me, slowly, passionately, deliciously. My tongue played with his. Our rhythm was instantly and perfectly in sync, our bodies seamlessly folded into each other. I didn't want him to let go, ever.

My mind reeled. I knew how stupid this was. I pulled away, both of us flushed. I was shocked, scared, and elated. I tried to pry myself from his arms, but he held me securely, possessively.

"I've been wanting to do that since the first time I met you." Our faces were close as he confessed his feelings.

"If I remember correctly, your first impression of me was of an overwrought *mum*."

"Did I forget to add the word hot in front of that? My bad." His eyes crinkled when he smiled.

I sighed in the pleasure of his words and the scent of his body. He smelled like summer—suntan lotion and sweat. The opposite of the expensive colognes Ronnie had started to wear once he made partner—the smell of his success. "Well, you've proven me right, you're indeed the most charming rogue I've ever met."

His smile was beautiful, but tonight his face was radiant, practically glowing. I couldn't stop myself even if I wanted to, and at that moment I didn't want to. He was taller, broader than Ronnie, and I was on tippy toes, wrapping my arms around his sunburnt neck. I had forgotten how enjoyable kissing was, just kissing when done passionately.

Teddy nipped my ear and whispered, "Now what?"

Half of me was ecstatic and the other part was terrified. I wrapped my arms around his waist, putting my head against his chest. The pounding of his heart mimicked mine. I wanted to scream yes. I wanted to cry no.

He looked deeply into my eyes. "I wasn't looking for this, and I know you weren't either. We can go back to the way things were, but now that I've kissed you, I don't want to stop."

I didn't say anything. I didn't want to think. All I wanted was his mouth on mine.

Lying in bed, I couldn't help but wonder about Teddy's timing, confessing his feelings for me the night before Visiting Day. I was going to see Ronnie tomorrow. Was it intentional? It didn't matter. I had allowed it to happen. Was it payback for his late nights and weekends at work and for standing me up? Or was it the thrill that Teddy was attracted to me? He made me feel like I was the smartest, sexiest woman he'd ever met.

# 24
# Greece Lightning

Sunday morning, Visiting Day, I was stationed between the parking area and the football field, delivering parents to their children. I kept an eye out for Ronnie. As the stream of cars lessened, I walked up and down the rows of cars looking for him, wondering how I'd feel when I saw him after five weeks apart. I felt my cheeks blush, thinking about kissing Teddy.

I found him sitting in the car glued to his cell phone. I tapped on the window, and he held up one finger.

Even though it was the one day out of eight weeks that he could see his children, he was, of course, on a business call. Not to mention it was Sunday. I shrugged, making a face at him that I was sure showed my disappointment, and walked off.

"Lori, Lori, wait up."

I stopped and turned around, my hands on my hips.

"Sorry about that. It's so frustrating. I have no reception here. I don't know how you handle it."

I wanted to say I like that we can't easily speak, but instead I said, "I find it liberating."

He slipped his phone into one of the many pockets of his cargo shorts, gave me a perfunctory kiss on the cheek, and said, "You're looking well."

I could tell by the purple circles under his eyes how many billable hours he must have been logging. Usually when we were apart, it was because Ronnie was on a business trip. This was the first time that we'd been separated because I was away. We stood awkwardly staring at each other.

Ronnie looked over my shoulder, breaking our silence. "Where are Zelda and Hazel?"

Out of five hundred campers, there were only five kids still waiting, and two of them were ours. My heart sank—I wondered if they had thought their dad wouldn't show. Zelda's arms were crossed, resembling her impatient dad; Hazel appeared dejected. But as soon as they saw him, they flew across the field and jumped into his arms. They were hugging and talking over each other, vying for his attention.

All activities were open to the families. I couldn't spend the morning with mine because I had to be available to chat with the parents. For the past week, the Bergers had pounded into us that the most important job of the day was leading the parents to the office so they could re-up for next summer.

"I'll see you at lunch," I said.

"You're not coming with us?" Ronnie seemed surprised.

"I can't. I'm working."

"Can't you take the day off?"

I tried not to sound sarcastic when I said, "You, of all people, should know how difficult it can be to change a schedule."

He gave me a feeble smile and turned to the kids. "So, what should we do first?"

Abby and I met up to search out parents to schmooze.

"How's Barry doing?" I asked.

"Honestly, I'm shocked he's not complaining. I think he

misses us so much that he's on his best behavior," Abby said.

"Ronnie's thrilled to be with the girls. It's also good for our husbands to see what we do and where we do it."

"You're right, I'm pretty sure Barry thinks I play mah-jongg all day."

The campers were spread throughout the grounds with their parents in tow, so we decided to start at the gymnastics shed and work our way back up the hill. We walked down together, smiling, in our matching uniforms with our name tags prominently displayed. We were told to boast about how wonderful camp was, how happy their children were, and how lucky they were to be a part of the Woodlands family. Issues that we couldn't handle would go to Bethany.

"I'd be surprised if there were problems we couldn't solve. I mean, no one knows them better than we do," Abby said.

"I'm relieved. I don't want to be the reason a family decides not to send their child back next summer."

"Yeah, I see your point."

There were sneakers, sandals, and a pair of stilettos piled up outside the gym. Why anyone would wear heels to walk around a camp was beyond my comprehension.

I saw the mother of the twins Rachel and Rebecca. She stood out from the rest of the parents in her long floral skirt and gauzy top. Her hair was dark with wiry gray strands running through. Her husband, who was mostly bald with a silver fringe that wrapped around the back of his head, wore trousers hiked up to his portly waist.

"I can't help but notice that my twins are no longer identical," she said.

"What do you mean? I sometimes have trouble telling them apart," I said.

"Can't you see how much bigger Rachel is than her sister?"

I knew exactly what she was talking about—yesterday at the lake when they were standing together in their matching bikinis, I noticed how much thicker Rachel was around the middle.

She gripped my arm, pulled me away from everyone else, and shrilly whispered in my ear, "Can't you see that Rachel has gotten fat?"

"I'm sure when you have them home, you'll get them back on track."

"You don't understand. They're bridesmaids in their cousin's wedding over Labor Day weekend. They must fit into their very expensive gowns." She put her fists on her hips and frowned at me, as though I personally made it my mission to shove sweets down her daughter's throat. "You're going to have to put Rachel on a diet."

I was relieved that this was one of those situations that were above my pay grade.

"You should go to the office and speak to Marilyn . . . she'll be able to help you."

As I walked up the hill, I thought about Teddy and felt my cheeks blush again. His ex wasn't coming today. Teddy thought Max would be okay with his mother being a no-show, that he understood the dynamics of his situation, but still it had to be difficult when everyone else's mother was here.

I continued to the soccer field, up to the volleyball net, then stood in the limited shade of the tennis courts, where I met Ashley's mom, who was petite and dressed in tennis whites complete with a sun visor and the requisite tennis bracelet. I couldn't help but notice the charm hanging around her tanned neck—the spherical diamond set on a gold racket sparkled in the sun. With her slim muscular arms, she looked more like a tennis pro than the camp's coach did.

"I'm guessing you're a tennis fan," I said.

She had a squeaky giggle. "I am pretty obvious."

I was enjoying our chat when out of the blue, she asked, "Is Ashley sleeping okay? She was afraid that she wouldn't be able to with so many other people in the room. She's the kid that never wanted to stay at sleepover parties."

"Really? Ashley isn't shy, she's always in the mix. But to answer your question, yes, she is sleeping well."

"How can you know? I mean, you don't sleep with her, or do you?" she asked.

"There are three counselors who sleep with her and report to me every day about what happens in the bunks."

To my surprise, she started sobbing. "It's just, it's just that I miss tucking her in every night and waking her in the mornings. She's having a wonderful time and, well, I just miss her more than she misses me."

I put my hand on her shoulder. "Thank you for trusting me to be the person who tucks your daughter in each night and gets to see her smiling face in the morning. I promise to continue to take good care of her."

She wiped her tears on her terry wristband. "Thank you, Lori. I'm so embarrassed I cried. But you have definitely reassured me. I'll sleep better after having met you."

My next stop was the arts & crafts studio. I saw Kacie's parents; I tried edging out. I didn't like to have favorites, but it was easy picking out my (I didn't want to think "least favorite," so instead I thought) "most challenging" camper, and that was Kacie. She and I argued over the stupidest things: If I said orange, she would say red just to contradict me. She seemed to get enjoyment out of being contrary, seeing how far she could push people, especially me.

I'd say, "Kacie, you need to put on your slicker, it's raining out."

"No, it's not," she'd say.

I'd drag her outside with me and we'd stand on the porch steps until we were wet, and *still* she'd argue.

I saw her parents with Maggie and thought, *Good luck getting Kacie through her teens.* I didn't want to interrupt their conversation, so I turned to go, when Kacie yelled from across the room, "Lori, don't leave, I want you to meet my parents!"

I made sure I had a smile on my face. "Hi, I'm Lori, Kacie's division leader."

Kacie looked like her dad, round face with intense dark eyes that seemed to question everything. Her mom, who had an open and warm demeanor, rushed toward me throwing her arms out for a hug. "Kacie can't stop talking about how you're her favorite adult at camp," she said.

"That's so nice to hear. Thank you, Kacie."

Kacie didn't look me in the eye. Maybe she hadn't actually uttered those words. Or, it could be true because I was probably one of the few people who didn't put up with her nonsense.

"Kacie says that you're the only one here with half a brain," her father added.

I laughed. "That's the nicest thing anyone's said to me all day." Kacie let me hug her.

I caught up with Ronnie a little before lunch.

"You seem different," he said. "More confident."

"Thanks."

"So, tell me exactly what it is you do all day aside from play."

I decided to ignore the sarcasm in his voice. "I'm glad you asked. Each day feels like an eternity and then poof, five weeks fly by in a flash. I mean, just walking around getting the campers to activities, phone calls to parents, daily paperwork, dodging Jack and Marilyn—"

Ronnie interrupted me. "Now you can appreciate what it's like for me when I put in long days."

"I absolutely appreciate how hard you work. I just want to share with you what *my* life has been like since I got here. I'm in charge of the daily well-being of forty-eight eight-year-olds and twelve twenty-year-olds. I wake them up at 7:30 a.m., and I tuck them in at 9:00 p.m., and I'm responsible for everything that happens in between."

"I get it. You're a babysitter."

I stopped walking. Even though what he'd said was hurtful, I didn't want to start an argument. I wanted to show a united front for our children, so I smiled and said, "Right, I babysit spoiled children, and you babysit entitled adults."

"Touché." He reached into a side pocket of his cargo shorts and handed me a letter-sized envelope with his law firm's name embossed in the upper left corner. "This is probably going to surprise you . . ."

My heart skipped a beat. "Are you serving me divorce papers?"

"What? No. Wow. Are things so bad between us that you think I came here on the one day I could see my children to divorce you?" He looked honestly shocked. "Open it. I think it will change how you've been feeling about me."

Inside were two tickets to Athens. I pulled them out and stared at them in disbelief. I was tongue-tied, trying to sort my feelings.

"I know you wanted to go to Greece this summer, and I stupidly refused. I don't know what I was thinking, but I'm rectifying the situation. We leave on Tuesday."

Tuesdays were the weekly campfires. I couldn't miss that or the upcoming dance, or the carnival.

"I can't leave in two days. My job doesn't end for another month."

"I know, but this coming Tuesday was the first day that worked for me. I have it all planned out, you'll leave with me tonight, and that will give you a day and a half to pack us up." He tousled my hair. "And hopefully Zito will have a salon appointment for you. I can't wait." Ronnie grinned from ear to ear.

This wasn't about romance. It was clearly Ronnie trying to manipulate me and restore control over our relationship. I would've naively fallen for the idea a month ago, but not now. My time away from him had given me clarity about the dynamics of our marriage, and I wasn't going to let him make any decisions for me ever again. No, the tickets did not change the way I felt about Ronnie—they validated my feelings.

"I made a commitment to work at Woodlands for the entire summer."

"I don't understand, I thought this was what you wanted."

I handed him back the envelope. "Yes, but you're six months late."

Zelda and Hazel had found a shady spot under a tree, and we joined them with plates filled with hamburgers, hot dogs, coleslaw, and potato salad.

The girls told me about what they did with their dad that morning: gymnastics, archery, and volleyball.

"I used a bow and arrow for the first time. I missed the bullseye by a mile," Ronnie said.

Hazel seemed to be jumping out of her skin. "Dad, did you give Mom her present?"

"Do you mean the tickets to Greece for this coming Tuesday?" I asked.

"The tickets are for now?" Hazel asked. "That can't be right, who'd take care of the girls in Mom's bunks?"

Zelda crossed her arms. "You always say we can't quit after we've made a commitment. How can you think Mom could pick up and leave in the middle of her job just because it was good for you? That's really inconsiderate."

Ronnie's mouth hung open, but no words came out.

I was thrilled.

Before we could continue the conversation, a mother of one of the Cubs came over to talk to me. "Sorry to bother you while you're eating . . ."

Smiling, I looked up, shielding my face from the sun, and said, "Give me one second." Facing Ronnie, I said, "Let's talk more about this later. I'll catch up with you guys down at the lake."

Zelda and Hazel were in the water splashing around with their friends. I stayed in uniform, and Ronnie wore tropical print trunks with a matching rash guard swim shirt and a baseball cap.

I expected he would've gained weight, ordering in, noshing on chips and candy in the office late at night. "You're looking slim."

He stood straighter. "You sound surprised."

"I figured since I wasn't home to take care of you, you'd be eating junk all day."

"Jana orders in food from healthy places and keeps things like carrots and hummus around to snack on." He tugged at the elastic of his trunks to show it was loose. "All the attorneys on my team have lost weight since she's been ordering."

"I'll have to remember to thank her for taking care of you while I'm away."

We stood next to each other watching the girls from the shoreline, our toes in the water. There was so much I wanted to say but didn't know where to begin.

Mike came by in a white Speedo with "Lifeguard" written across his butt in green. He put his hand out to shake Ronnie's. "You must be Lori's husband. I'm Mike, I run the show down here."

It was comical watching them size each other up.

Ronnie sucked in his gut and threw back his shoulders, standing straighter. "Ron. Nice to meet you."

"I hope Lori told you how I saved her ass." Mike actually glanced at my butt. He picked up the whistle hanging around his neck. "Lori, you're not wearing the one I gave you."

"I didn't think I would need it today since I have you *and* my husband watching out for me."

Ronnie threw his arm around my shoulder, pulling me into him. "I don't think my wife mentioned you. But it's nice to meet you."

I wasn't surprised by Ronnie's demonstration of possession. His interest in me might have waned, but he still needed to piss around me.

Mike gave Ronnie a bemused look and said, "Sure, buddy." And swaggered back to his post.

When Mike was out of earshot, Ronnie said, "He seems very fond of himself, strutting around in a miniscule Speedo. His ego must be as swollen as the rest of him."

"Di, one of my housemates, says it's his budgie smuggler."

"I saw the way he looked at you . . . has he come on to you?"

"You know the type, he's like that sleazebag in your firm who always flirts with me at office events."

Before we could continue our discussion, Teddy appeared with Max and I froze for a second. They looked adorable in their matching board shorts. I hadn't ever seen Teddy without his soccer shirt on. The broad shoulders were obvious, but until then I hadn't seen the lean, long, well-defined torso that was hidden under his clothes.

"Ronnie, this is Ted, the soccer coach, and his son Max."

Teddy's demeanor didn't change. "You're one fortunate man to be married to Lori."

"A Brit? You're a long way from home."

"Woodlands feels like home to me and Max." He squeezed his son's shoulder. "Well, nice meeting you. Enjoy your visit." Teddy caught my eye and gave me a subtle nod as he walked off, hand-in-hand with Max.

"I had no idea that there would be so many men, I mean adult men. I figured they'd be kids, you know, half your age."

"I was also surprised."

"And they're all so fit."

Parents kept interrupting us to say hello and to tell me how happy their daughters were.

"You weren't kidding when you said you're never alone at camp," Ronnie said.

"Now you see why I can't leave my job in the middle of the summer."

"When I bought the tickets, it made complete sense to me. You say I never do anything romantic so when I did, I thought you'd *jump* at the chance to be with me. But I see that you have responsibilities where people depend on you, and you can't just walk out."

"I can't leave because of the commitment I made. Plus, I'm enjoying my job. I've been learning about myself, how resilient I am, how capable I am. After all our disagreements about camp, it probably worked out for the best because now I can keep an eye on the girls and watch them having the time of their lives."

I smiled as Zelda and Hazel held hands jumping off the docks, exactly as the kids did in the Woodlands video we'd watched back in February.

"You and I are living separate lives," Ronnie said.

"We did agree to try a separation this summer."

"I'm feeling really disconnected from you, Zelda, and Hazel."

I turned to face him. "That is exactly what I've been telling you about how I feel when you're in the middle of a case. You may be physically present, but you're mentally absent."

"This is how I make you feel?"

Now that it affected him, he was finally hearing me. "Most of the time, yes."

"But I'm home every night, if not for dinner at least for dessert."

I scoffed. "It doesn't matter what you think. I'm telling you how I feel."

"It isn't my intention to hurt you," Ronnie said.

"I never thought it was . . . but you do. The truth is that I no longer feel like your partner or best friend. I feel more like the hired help you occasionally sleep with."

He looked off into the distance for a moment and then turned to face me. "I had no idea you felt that way."

I looked down at the water washing over my feet and shook my head in disappointment. He hadn't paid any attention to a word I'd said in the past six months.

He put his arm around my shoulders and kissed the top of my head. "I'm going to make it up to you starting tonight."

"Part of being separated means that our bodies don't entangle. But aside from that, do you really think that one night of sex will magically make all our problems disappear?"

Ronnie saved a seat for me in the theater while I stood outside, chatting up more parents. I slipped in next to him and noticed two small gift bags at his feet.

"What're those?"

"I bought a bracelet for Hazel with a comedy/tragedy charm, and one for Zelda with a basketball charm." I could tell he was impressed with himself.

"How'd you come up with the idea and know where to buy them?"

He reddened. "Actually, Jana and I brainstormed and then she picked them up for me."

I'd been hearing quite a bit about Ronnie's assistant Jana. "I'm sure the girls will be thrilled. I'll have to call Jana to thank her."

Genie stepped out from behind the curtains dressed in black. She introduced herself and with the biggest smile said, "Welcome, Woodlands families, to our version of *Grease*!"

The curtain went up to applause as the music started and the singing began.

Hazel's hair was pulled back into a high ponytail. She wore a pink satin bomber jacket, a poodle skirt, and saddle shoes, and she was grinning from ear to ear.

Whenever Hazel was front and center, Ronnie squeezed my hand.

When it was over, the cast came out and bowed to thunderous applause.

From stage left, Connor appeared with a bouquet of flowers and presented them to Genie. Her dimpled smile lit up the humid theater. She had chosen her first summer love well.

We found Hazel outside standing in a group with the other pink ladies, having their picture taken. When Hazel saw us, she ran to her father and jumped into his arms. It made my heart swell. My family. I loved them. Things weren't perfect, but if Ronnie and I put in the work together, we could make it better.

But the kiss I shared with Teddy last night had broken, no smashed, one of my rules: If any of my flirtations crossed a line where I felt uncomfortable sharing the encounter with Ronnie, I'd immediately stop. But we were separated, so was I technically guilty of anything?

"You were the star of the show," Ronnie told Hazel. He handed her the gift bag. "I bought you a present."

She tore the bag open and was excited to see the bracelet. I helped her put it on and she ran off to show her friends. Ronnie handed the other bag to Zelda, who jumped on him and gave him a big hug.

"I have to go to the parking field to say goodbye to the parents," I said. "Why don't you go to my room? You can shower and take a nap."

"Good idea. This day's been exhausting. How do you do it every day?" Ronnie asked.

"Practice."

"I hate coming home to an empty apartment. No one at the door to greet me. I really thought I'd walk out of here with you today."

"The fact that our expectations haven't aligned for quite a while was one of the reasons we decided to give each other some space. But if we can work out our issues, you will be taking me to Greece, and I'm not talking about the play."

When I returned to my room, Ronnie was propped up in my bed looking refreshed, but frustrated, as he tried to get service on his BlackBerry.

"How do you sleep in this bed? It's so uncomfortable, and it sags in the middle."

"I'm so beat at the end of the day, I basically pass out."

"After you shower, let's go into town for dinner. I saw a place that looked like it could pass for fine dining."

"I know the restaurant you're talking about." I didn't mention we'd had reservations there the night he stood me up. "But I can't leave."

"What do you mean?" Ronnie asked. "I get that you can't take the trip with me, but I can't take you out for two hours?" He stood reaching for the doorknob.

"Where are you going?"

"To tell Jack that I'm taking *my wife* out for dinner."

"You do that, and I'll call your managing partner the next time you miss a family meal because of work obligations."

Ronnie had that look of astonishment on his face that appeared when he didn't get his way.

"Today is about you spending time with Zelda and Hazel. I made special arrangements for you to have a dinner date with them at the Pizza Joint in town, but they must be back for the evening Flagpole."

His eyes unfocused, which meant he was figuring out his next move. He looked at his phone and then at me.

"I thought you'd leave with me, and the truth is, I have a bunch of deadlines I have to meet. My team is waiting on word from me and, well . . ."

I knew where this was going. "Well, what?"

"I think that it makes sense for me to leave right now. This way I can drive home before it gets late and get some work done tonight."

I wasn't surprised. Honestly, I was relieved. He didn't belong in my camp world. He didn't fit in with my friends. Thank goodness I hadn't mentioned the dinner plans to Zelda or Hazel. When I thought about the stink he'd made over his kids abandoning him for the summer and the makeup sex we were supposedly going to have, I was smacked in the face by his hypocrisy.

I shrugged. "That makes sense."

"You're okay with me leaving?" He sounded surprised.

I was sure he expected me to have a hissy fit and try to make him feel guilty. But I was having mixed feelings about having sex with him. It was better that he decided to leave. "I'll walk you to the car."

"No need. I know you're busy." He pecked me on the cheek and picked up his overnight bag.

When the door closed, I realized he hadn't told me what he wanted to speak about the night he stood me up and I had forgotten to ask. I plopped on the bed and exhaled a huge sigh of relief.

Abby knocked on my door. "Can I come in?"

"Sure."

"Your husband left?"

"Yeah."

Before I could explain why, Abby said, "Too bad he couldn't take Barry with him."

# 25
# Second Base

Getting the campers tucked in after they'd spent the day with their parents was a formidable task. The girls who weren't homesick became homesick. Plus, I noticed some of the counselors were weepy. If they lost it, I'd lose all control. I had to nip that before they led the campers into a crying orgy. I gave reassuring hugs and promises of lots more fun events that they wouldn't want to miss, and that was to pacify the counselors. Then I spoke with each camper, letting them tell me one interesting thing that happened during the day. Once everyone was refocused, the temperament in the cabins calmed down.

I was especially worried about Leah, the worst homesickness case that Mindy said she'd ever seen, but her parents had told her if she stopped crying, they'd buy her a dog when she got home. The bigger issue that night was Chloe. She seemed fine during the day, hanging out with her mother and grandmother, but when I went to place my hand on her back, she was trembling and sobbing into her pillow. I knelt down beside her and she latched on to me, bawling into my neck. I picked her up and carried her outside. We sat down on the porch steps, and I let her cry into my shoulder. I rubbed her back, trying to soothe her. When she calmed down, she told me how awful things had been since her parents divorced.

"It's all my fault," she said, rubbing her eyes.

"Chloe, sweetheart, that's not true. I'm 100 percent sure the divorce has nothing to do with you." I picked her chin up to look me in the eyes, pulling her onto my lap. "You are wonderful." I held her until I heard her rhythmic breathing, then I tucked her in.

Kacie was the last girl in the last cabin that I spoke with. "Tell me the one thing you liked best about today."

"That my parents got to meet you."

"I was happy to meet them too."

"My dad told them he would only sign me up if you'll be my division leader next summer."

I was astonished that anyone was counting on my return. "Kacie, tell me, why do you disagree with everything I say?"

"I don't do that."

We both laughed.

For a second, I considered not going to Mindy's because I'd be the only one there without a spouse. Well, except Teddy, and I *needed* to see him.

I nursed my drink, half listening to the conversations. It was standing room only, crowded with all the other spouses staying the night.

Teddy joined me. "I don't see your husband."

"He left a couple of hours ago."

I thought I saw him smile, but it was gone in an instant.

"Is that okay with you?" he asked.

"Yeah. It's for the best."

"In that case, I look forward to our rendezvous later. I mean, if you're up to it?" His smile improved my mood.

"How about now? I don't think anyone would notice if we slipped out."

By the laundry shack, Teddy took out his cigarette case. I

grabbed his wrist before he opened it and threw my arm around his neck, pulling him in for a kiss. I heard the case drop as he wrapped himself around me. The passion I felt when he held me was exactly what I wanted and needed.

I whispered, "Do you want to know—"

He put his lips back on mine, cutting me off, then whispered, "You're here with me. That's all I need to know."

When we came up for air Teddy picked up the cigarettes, lit two, and handed me one asking, "When are you off next?"

"This coming Wednesday, from six until Flagpole Friday morning."

"I can rearrange my days off so we can be together, if that works for you."

"You can do that? I thought these things were set in stone, planned months ago."

"I'd move heaven and earth to spend thirty-six consecutive hours alone with you." He tossed his butt and drew me in, his hands caressing my ass while devouring me with kisses.

It thrilled me that Teddy was willing to reschedule his life to be with me while my husband couldn't manage to stay for dinner with his children.

I leaned back. "Where? How?"

"I have an idea. Give me a day to figure out the details. I promise you a romantic getaway—the two of us, no work, no prior relationships, no children. Thirty-six uninterrupted hours, you and me in the present, getting to know each other better."

The expectation of being alone with Teddy for two nights made my pulse race. I looked him in the eyes, and I believed him. Teddy was a person who wouldn't disappoint me.

"I have only one request," I said.

"Yes."

"Please don't make me sleep in a tent."

He chuckled. "It will be much grander than that."

26

# Field Trip

I hit the brakes, my heart pumping in time with the turn signal. Once I made the left onto the dirt road, there was no turning back. The angel and the devil in my head were both making their case, but I decisively drove the car toward Teddy. We were meeting at the home of Herman and Estelle, the prior camp owners. They were visiting their grandchildren and had asked Teddy to keep an eye on the place.

My palms started to sweat—the steering wheel almost slipped through my hands. The sun flashed off the gold of my wedding band. I twisted it off and placed it in the cup holder, sliding the cover closed.

I passed several large houses on the opposite side of the lake from the camp. The fifth one was a two-story monstrosity of different kinds of architecture. It was as if the builder couldn't decide on a style so included them all: beach house, ski chalet, and log cabin. There was a wooden plaque above the garage that read, THE HOUSE THAT CAMP BUILT.

When I pulled into the driveway, Teddy was leaning against the stone fence, his face illuminated by the late afternoon sun. He looked like a golden Adonis. I didn't get to go to Greece, but I was about to have a Grecian fantasy. He wore a plaid short-sleeved button-down shirt with tight, low-slung jeans, and his ever-present green converse sneakers. No socks. He also wore the same roguish grin as the first time we'd met.

Every fiber of my body was on fire.

He strolled over to the car, opened the door, and took my hand, helping me out. He brought it to his lips and kissed my knuckles. I felt a vibration move from my hand and spread through my veins. He reached into the back seat, grabbed my overnight bag, and threw it over his shoulder. He took both my hands in his and we stood in front of the house, gazing at each other.

Teddy broke the silence. "How'd I do?"

"Is it just us?"

"Just us." He nodded toward the door. "Shall we?"

I didn't answer right away. I took a deep breath. "I'm nervous."

He smiled. "Why?"

"I haven't been with . . . I haven't had as many partners . . ."

He squeezed my hands. "If the way we kiss is any indication, I think we'll be just fine."

He put his arm around my waist, and we walked into the house. The sun shone through the large picture windows that looked out onto the lake, and the room glowed. I paused in the living room, glancing at photos and tchotchkes on a table behind the couch. There was a fireplace with a weathered Woodlands sign hanging above it. I felt Teddy watching me as I walked out onto the porch, stalling. I gripped the handrail, trying to compose myself. Behind me I heard cabinets and drawers opening and closing.

Teddy joined me carrying a bottle of wine and two long-stemmed glasses. "Herman doesn't drink, but Estelle loves her wine." He set everything down on a table against the wall, slid a corkscrew out of his back pocket, and skillfully uncorked the wine. He handed me a glass and said, "To us."

We clinked, and I took a gulp.

He put down his wine, took my chin in his hand, and tenderly kissed me. Our first kiss had ignited something, or should I say reignited something, that I hadn't felt in a long time—desire. Even though my mind was screaming *Stop*, I had no control over how my body responded to his scent, his nearness, his kiss. I placed my glass next to his and threw my arms around his neck, passionately kissing him back. He lifted me, holding me the way he did the night of the break-in.

We continued kissing as he carried me upstairs. He gently put me down in front of the king-sized bed. The room was cavernous with two large windows and a skylight. It was decorated in early American Holiday Inn, but instead of mass-produced landscapes there were photos of grandkids interspersed with kitschy signs lining the walls: No Life Like Lake Life, Relax, You're on Lake Time Now, and Memories Made at the Lake Last a Lifetime.

We faced each other expectantly. If I was doing this, I was going to own it and enjoy myself.

I started unbuttoning his shirt as he lifted my sundress over my head. I felt nervous about my body. Since working all day at camp, I was in the best shape I'd been in a long time, but no one besides Ronnie had seen me naked in over fifteen years. I had stretch marks, and worse, Teddy was about to uncover that I wasn't a natural redhead.

I began fumbling with his jeans, but he stopped me, pulling me into him and nimbly unhooking my bra. Then he stepped out of his pants, took a condom from his pocket, and tossed it on the bed.

Contraceptives—something I stupidly hadn't thought about. I looked at the shiny wrapper and laughed.

"Did I miss something?"

"The condom. I haven't used one of those . . . I'm thinking since I was in college."

"A necessary precaution." He kissed my wrist and said, "I have a confession to make."

"I'm listening."

He looked mischievous. "I looked up your skirt the night of the diner caper."

I smiled. "I guess you must have liked what you saw."

He motioned to me to sit on the bed. "Since that night, I've been fantasizing about how your naked arse would feel in my hands." He deftly tugged my underwear off, then stepped out of his and pulled me up. "Yes." He gave it a squeeze. "It has more than lived up to my expectations."

I did the same to his and felt him pressing against my stomach. An electric pulse surged through my body. "Here's *my* confession. When I saw you at the lake with your shirt off, all I wanted to do was . . ." I placed my face against the hair on his chest, inhaling his scent—suntan lotion and musk.

He lifted me onto the bed as we kissed. Once I was naked in his arms, all my inhibitions were gone. We took our time licking, nibbling, and caressing. He brought out a passion and excitement in me that I'd never felt before. He rolled on top of me, and I officially became an extremely satisfied and *separated* woman.

I lay on his chest while he ran his fingers through my hair. I wanted to tell him in detail how he made my body tremble and climax in a way I had never experienced. But he said this time together was just about us, in the moment, so instead I said, "That was worth waiting for."

"Yes. Yes, it was."

I was enjoying the afterglow when he asked, "Are you hungry?"

I rolled over and kissed him, slowly, tenderly. I could feel his excitement, which aroused me again. "For you."

Half awake and somewhat disoriented, I had no idea where I was, but I was filled with a sense of serenity. Opening my eyes, I remembered: I was on a furlough from my life. I was naked in an enormous comfy bed. I hadn't slept in the nude in years.

Smiling, I reached for him, but he wasn't there. I heard noises coming from downstairs. I went to shower. As the water washed over me, I thought about what I'd experienced last night—passionate sex, several times, with a man who was not my husband. I couldn't wait to do it again.

I toweled off in front of the mirror, trying to look at myself objectively. Farmer's tan, tits still had some perk—thank you, yoga. I turned to look at my ass and blushed, thinking about how Teddy admired it, when I heard footsteps on the stairs.

Teddy walked in carrying a steaming mug in each hand. "Good morning, my love."

Those four words were wonderful to hear, but even more so in his British accent.

I fluffed up the pillows, tossed the towel, and sat on the bed, my back against the headboard. "It is a good morning. Coffee in bed delivered by a handsome bare-chested man."

He placed the cups on the night table and sat next to me, taking my face in his hands, and gently kissed me. "I have no idea how you take your coffee, so I guessed." He had on his impish grin. "Hot and sweet."

I burst out laughing and scooched over so he could slip in next to me. We were sipping when I asked, "Should we make a plan for today?"

He put his mug down and said, "Well, since we're still in bed . . ."

I couldn't remember the last time I'd had sex first thing in the morning.

We were entangled in the sheets and each other when I said, "What a lovely way to start our day."

He drew me in closer. "It is, isn't it?"

My stomach growled. "You sent me to bed without any supper."

He nibbled my ear. "Come to think of it, I'm famished. Let's go raid the kitchen."

I saw his button-down shirt crumpled on the floor—I picked it up and put it on. It was soft against my skin and smelled like him.

He smiled. "That shirt never looked so good."

We went downstairs and I turned on the faucet. "I'm thirsty. You must need a glass of water too. We have literally been sucking all the moisture out of each other."

He smiled as I handed him a glass.

I was refilling our coffee cups when Teddy asked, "Why do you suppose they call these English muffins? There's nothing English about them."

I squeezed his butt. "The only English muffins I see are yours."

We took our breakfast out to the screened terrace overlooking the lake and sat next to each other on Adirondack chairs. The lake and ski dock were barely visible through the cover of weeping willows that lined the back of the property. That was good—if we couldn't see them, they couldn't see us. We were so close to the camp but so far away.

He took my hand and kissed it. "I've been a cad, seducing you and taking you to bed. I hope you're not feeling remorseful this morning."

"I made a choice." I squeezed his hand. "And I'm delighted with the outcome."

The relief that washed over his face gave way to a huge grin. "In that case, I was wondering, if I could arrange to change my days off to match yours for the rest of the summer, would you join me here again?"

"I don't know. Would you expect me to put out?"

He chuckled. "And be naked the entire time."

"I'm not sure, that's a lot to ask. I mean, I do look stunning in your clothes." I tugged at the collar of his shirt.

"You look glorious out of it." He put his hand on my knee.

"I suppose I could squeeze you into my busy social calendar."

"Let me take you out to dinner tonight."

"You mean like put clothes on and be with other people?"

"I think if we went to a restaurant, then yes, clothes would be mandatory."

"All I want is you, naked, holding me."

"A much better idea. Although I will have to put some on to go to the market—I'm afraid the cupboards are bare."

"You should probably drive into town by yourself in case you run into anyone."

"I hate that we have to hide," he said.

"I think it's sort of sexy and mysterious. Sneaking around. Having a secret."

I could tell he wasn't buying it either.

After Teddy left to go shopping, I sniffed the collar of his shirt. I loved his natural aroma. A friend told me that when she met the man she eventually married, she knew he was the one because of his scent. I had never thought about smells that way but now I understood.

I poured another cup of coffee and went back outside.

A motorboat circling with water-skiers and the laughter of campers drifted up from the lake. I wondered if Zelda or Hazel were one of them. I found a pair of binoculars on the side table. If I walked to the left-most part of the porch and stood on my toes, I could see through the willow trees. The lake was filled with boys. I tried to locate Max, but I couldn't find him.

Max was between my girls' ages. I allowed myself to daydream about our kids growing up together. But where? There was no way Ronnie would ever let me take the kids to live in another country, and I was sure Teddy and Max couldn't come to New York.

In my imagination, the five of us would live in this house and have the camp as our playground. It was an impossible dream.

Divorcing Ronnie. Could I? Would I? It seemed as if we'd lost our passion for each other. He said he wanted to work on improving our relationship. How would I go about doing that when I'd started one with another man? So many emotions were whirling around my brain—mostly confusion, uncertainty, despair, and a little guilt. *Hell, why should I feel guilty?* Ronnie never showed signs of remorse when he did things that hurt and disappointed me.

I let my mind play out more scenarios and all of them came to dead ends. Hazel was the youngest—ten more years until she started college. A lifetime.

I closed my eyes, transported to a hammock hung between palm trees, drinking a mai tai with Teddy fanning me. I heard three low whistles in the distance. Was I daydreaming or was Teddy back? What I knew for sure was that I felt a tingle throughout my body.

I felt the gentlest kiss on my head and Teddy's hands on my shoulders. I placed my hands over his and sighed.

"Lunch is ready for you, my love."

I stood up and surprised us both by taking Teddy's hand and placing it between my legs. "This is what happens when I hear your whistle."

The way he looked at me, full of desire, made my body tremble. He scooped me up, brought me inside, and put me down on the couch. I lay back panting.

"I do that to you, just by whistling?"

"Every time," I said.

He kissed me forcefully, passionately.

"You've got me well trained," I said, "like Pavlov's puppy. But now it's your turn. Tell me how you'd like your afternoon orgasm served?"

He leered at me, squeezing my butt with both hands.

After, as we lay strewn across each other on the couch, I said, "I think we are in need of a new rule."

"What's that?"

"For every two orgasms, we eat."

He laughed. "To be clear, are those yours, mine, or a combination of both?"

I laughed with him. "All of the above."

"Okay, as I said earlier, before I was, ahem, interrupted, lunch is waiting."

In the kitchen, a platter of food sat on the counter and a single majestic sunflower stood in a water glass.

"I love sunflowers," I said. "They make me think of summertime. From now on they'll always make me think of you. Thank you, it's perfect."

"Like you." He squeezed me into him.

"And look at this impressive spread." There were meats, cheeses, fruits, olives, and a freshly baked baguette.

"I realized when I was in the market that aside from this morning's poor excuse for a breakfast, we've never eaten a meal together. I'd no idea what you liked, so I bought a little bit of everything."

"Uh oh, you broke my number one rule."

"And what would that be?"

"I don't sleep with a guy unless he's at least bought me dinner. How'd you manage to get away with that?" I asked.

"Aren't I a clever lad?"

After a decadent late afternoon nap, Teddy threw dinner together.

"The gourmet market in town is owned by a fellow countryman. He carries two of my favorites from when I was a boy, Heinz Salad Cream and Branston Pickles." He held each in a hand. "Nan used to make a special sandwich for me in the summertime, and now it's one of Max's favorites. I hope you'll like it."

"The nan who called you Teddy?"

He raised an eyebrow. "Yes, the only other person who got away with calling me that."

Teddy had cut the remainder of the baguette lengthwise and toasted it. Then he slathered the bread with the salad cream, filled it with the leftover meat and cheeses, and generously dispersed the pickles throughout.

"Here in the US, we call this a hero or a sub."

He poured what was left of last night's wine. "Are you Yanks familiar with the Earl of Sandwich? When I saw the condiments, I thought it would be fun to share something from my childhood with you, though it's probably not up to your New York City gourmet standards. I'll be better prepared next week."

"I don't consider myself a food snob. I mean, come on, I've managed to eat whatever the camp cook dishes out, and if this is your favorite, I'm sure I'll like it. I'm touched that you wanted to share it with me."

There was too much of the thick dressing for my taste, but I wasn't complaining. A hot man who wanted to cook for me and couldn't keep his hands off me—I was good.

We quietly ate until I broke the silence. "I just realized we didn't smoke last night, and we both survived."

He hesitated a moment. "I need to come clean. I hope you won't be angry with me."

"What is it?"

"Do you remember the first time you caught me smoking, and I told you I don't do it every day?" he asked. "Generally, I only smoke when I'm stressed or upset. At the beginning of camp, my ex was driving me barmy. I needed to be alone, to think and unwind. But then you showed up and everything got better. You listened to me, and because of you, I was able to do something I was never fully able to do with anyone else—express and share my feelings. Talk things out." He chuckled. "Listen to me, I'm evolving before your very ears."

I smiled and Teddy continued, "I was running across the soccer field and had trouble catching my breath. I decided, no more cigarettes. But that night in bed I thought, *Idiot! No smoking means no Lori.* Smoking became an excuse for me to enjoy your lovely company." He reached across the table and took my hand in his. "I swore that night I'd meet you anytime, anywhere."

I laughed. "That's funny and sweet. I don't want to smoke either." I wrapped my other hand around his. "Can we stop and still meet every night?"

"Perfect. I need to keep my body healthy, so I can do my job and still have the energy to properly shag you into our old age."

My body was covered in goosebumps. I was simultaneously thrilled that he planned on screwing me for the rest of my life and scared that he planned on screwing me for the rest of my life. From every angle, I was screwed.

"Truth. Honesty. From now on, you and me, always." I stuck out a finger. "Pinky promise." We hooked pinkies as he ogled me from across the table and took our entwined fingers in his mouth. I pushed my half-eaten plate away and pulled him to his feet, heading for the stairs.

Teddy grinned. "What about dessert? I bought you pie and ice cream."

"Bring it."

The sun woke me as it peeked through the windows. My head was on Teddy's chest, his arms securely around me, his eyes closed. I wondered what I expected to get out of our time together. My vision was short-term, blurred by the idea of sex with Teddy, an athlete, a jock, the kind of guy who'd never given me a second glance in high school. Was my fantasy over, or had it just begun? The reality of our fling, who was I kidding, our affair, far exceeded my expectations. Now it was hard to see my life without Teddy in it. At the same time, I couldn't picture my life without Ronnie in it.

What I'd thought would be a summer thing—what happened at camp stayed at camp—was morphing into so much more.

We were up early, cleaning, throwing our things together. No more lazing in bed. Teddy's day started earlier than mine; he had to be at the Bergers' morning meeting where he'd be briefed about what happened while he was off cavorting with me. I didn't have to show up until breakfast. The plan was I'd wait fifteen minutes while he jogged back to camp, then I'd drive over and meet my coffee klatch.

He leaned against my car, his hands on my ass. I felt like I was in high school dating the captain of the football team, *American* football. The fact that we wore sneakers, shorts, and T-shirts only added to the vibe.

"Thank you for bringing excitement back into my life," Teddy said.

"What does that mean exactly, you know, for us?"

He held my gaze but didn't answer right away. "I guess, well, considering our circumstances, it means that when the summer's over, so are we."

Disappointment and relief flooded my senses simultaneously. "Then we'll have to make the most of our time together."

"I'm already thinking about the different ways I want to make love to you next week."

It was a good thing Teddy was holding me because my knees went weak.

I watched him walk away, no swagger, looking like a half boy, half man in his soccer uniform. He glanced over his shoulder knowing full well I'd be checking him out, and he gave me that look, that look that made me blush. He took my breath away. I had to lean against the car for balance.

I was in deep. I turned the key in the ignition and thought, *Let the lying commence.*

Reluctantly, I drove back to camp. I needed to focus on the day ahead and let go of the erotic time I'd had with Teddy. If anyone asked how my time off was, I'd say it was relaxing and I'd spent most of it in bed. This way I'd keep my fibbing to a minimum.

Abby, Maggie, and Roger were in their usual seats sipping coffee.

"Anything interesting happen while I was off?" I poured myself a cup and joined them.

"Drama free," Abby said.

"Zelda and Hazel good?" I asked.

"I had them both in the studio yesterday. They were enjoying themselves. I don't think they realized you weren't here," Maggie said.

I was back into the mundane, but things were never going to be the same.

At breakfast, I walked around the Cubs tables to say hello.

"Lori, I missed you. Where were you?"

"I had my day off."

"Did you get to see your parents?"

If only I could. "Unfortunately, no."

"Did you bring me anything?"

I laughed. These kids really did think of me as their mother. "Sorry, no."

Most of the counselors told me they missed me. Their job was more difficult when I wasn't there to run interference.

Amber stood up, unclipped the radio from her pocket, and bent at the waist, holding her arms forward as if it were a sacred offering. "Lori, thank you for entrusting me with the responsibility of being in charge."

I hugged her. "No, thank you, Amber, for allowing me to be off without worrying."

That night I got to Mindy's room on the early side and ran through the evening ritual of mixing drinks. I wanted to catch up with my friends but was anxious to see Teddy. He walked in with Bob about twenty minutes later. I barely looked at them as I prepared their drinks.

Teddy smiled. "Thank you, Lori, I missed your G&Ts when I was off."

I gave the other to Bob. "I missed them too—Lori was off the same days as you," he said.

"I hope you enjoyed your time off as much as I enjoyed mine. Cheers," Teddy said.

It took every ounce of willpower to keep a straight face.

"Ted, tell us what you did. You haven't looked this relaxed in years," Mindy said.

"Yeah, you're right. I caught him daydreaming with a grin on his face this afternoon," Bob said. "He only smiles when he's with his son, and Max was not around. Come on Ted, spill, who is she?"

"I have not come here this evening to be interrogated. I've come to enjoy the company of my peers." His upper crust accent stopped that conversation.

"Sooner or later, the truth always comes out," Bethany said.

Since Teddy wasn't talking, the subject changed.

"Isn't Chip due any day?" Mindy asked.

"Yep, usually comes a week or so into the second half. So, yeah, soon," Bob said.

"Who's Chip?" Abby asked.

"Silent partner in the camp. The money guy," Bob said.

"Jack and Marilyn don't own the camp?" Abby asked.

"Part owners," Bob said.

They were telling stories about Chip; I wasn't really paying attention to anything but my inner thoughts. Out of the corner of my eye I saw Teddy nod his head slightly. I stood up and stretched, said my goodnights, and headed to my cabin.

# 27

# Carnival

The days melted into each other. If it weren't for the calendar tacked to the wall in my room, I'd have no idea what day it was. As long as I got the campers to where they were supposed to be on time, I was golden.

I highlighted my days off. I certainly didn't want to miss those.

Sunday rolled around once again, and the temperature promised to hover in the nineties. Since the specialists were off, there would be no waterfront activities.

The daily sheet listed the one morning activity as prepping for that afternoon's carnival. The sun was relentless, and shade was at a premium. The cabins felt like saunas, so all the girls were outside trying to stay cool. It was going to be a long day.

Gilda handed me a bag of white T-shirts and one set of colored Sharpies.

"What are these for?" I asked.

"The campers are supposed to decorate the T-shirts and wear them at the carnival. This year's theme is superheroes."

"This is supposed to keep them busy all morning?"

"That's what the bosses say."

"Can you explain to me how one case of twenty-four markers is supposed to keep forty-eight campers entertained? And let's be real, no one uses gray or brown."

"I wish I had more."

"You'd think for the price of enrollment they could afford to buy three more packs," I said.

I headed to the Cub cabins with my meager supplies. Fortunately, most Cubs had brought their own art materials with them: gel pens, crayons, and, of course, Sharpies. After I explained the project, the girls went about getting ready for the carnival and were finished in less than an hour.

Tetherball was popular, and there was a lineup for the swings. Some girls drew, read, or polished their nails in clusters, either on the porches or under the few trees dotting the hill.

I parked myself outside in the middle of the bunks so I could easily be found. Lying on the hill, my arm covering my eyes, I was close to falling asleep from a combination of fatigue, boredom, and heat, but I had to pee. It was too hot to trek all the way back to my cabin, and I certainly didn't want to use the toilets in the bunks. The one time I'd walked inside a stall I gagged from the wet seats and toilet paper on the floor. My default was the OD shack. It was close, clean, and private. While washing my hands, I noticed a spigot attached to the wall. I rummaged through the piles of junk strewn in the corner of the adjacent room. Underneath random lost and found items was a garden hose. Hmmm. I untangled it and hooked it up to the spigot, and when I turned the knob, water sputtered out.

Unraveling the hose, I pulled it into the sunshine. Placing the nozzle on the grass, I went back inside and turned it on full blast. I walked as far as I could toward the hill, held the hose high, and placed my thumb over the nozzle so that water sprayed out in a beautiful cold arc. Within seconds I had throngs of giggling girls running through the DIY sprinkler, cooling off.

Gilda's office abutted the OD shack. "I heard shrieking, so I came by to find out what was going on."

"Everyone was so hot and lethargic, I thought this would shake things up a bit," I said.

"Did you ask Marilyn or Jack if you could do it?"

I felt dread in the pit of my stomach. "I need permission to make sure the girls are having fun?"

"You shouldn't, but if you look up micromanager in a dictionary, you'll see a picture of Jack."

"I'll worry about him later." I turned my attention to the happy campers slipping and sliding in front of me.

The sheer joy on their faces was infectious. Within half an hour, all of Girls Camp was exhilarated and soaking wet.

I had to stop so that everyone had time to change into dry clothes before lunch. As I wrapped the hose around my arm, I saw Zelda and Tara, her camp BFF, walking back to their cabin.

"I wish my mother was as cool as yours," Tara said.

I looked over my shoulder to see Zelda's reaction. She seemed to be digesting what was said. "Yeah, I'm lucky."

My heart soared.

The radio crackled as I placed the hose back in the corner. "Lori, come in for Jack; Lori, come in for Jack."

The dread I had let go of earlier instantly returned. "Lori here."

"I want to see you in the office ASAP."

"On my way."

I took a deep breath, confident in the knowledge that I'd done nothing wrong.

When I walked in, I was met by the chill of the air conditioner against my wet clothes and an apologetic look from Nicole. Both made me shiver.

"I heard you hosed down Girls Camp without asking my permission," Jack said.

Marilyn sat at her desk staring intently at her computer.

"Yeah, it was spontaneous. I was in the OD shack and saw the hose, and it was so hot, and there was no shade, and it didn't occur to me to ask, but the girls loved it."

"How many times do I have to tell you that you do not run this camp?" he barked. "It's my camp and I make the rules."

I was about to say something in my defense when Bob walked through the back door. His hair was plastered against his scalp, and he had water stains on his shirt.

"Hey, Bob, how'd you get so wet?" I asked before Jack could say anything,

"We had an impromptu water balloon fight on boys' side. It's so hot out there, and it cooled the boys down. They had a blast," Bob said.

Jack's face turned beet red.

"Did you ask Jack's permission to do that?" I asked.

Bob shrugged. "Why would I need his permission to keep the boys cool?"

"That's my thought exactly." I turned to face Jack. "If we're done here, I would like to get out of my wet clothes before lunch."

Bob would get two lime slices in an extra strong gin & tonic later.

Marilyn looked away from Jack to hide the smirk on her face.

Jack turned his rage toward Bob. "Why are you here anyway?"

"To tell you that the carnival people are setting up."

Jack got up in a huff. "Finally!" He stormed out the back, slamming the door behind him.

I had won a small victory. Despite Jack's efforts to undermine me, he was having the opposite effect. I felt empowered after each confrontation.

After lunch we let the campers loose at the carnival. The superhero theme was apparent on the older girls who wore bikinis with hand drawn six-packs on their stomachs—a use for the brown Sharpies. They had ripped their T-shirts and fashioned them into capes which fluttered behind them as the girls ran as fast as they could toward the games, rides, and candy. With the entire camp together, there were well over five hundred campers and counselors dressed in bathing suits, costumes, and flip-flops.

Arcade games were set up under a tent—shooting water into a clown's mouth until a balloon popped, ring toss onto pegs—all to win cheap keychains that were inferior to the lanyards the campers made themselves, but a trophy was a trophy. There were two of those machines where you tried to pick up stuffed toys with a mechanical claw, and right outside the tent sat a dunking booth.

Cotton candy, popcorn, and slushie stands had long lines, but the campers didn't seem to mind, particularly those who used the time to flirt—the carnival was one of the few events where the boys and girls mingled.

A Slip-N-Slide sat in the middle of the field, but the longest line was for the Tilt-A-Whirl.

Maggie had wrestled with staying at camp on her day off to attend the carnival, but Roger was adamant about getting the hell out. She asked if I wouldn't mind supervising the craft table during the event. She had purchased paper masks to complement the superhero theme.

The table was set up in the middle of the football field where I could keep an eye on Zelda and Hazel and watch the comings and goings of the Cubs. It was interesting observing the creative process—the girls took their time picking out colors, gems, and feathers, gluing them perfectly in place, whereas the boys grabbed whatever Sharpie was nearby, drew a lightning bolt or wrote the name of their superhero, and were done.

After my shift was over, I walked toward the center of the activities and saw Teddy. My body flushed, thinking about our two nights together. I took a deep breath, remembering not to act too familiar. He was talking to a counselor right next to the marriage booth. When he saw me, he pointed to the booth and said, "Hey, Kramer, let's get hitched."

"Why not? I already consider you my summer husband."

Gilda's daughter Zoe performed the ceremony. She wore a tuxedo T-shirt and held a hardcover copy of *Atlas Shrugged* in place of a Bible.

"That's a hefty summer read," I said.

Zoe shrugged. "Tell me about it."

We both laughed.

She held out the book for us to place our hands on. "Do you solemnly swear to be married at Camp Woodlands for the rest of this summer?"

Teddy looked totally embarrassed even though it was his idea.

"Aw, are you having cold feet? Don't you trust me to have your back?" I asked. "Because I completely trust you."

"Well, yeah, yes, sure." He looked at Zoe. "I do."

We were given a choice of woven friendship bracelets, which we tied on each other's wrists, then walked away so the next couple could get camp hitched.

"That was fun. Will I see you later, summer husband?"

He leaned into me whispering, "I can't wait to consummate our marriage."

I stood on the small hill on the sidelines watching the mayhem. I noticed that the carny, a young guy controlling the Tilt-A-Whirl ride, was flirting with a counselor and not paying any attention to the kids. When I looked to see if any of the Cubs were on the ride, I saw a cape, worn by one of the campers, caught on a link in the chain that attached the car to the mechanical arm. The camper tugged on the cape, but it didn't come loose. He tried to get the attention of his friends, but no one noticed. His face became pale. I saw him open his mouth in a scream, though I couldn't hear it over the ruckus.

I realized I was the only one who saw what was happening and ran toward the carny shouting, "Stop the ride, stop the ride!"

The carny looked at me like I was a lunatic.

Pushing him aside I said, "How do you turn this thing off?" The control panel had a big red emergency button, and I slammed it with my palm. The ride screeched as the tin-can cars slowed, shuddered, and finally banged to a full stop.

The campers shouted to turn the ride back on.

The carny yelled, "What the fuck, lady!"

As I ran toward the kid, I shouted, "Radio the infirmary, and call 911." I ducked under the support bars to reach the boy whose lips had begun turning blue.

Holy shit, it was Nate, Bethany's son. I couldn't untie the cape—it was pulled too tightly around his neck. I was trying to rip it without putting more strain on his throat when I remembered I had a pair of crafting scissors in my pocket. Quickly but carefully, I snipped away at the fabric until he was free. Nate slumped in his seat, and I instinctively slapped his back. He coughed and grabbed his throat. He was pale but his lips were no longer blue.

Teddy appeared by my side and unclipped the seatbelt. "Nate, buddy, you're gonna be fine. The doctor's on her way."

The camp medical team surrounded Nate and immediately began checking him, carefully inspecting his neck and listening for any difficulty with his breathing. I noticed his throat beginning to bruise. I wanted to stay to make sure he'd be okay, but the medical team had everything under control. Bethany appeared, murmuring in Nate's ear and holding his hand.

Teddy put his arm around my shoulder. "Come on, we're in the way here. We need to let the professionals do their job."

As we walked, I started to shake, and when I saw the concern in Teddy's eyes I began sobbing.

Teddy said, "Let's get away from the crowd. The infirmary's probably empty since everyone's with Nate."

He led me into an examination room. I couldn't control my shaking. Teddy held me against his chest while rubbing my back, his head resting on top of mine. He let me cry. I hiccupped trying to catch my breath.

"Here, sit down. Try taking slow, deep breaths. I'll get you some water."

He handed me a cup, and I slowly drank, trying to collect myself, but only one word came out. "Nate."

"You saved his life."

A deep shudder racked my body. Teddy stood directly in front of me. His calm presence and his hands firmly on my thighs grounded me. He said, "Bethany and everyone at Woodlands are lucky you're here this summer."

The screen door slammed, and Nurse Ella yelled, "Is someone in here?"

"It's us, Ted and Lori . . . she needed a moment. How's Nate?"

"Fingers crossed that the worst case is a sore throat and a bit of bruising, but we decided it was prudent to send him to the hospital to make sure he'll be okay. Thank goodness you saw what was happening."

I started crying again.

Ella took my wrist, checking my pulse. "I know what happened was a lot. You may be in shock. Would you like a sedative?"

I shook my head. "No. No, I'll be fine."

Teddy looked at his watch. "There's still time before dinner. I'll walk you to your cabin, so you can rest."

We heard sirens and watched the EMTs lift the gurney Nate was strapped to into the ambulance. Bethany climbed in after him. Teddy put his arm around my waist. It seemed natural and uncomfortable at the same time. Even though we took the back way, it wasn't smart walking with his arm around me, but I needed the comfort he offered.

When we stopped in front of my cabin, I said, "I hope Bethany and her son will be okay."

"I do too. But right now, I want to make sure you're okay. I mean, a lot has happened today, and, well . . ."

"Let's see, we got married." I held up my wrist and flashed my bracelet. "And I saved a boy's life. You know, another typical day at camp."

He chuckled. "Nothing this summer has been typical. I'll check in later to see how you're doing. Radio me if you need anything."

# 28
# Camp Lessons

I was a few minutes late for dinner, but when I walked through the dining hall door, a hush came over the room. And then the entirety of Girls Camp stood on their chairs, applauding and singing, "*Lori* is Camp *Queen*—the *best* we've ever *seen*. Her *spirit* lights up *everywhere* that she has ever *been*!" It was the song only sung for the camper of the week, the highest honor at Woodlands. It took a moment to register that they were giving me a standing ovation. I was covered in goosebumps. Zelda and Hazel were clapping and foot stomping more enthusiastically than everyone else. The pride I saw in their eyes made my heart swell, and tears streamed down my face.

Marilyn flicked the lights, getting everyone's attention. "Okay, that's enough. Let's start dinner."

She couldn't take the moment away from me because girls were patting me on the back and giving me high fives. I was ambushed from behind—it was Zelda. "Mom, what you did today was awesome. I already started a letter to Dad telling him how you're the camp hero."

She hugged me in the middle of the dining hall for everyone to see. I breathed her in, savoring the moment. Hazel was right behind her. "Mom, wow, everyone is talking about how you're a hero."

"What do you say to them?"

She smiled from ear to ear. "Yup, that's my mom."

After dinner, I knocked on Bethany's door before opening it a few inches. Nate was lying on his back sleeping, his neck in a brace.

"I wanted to check on the patient, and you."

Bethany looked at Nate before she stepped outside. She grabbed my shoulders and said, "I don't know how I even go about thanking you."

Tears ran down both our faces as we hugged. My emotions were erratic—I'd been crying on and off all afternoon. A few hours ago, I'd cried out of fear, then joy, and now relief. Since I'd begun this job, there had been lots of tears.

"Tell me what happened at the hospital . . . what's his prognosis?"

"They said he has a neck strain, and there will be bruising and swelling. We have to wait to see if there will be any damage to his vocal cords, but even if there were, they didn't think it would be long lasting. Keeping our fingers crossed."

I hadn't even thought about his voice, and I wasn't about to bring up the psychological aspect of the injury. No reason to add to the list of worries that were probably plaguing her right now. "Are you and Nate leaving camp?"

"My husband's on his way right now. We'll discuss our options when he gets here. I'm sure if Nate can, he'll want to stay."

I had mixed feelings about Bethany leaving; a week ago I would've said good riddance, but now that we'd made a real connection, I hoped she'd stay.

Bethany asked, "Lori, can you please run the evening Flagpole?" She handed me her clipboard with the announcements and activity information.

"Me? Are you sure?"

"Yes. I'm sure."

I felt like a child whose mother was letting her cross the street for the first time.

The campers were already in formation surrounding the flagpole. Mindy and Marilyn were waiting, I guessed, for me.

Before I started the evening ritual, I quietly said, "Bethany asked me to conduct the Flagpole but before I do, Marilyn, would you like to address the campers?"

I was putting her on the spot, but if she were any kind of leader, she'd be ready with comforting words.

Looking uncomfortable, she spoke softly, "Jack doesn't think it's a good idea, too many letters home . . ."

Mindy didn't seem surprised by Marilyn's response. "It's always best to be direct, otherwise, you're responding to gossip and rumors."

Marilyn indecisively shrugged her shoulders, opting to leave the next move to the hired help.

Mindy stood front and center and, in a voice loud enough that everyone could hear, said, "I want to let you know that Nate is well and doing fine."

Everyone applauded and cheered.

"But now I want to thank Lori for her fearlessness, quick thinking, and life-saving actions!"

There was more applauding and cheering.

*Fearless?* I thought. *No, you're wrong—there are so many things I was afraid of, bears, snakes, the bottom of the lake, my feelings for Teddy.*

I smiled, looking out into the crowd wondering—*Is it still a standing ovation if everyone was already standing?*

After Flagpole, Jack radioed me to come to the office. I wondered when he'd get around to speaking with me.

Before I was through the door, Jack nodded toward his wife and said, "Marilyn tells me that your approval rating has skyrocketed."

Was that Jack's attempt at humor?

He sneered. "I hope all the acclaim doesn't go to your head."

I gawked at him. I knew better than to expect gratitude, but I'd naively thought I'd get an acknowledgment.

"What's that supposed to mean?" I asked.

"I don't want you to think of yourself as some kind of savior. You happened to be in the right place at the right time."

"You called me in here to insult me?"

Jack scoffed. "There you go again, twisting my words."

The only thing twisted was his brain. I didn't have to stay and listen to him. I looked over my shoulder as I walked out and said, "While the two of you sit in your air-conditioned office, I'll be outside with *your* campers."

Back in my room, I thought about how it took attending sleep-away camp—okay, thirty years late—to finally have the courage to stand up to a bully.

I wondered if Teddy would have time to meet. Boys Camp was freaking out, and if anyone could soothe the campers, it would be Teddy and Bob.

I hoped he'd show up because I needed to unload on someone I trusted, who respected and understood me. Sadly, that person was not my husband.

I must have dozed off, but I woke smiling when I heard three low whistles.

# 29
# Flagpole

The sun was burning off the morning mist as I stood alone at the edge of the lake by the ski dock doing sun salutations. It was a glorious way to start the day, getting lost in the beauty of the morning, watching the light shimmering on the water. I felt blessed to be able to enjoy this view—it sure beat the hell out of a yoga studio. I'd just swan dived over my legs and swayed, loosening my mind and my back, when my radio sounded. It was Marilyn. Talk about a zen kill.

I fought a head rush from standing up so quickly. "Lori here."

"What's your location?"

"The ski dock."

I heard some murmuring in the background.

"Why are you at the ski dock? You're supposed to be at the morning meeting," Marilyn said.

I stared at the radio for a moment. "No one told me. I'll head right up."

Even if I ran, it'd take at least twenty minutes. It was a good two miles to the office, the last quarter mile a steep hill.

"Ted offered to pick you up in a golf cart." Marilyn sounded annoyed.

"Okay, I'll start heading back to meet up with him."

I racked my brain trying to remember if someone had

mentioned the meeting to me. Bethany asked me to take over Flagpole last evening. She'd driven home late last night with her husband and Nate, but she hadn't said anything about a meeting. Maybe it was implied, and I'd somehow missed it.

I'd walked out on the Bergers yesterday, now this morning I'd have to sit in the same room with them to get instructions about new responsibilities. I should've been proud to be trusted with some of Bethany's duties on top of my own, but that placed me in the Bergers' direct line of fire. I took a deep, cleansing breath and braced myself.

Teddy honked the horn when I was between sail and ropes. He had a playful look on his face.

"Hop in, Kramer."

I slipped in next to him and smiled when he placed his hand on my thigh. But before starting the cart, he pointed at the willow trees across the lake.

"Over there, through that curtain of branches, is where we got to know each other better." He was irresistible when he blushed.

Squinting, I could barely make out the porch.

"Let's get out for a second. I've been wanting to do this and now's the perfect opportunity." Teddy took my hand and led me onto the dock where he wrapped me in his arms, kissing me in broad daylight. "That's how we should start every day."

I could tell he was pleased with himself. "I'm not so sure. Do it again, and I'll let you know."

"Cheeky."

My morning had just gotten a lot better.

"We should go before they wonder what took us so long," Teddy said.

"I'll tell them that Ted and I were snogging down by the lake."

Mike was at his usual morning post outside his Airstream, sipping a cup of coffee. I waved as we drove by, laughing at the confusion we saw on his face.

"Is he still making passes at you?" Teddy asked.

"Yes, but I look at it as a game, my daily sparring with Mike. I've come to enjoy our banter. I like to think he's exercising his mind, keeping up with my retorts."

"Having spent the past weeks trying to keep up with you myself, I'm not sure that lunkhead is up to the task."

"You'd be surprised. He's landed a wisecrack or two that were pretty impressive."

Teddy looked at me. "I see you're wearing the whistle he gave you."

"You mean this?" I held it up. "Our engagement whistle?" We laughed.

As we continued up the hill, I asked, "Tell me what I need to know before we enter the conference room."

"We review the counselors' paperwork from the night before. Talk about what worked and what didn't. Then we go over today's schedule."

"That means we'll be talking about the carnival," I said.

"I'd think it would be the main topic."

"I have to brace myself for the obnoxious remarks Jack will hurl at me," I said.

"I wouldn't worry—you've proven you can handle whatever foolishness comes out of that man's mouth."

Girls Camp was peaceful with everyone still asleep. I placed my hand on his knee. "Thanks for having faith in me."

"Lori, I'll always have your back." He covered my hand with his and I believed him.

As he pulled into the parking area in front of the office, I said, "This is the exact spot where we met."

"No, Nicole introduced us in the office. This is where I teased you for the first time."

"We've come a long way since that day."

We gazed into each other's eyes. "We have, haven't we."

We sat there for a moment. Teddy took a deep breath and said, "I jumped at the chance to pick you up, but now I see I brought you to a hornet's nest."

"Don't worry. After yesterday, they don't scare me anymore. Plus, what's the worst they can do? It's not like they can fire me. After all, I'm sure you've heard, I'm the camp's national treasure."

No one acknowledged us when we walked into the meeting, which, thankfully, seemed like it was mostly over. I sat next to Mindy as she pushed some handouts in front of me.

"Lori, just so you know, Bethany will be back Wednesday at the earliest, maybe as late as Friday. You'll be covering for her while she's gone," Jack informed me.

"That means you need to attend the morning meetings." Marilyn's voice dripped with attitude.

It dawned on me that she was probably the person who was supposed to tell me about the meeting and hadn't.

I could've called her out, but what good would it do to make Marilyn look bad? Though she hadn't done anything to gain my sympathy, I felt some for her, having to deal with Jack 24/7. I nodded and said, "Understood."

"Where's your knapsack and clipboard?" Marilyn snapped at me, probably the way Jack snapped at her.

"I left it at the arts & crafts studio where I pick it up on my way back from my morning walk." I assumed Abby heard Marilyn radio me. Otherwise, she'd be worried I met up with another bear.

"Well, you'd better make sure you're prepared for tomorrow's meeting."

Any feelings of sympathy had just gone up in campfire smoke. "Will do."

As the meeting broke up, I looked directly at Jack and asked, "What's Nate's diagnosis?"

"He should have no lasting effects from the accident, but we'll know more later today." Jack looked at his clipboard as he spoke, as if he might melt if he looked me in the eye.

I picked up the paperwork, left the table, and stuck my hand into my mail slot to see if there were any messages. I also checked Bethany's box. As I walked by Nicole's desk, she gave me a supportive nod, which I returned. Bob and Teddy were waiting outside.

"Don't pay attention to the Bergers. They're in particularly bad moods, having been reamed by their partners after yesterday's disaster," Bob said.

"You're a bloody hero, and they have the nerve to accuse you of being unprepared," Teddy said.

"I'll be fine. I'll figure it out."

Abby and Maggie intercepted me on the way to breakfast. Roger was a step behind them carrying my knapsack.

"I brought you some dirty-water coffee." Maggie handed me my cherry blossom covered thermos.

"You're a life saver! This is exactly what I need." I took a gulp and, as usual, a drop fell smack in the middle of my clean white T-shirt.

"How'd you forget to go to the morning meeting?" Maggie asked.

"Marilyn forgot to tell me, and she made it out to be my fault."

"Typical," Abby said.

Roger handed me the bag. "When did you become so important, you get to hang out with the big kahunas?"

"My theory is that in the Bergers' warped way of thinking, since I was the one who saved Nate, I should be the one to cover for Bethany," I said.

"'Warped' being the operative word," Maggie said.

"She was aggressively obnoxious about it. I figure Jack gets kicked by the partners, Jack kicks Marilyn, Marilyn kicks me," I said.

"So, who are you kicking?" Roger asked.

"Not my style," I said.

# 30
# Job Wheel

The forecast was for sunny skies and temperatures in the high seventies. At least the weather was on my side. I had mixed emotions as I stopped at the OD shack to pick up the flag. It was exciting and nerve-wracking to lead; whatever I did would be scrutinized. I needed to be on my toes. I took a deep breath, positive I was up to the challenge.

The flag was against my chest as I stood in front of the campers, assembled for the morning announcements. I heard murmuring in the crowd, scanned the line of girls spread out like a fan, and made eye contact with my kids—who were grinning and giving me the thumbs up.

Smiling, I said, "Good morning, campers."

They roared back, "Good morning, Lori."

"It's so nice to see your happy faces straight on instead of off to my right." I pointed to where I usually stood each morning.

There was a smattering of laughter.

"I'm going to be standing in for Bethany while she's home taking care of Nate. We're hoping they'll be back to dance with us this Saturday night at the Disco Party."

While the girls cheered, I grabbed Abby and twirled her around.

"The Chipmunks have canteen this afternoon."

They hooted and sang out in unison, "You scream, I scream, we all scream for ice cream."

"Tonight's movie is *The Parent Trap*."

I turned to Abby, who had a birthday tiara in her hand. She announced, "Today is Zara's birthday and she gets to raise the flag."

As Zara claimed her crown, her bunkmates chanted, "She's got *spirit!* She's got *spunk!* That's because she's in our *bunk! Yay, Zara!*"

The flag went up, we said the Pledge of Allegiance, and the campers dispersed to do their chores before the start of first period.

Mindy was by my side. "Well done."

"Why wasn't Marilyn here? Do you think it was a snub? You know, I didn't show for her meeting, so she's not showing for mine?"

"That'd be petty and would make her look bad." Mindy stopped for a moment. "So yeah, knowing her, that could very well be the reason. What are you going to do now?"

"I was going to return some phone calls, inspect the Cubs' bunks, and then walk the campus to check out all the activities."

"Sounds like a plan. Here's the key to Bethany's golf cart. I know you prefer to walk, but you've got a lot of terrain to cover."

"Thanks. I think I'll make the calls from Bethany's room; no reason to go into the office."

"Smart move. I'll catch up with you later."

It was fun zipping around camp on a golf cart. The best part was that since I was the temporary head counselor and needed to be everywhere, I could watch Zelda and Hazel participate in activities. Zelda's group had soccer, and it was my good fortune that Teddy was refereeing the game. I pulled up next to the field—the ball was in play at the opposite goal.

Zelda's team had control of the ball. Tara kicked it to Zelda who scored a goal. Teddy blew his whistle and ran over to Zelda, who was beaming, and gave her a high five.

When the match was over, Zelda and Tara ran to Teddy. Zelda jumped onto his back while Tara blew into his whistle. They were laughing and easy with each other.

Ronnie rarely made it to our children's games, even on weekends. He barely had time to listen to the girls when they told him about their days. Here was a man we'd just met, delighting in Zelda's achievements.

Teddy noticed me watching and stopped for a second, grinning. He tapped Zelda on her shoulder and pointed. Both girls came running over.

"Did you see me score?" Zelda, despite her claims of not wanting me around, was excited to see me.

"Yeah, I did!"

Zelda let me hug her for a hot second before she pushed away.

"Hey, Tara, great passing. Good game." We high-fived.

"You're in charge?" Tara asked.

"Yeah, I guess I am."

"Then do you think we could get canteen today?" Tara asked.

I laughed. "It's not like I have superpowers."

Teddy joined us. "These two were today's soccer stars. Impressive footwork and teamwork." He fist-bumped them.

"Your group is getting ready to move on. I'll try to catch you at another activity," I said to the girls.

When they trotted off, Teddy said, "Hey, Kramer, nice surprise. Did you come to check me out?"

I adored his boyish grin. "Ha, as if! Since I've been put in charge, I thought I'd use the opportunity to see what my kids were up to. You, Mooney, were a bonus," I said.

"It's not at all surprising that you have great kids. Athletic, fun team players, and beautiful—they obviously take after you."

"You sweet talker. If we were alone, I'd be the one jumping on your back." I was typically not a fan of grown men who wore sports jerseys, but he looked so incredibly hot in his shiny soccer uniform.

He was smiling. "You're undressing me with your eyes, aren't you?"

"I would like nothing more than to lick the sweat off your body right here, right now."

It was arousing to make him moan without even touching him. He took a deep breath and asked, "Since you have the golf cart, can you drive me over to boys' side?"

"Of course—it's the least I can do since you were gallant enough to pick me up earlier."

Teddy slid in next to me, his leg resting against mine.

"Do all the kids jump on you like Zelda did?" I asked.

"Only the ones I bond with."

I didn't think it was possible to admire him more than I already did. "Hazel?"

"I was with her last week. Her age group was scheduled when I was off, playing with you." He tapped my knee, both of us smiling.

"I feel like I'm missing out. I don't really know Max at all, and I have no idea how to remedy that."

"He's a good kid. I think you'd like him, so yeah, it would be nice if you got to know him. Let me think how I can make it happen."

I was about to suggest trying to get the five of us together, but why? What would I tell my daughters? "I want you to meet Max because I've been having romantic liaisons with his dad"? I changed the subject. "This morning, when Jack said Bethany may not be back until Friday . . ."

"We wouldn't be able to meet up. I came to the same conclusion. I know Nate, and he's going to want to get back to camp as soon as possible," Teddy said.

"It would be too obvious if you asked to change your days off again to match mine."

"There are no secrets at camp, but at least we could fool ourselves into believing we're covering our tracks."

"But what if they're not back by Wednesday? All I think about is the next time I can fall asleep in your arms, and now that may not happen at all this week," I said.

Teddy didn't say anything as I pulled up next to the boys' soccer field. When I looked into his eyes, I could feel that he wanted me as much as I wanted him.

The boys started filling the field, and one of the counselors yelled to him, "Hey, Mooney, unlock the door so we can get the gear out."

"Be there in a sec," he shouted back.

As he got out, he bent close to me and whispered, "No need to worry, nothing is going to keep us apart, I promise."

He turned away and I watched him jog over to the equipment shed. The same feeling washed over me as when I'd left the lake house—I was in deep.

To be honest, I enjoyed being in charge—well, at least some parts. Now I got to start and end my day with Teddy. I also liked the freedom of driving around in a golf cart and seeing the big picture—how the whole camp ran.

The downside was the agony of the morning meetings. It was bad enough just being in the same room as Jack, but he seemingly took perverse pleasure in pointing out everyone's mistakes and faults—not unlike how Ronnie had been treating me for the past few years. I was no longer going to allow either of them to make me the center of their disdain.

I started to appreciate Bethany in a whole new light. At the beginning of camp, she was quick to criticize my mistakes, but I now realized it was probably because of how Jack treated her. After my conversation with Mindy, Bethany became more supportive of me and the other DLs. It was becoming apparent to me that Bethany and Mindy needed to rely on each other for the support they weren't getting from the Bergers.

At the meetings I positioned myself near my allies. I sat next to Mindy, who whispered witty comments in my ear. I knew she wanted me to succeed and offered her assistance at every turn. Teddy sat across from me.

I was doing my best to stay afloat, juggling Bethany's responsibilities and my own. My counselors stepped up, reassuring me that they and the campers would be fine. It seemed that everyone wanted me to succeed except Jack. It made no sense.

Even though he hired people who were smart and resourceful and dedicated to the happiness of the campers, he micromanaged and undermined his staff. On top of that, he had no idea that his constant criticism and verbal lashings worked against him. If he simply let his capable employees do their jobs, everyone would've been much happier.

Fortunately, things had been calm since the carnival. Hard to believe that was only two days ago—it felt like a week. Time moved differently at camp.

I caught up with Hazel's group at gymnastics. There were twenty-four nine-year-olds wearing camp-issued green and white leotards, running around barefoot with their hair pulled back in high ponies. It made me think of nine-year-old me taking lessons at Miss Doris's School of Dance, positive that I belonged even though I had no natural ability.

They were in various stages of a gymnastics obstacle course, which required them to walk the balance beam, dismount, jump onto and off a pommel horse, swing on the lower parallel bar, dismount into a somersault, and end with a cartwheel. And for the big finish: stand straight with their hands above their heads, smiling.

I positioned myself in front of Hazel so she'd see me after her flourish. I applauded, thinking how lucky I was to be here and to see her happy and self-assured. "Great job! I'd give you a ten for sure."

She gave me a hug. I'd missed those so much. "You, too. How'd you get to be head counselor?"

"It's a bit unclear, but thanks for the compliment."

"You do a great Flagpole—I'm really proud of you. I wrote to Dad and told him all about it." Hazel had a big grin on her face.

"Have you gotten mail from Dad?"

"Yeah, but his letters are kinda weird. They're typed and say things that he never says."

"Like what?"

"I don't know. 'Love you forever.' 'Can't wait to play with you.'"

Jana was probably writing them and having Ronnie sign them. Typical. I wondered if he even read them. I couldn't imagine him signing a letter to a client without it undergoing at least three revisions.

"I'm sure he's trying his best. I mean, he's never written you a letter before," I said.

She shrugged. "I guess. See you later." Then she whispered, "Mom."

Jack started the Wednesday morning meeting by letting us know that Bethany and Nate would be back at camp before dinner.

I avoided making eye contact with Teddy during these meetings, but I was so excited I couldn't help myself. Teddy's face was down but he subtly shifted his head toward me and I saw the twinkle in his eyes. The dread I'd felt when I walked into the room evaporated. We wouldn't have to miss our tryst. We both glanced at the clock at the same time. I wondered if his heart was pounding as hard as mine.

# 31
# Campfires

I'd let go of my anxieties and didn't hesitate to make the left turn. For the past week, my mind had kept drifting back to our time together at the lake house. I went to place a water bottle in the cup holder and saw my wedding band there—I hadn't noticed I wasn't wearing it. I closed the cover.

He was waiting for me, the sun shining on his bronzed face. So handsome, so sexy, I couldn't believe that this beautiful man wanted me. This time I wasn't nervous, only eager to be alone with him. Behind closed doors.

He grinned when I pulled into the driveway. I didn't wait for him to open the door—I jumped out, threw my arms around his neck, and kissed him.

"This has been the longest week of my life. I felt like a child counting the days until I could unwrap my Christmas gift," he said.

"But we snog behind the laundry shack every night."

"True, but undressing you and having you naked in bed with me is a whole other level of . . ."

He hesitated so I offered, "Intimacy?"

His grin grew wider. "Yes, let's go get intimate."

A bowl of peaches sat on the kitchen counter next to one filled with blueberries, and a single perfect sunflower stood in a glass vase.

"The sunflower is beautiful, tall and perfect like you." I had my arm around his waist.

He squeezed my hand. "I was toying with getting you a bouquet of—"

I cut him off. "I adore that you buy me a sunflower because it makes you think of me." I smiled. "I was about to say with no strings attached, but our rendezvous do have certain expectations."

He tilted my chin up. "And you've more than lived up to mine. This week I'm better prepared to properly take care of you. I hope I meet your expectations."

I hadn't been in the forethought of anyone's mind in a very long time.

We held hands as we walked up the stairs to *our* bedroom.

He pulled my shirt over my head and then stopped. "Maybe we should eat first?"

"Consider me the appetizer." I let my bra fall to the floor.

Satiated, he collapsed on me, both of us panting.

He propped himself up, looking at me. "You are very much worth the wait." He kissed me and plopped back down.

We stayed like that, sprawled on each other, my fingers massaging his scalp until he said, "That was two orgasms—it must be time to eat."

There were bottles of water on the nightstand and a bowl of grapes.

"I'm impressed. Not only did you buy food, you thought to bring snacks upstairs."

"I'm here to satiate every part of your body." He rolled off me, reached over, and picked up a small bunch of grapes. He pulled one off the stem, placed it between his lips, and kissed it into my mouth.

I laughed.

"Are you mocking me?" he asked.

"Quite the opposite. Sex with a beautiful man who feeds me grapes. All my fantasies are coming true without me even telling you what they are."

He popped another into my mouth. "Let's make some new ones together."

I sighed. "I'm pretty sure I'm living one right now."

"No more going to bed on an empty stomach." He was talking to me with his head in the fridge as he pulled ingredients out.

Teddy was indeed prepared. There were steaks that had marinated overnight and fresh local corn to barbecue. I tossed a salad while he grilled. There was also a lime next to a bottle of Tanqueray.

The meal was yummy, but I was more enamored that he'd shopped and prepared dinner. After we cleaned up, we sat next to each other sipping gin & tonics on the porch.

"Sitting out here with you, well . . . I feel relaxed and content in a way I don't think I've experienced before," I said.

"I've never felt this comfortable with another person, aside from my son. It's more than our time in the bedroom. I like sitting out here with you, talking about everything and nothing. I never really had that." He took my hand and kissed it.

"I want to thank you. I stood up to Jack, and you helped me do that."

"The only thing I did was point out your strengths. It was all you, your gumption, facing Jack, saving Nate, taking over as head counselor. I was merely a witness."

He was right. I had done all those things—by myself. "Thank you."

"For what?"

"Reminding me that I am a competent person."

"That's an understatement."

The evening turned cooler as we chatted. I reached for a blanket and draped it across my shoulders.

Teddy took my hand. "Are you cold, my love?"

"A little."

"Let's go inside. I'll build us a fire."

He helped me out of the deep Adirondack chair and kept my hand in his as we went inside. I admired his graceful movements as he skillfully stacked the logs in the hearth.

"Don't forget to open the flue," I said.

"Thanks for the reminder, already done." He brushed his hands together as the flames began to dance. "There we go."

Teddy took the blanket from my shoulders and laid it on the floor. His warm body was comforting as he hugged me into him, kissing me tenderly. I felt a tear slowly run down my cheek.

"Is that a teardrop?" He wiped it away with his thumb. "Have I upset you?"

"Being here with you, the fire, it's all . . . it's all perfect."

He pulled me down to my knees, facing him. "I agree." He laced his hands through my hair as we kissed.

We lay next to each other, feeling the warmth of the flames and each other.

He leaned on his forearms, hovering over me. The glow of the fire reflected in his eyes.

"I've never made love in front of a roaring fire," I said.

"Brilliant. Something we can experience together."

Teddy was propped up on pillows, the morning sun shining across his face as he read. He looked distinguished in his glasses. I was mostly awake, aware of him absently twisting my curls around his fingers while my head rested on his chest.

"Good morning, my love." He kissed the top of my head.

"Good morning, my Teddy."

He slid me off him, our faces inches apart. He smiled. "You smell a bit smoky this morning."

I returned his smile. "So do you." I stroked his cheek. "I was thinking, if it's not too much to ask . . ."

"Anything for you."

"I was hoping you could help me wash the smoke out of . . ."

He jumped up, playfully tugging me out of bed before I could finish my sentence.

After our shower, Teddy made me a proper English breakfast—bangers and beans with fried eggs. I had never had bangers, but I was open to trying anything when I was with Teddy . . . in and out of bed.

I speared a sausage with my fork and held it up. "There must be a joke in here somewhere . . ."

Teddy held my wrist and with a wry smile said, "I refuse to have you poke fun at that part of my anatomy."

We took our breakfast onto the porch; the August humidity had returned.

"By the way, you broke another one of my rules," I said.

"Let's see, I fed you after two orgasms. Not only did I buy you dinner last night, I cooked it for you. There's more?"

"My mother told me, 'Lori, *never* perform fellatio on a man unless he's buying you a house.'"

Teddy almost choked on his tea, then started laughing. "You're serious?"

"My mother was a real New York City broad, a ballbuster. She didn't hold back any thought or opinion."

"I admire that in you."

I bristled, but then a mixture of pride and elation overcame me. "I hadn't realized that I'd turned into my mother."

He gave me a dazzling smile and placed his hand on mine as we sat. I was basking in the sun, the afterglow of our steamy bathroom sex and making him laugh. What I experienced with Teddy was better than anything I could've ever dreamed up. I'd never felt as sensual or desired.

He broke the silence. "Woodlands has been my second home for over twenty years. It's the only place where I feel like my life is uncomplicated. Max loves it here. I met you here." He squeezed my hand.

I understood his feelings. My kids were having a great summer, and I could easily get used to sitting next to Teddy every day.

I lifted his hand to my lips and kissed it. "Yes, life is perfect at camp."

He turned on the radio and we danced around the kitchen while cleaning up. We decided to spend the remainder of the morning relaxing on the porch in our bathing suits to soak up the sun. I laughed when he pulled on a pair of very short trunks with the Union Jack across his delectable ass.

"What's so funny? I'm a proud Englishman." He shook his butt at me.

I gave it a squeeze.

"This is how we Brits dress when we're not surrounded by prudish Americans. Come on, join me. Throw on a bikini."

"I haven't owned a two piece in well over ten years."

"Why the hell not? You've got great curves you should be proud to show off. Next time I'm in town, I'm buying you one."

I wished I could see myself through his eyes.

He grabbed his knapsack. "I'm sorry, but I promised Bob I'd take care of some things for Color War. I don't want it to interfere with our day, so I thought this would be a good time. I'll get it done quickly, and then my attention will be solely on you."

I picked up the dog-eared book on the nightstand. "In that case can I read your book? Huh, I've never read John le Carré."

"My dad's favorite author. He introduced me to him when I was in secondary school, and now I read at least one each summer."

"Subterfuge, crossing lines, secrets. I can relate to that."

Settled back on the porch, we were serenaded by motorboats and the laughter of campers as the sun washed over us.

Teddy started working, but I couldn't focus on the book—I kept sneaking peeks at him. He was so engrossed in figuring out the rosters that he didn't notice me watching him. I was captivated by the way his eyebrows arched when he concentrated, the way he held the pencil as he scribbled notes. I wanted to remember everything about him, how he put his hand to his mouth when he was thinking, or absently ran his fingers through his hair, the mole on his left shoulder blade.

I took mental snapshots to store for when I couldn't be sitting next to him. I started counting down the days—not like the homesick campers, the exact opposite. I didn't want the summer or our romance to end.

In the background, the radio played golden oldies. Frank Sinatra crooned, "Fly Me to the Moon."

When he put his pencil down, I pulled him out of the chair. "Dance with me."

He grinned from ear to ear. "That's the second best offer I've had today."

Laughing, we swayed to the music. One of his arms securely held me, his other hand had mine next to his heart. I adored being close to him, our bodies touching.

"I like dancing with you." I bit his neck.

"We fit well together, horizontally and vertically." He sang into my ear. "In other words, please be mine." He spun and dipped me.

"Working at camp was the best decision I ever made," I said.

"And why's that?"

"Because I'm here dancing with you."

We locked eyes, our bodies melting into each other. Our kisses were slow, deep, and lazy on a cloudless August morning.

That afternoon I had an epiphany as I gazed at him. "You know who would be a natural at running this camp?" I asked.

Without hesitation, Teddy said, "You."

"Me? No, you."

"All I want is to play *soccer* every day."

"I've watched you coaching. You're incredible with the kids. You're respected. You're fun. You're an inspiring leader. I'd follow you anywhere."

"You come up with the zaniest ideas. First breaking and entering, and now running a camp, and somehow you coax me into being your accomplice."

I smiled. "I do, but I'm serious. You should buy Woodlands."

"Is it for sale?" he joked, but then he paused. "I have thought about it, but now the only way I'd even consider it would be if you did it with me."

I laughed. "It could work. Look at us, partners in crime and then partners in business."

"And then our partnership could grow into"—he hesitated—"something more."

Our conversation had taken an unexpected turn. My understanding had been that we were over when the summer was over. I must have had a confused look on my face because he quickly added, "I'm actually serious."

"Come on, that's crazy."

"We could do it. You said you were considering finding a career when you got home."

"I hadn't thought that buying . . ."

"And with Jack here, you won't return next summer. I can't have that." He looked genuinely distraught, but then excited. "Before I get carried away by this idea, I need to know if you're serious about us owning the camp."

He stared at me, waiting for my answer. I had no idea what to say. Would I want to make Woodlands my summer home, with him—for the rest of my life? Answering only with my heart, I said, "Yes, I believe I am."

"The two of us together would be unstoppable," he said.

"Unstoppable. I like that."

"Every time I've thought this through, I knew it couldn't work with me living in London from September through May. But with you in New York, it's possible. Of course, there's the small problem of the camp not being for sale." He laughed. "Although, that's a minor glitch. Then there's the issue of money . . ."

A humorous thought popped into my brain. Ronnie didn't want to pay for camp, would he want to pay for *the* camp? I'd figured out how to get the kids into a camp. Now I needed to figure out a way to finance my share.

"Money's always an issue. But we're resourceful people, we'll figure something out. Are you as excited about the possibility as I am?" I asked.

"Indubitably."

He drew me into him, and we kissed for a long time. He was such a fabulous kisser, focused and passionate. It made me think of Rhett's line to Scarlett, "You need to be kissed often and by someone who knows how." Teddy totally knew how, and our plan would have us kissing for years.

Back in my room, lying in my sagging bed, my head was filled with Teddy and Woodlands. I pictured us holding hands, walking the grounds together. Encouraging, inspiring, and participating in activities with the campers, mentoring and collaborating with the counselors. Then, each night after a long but satisfying day, falling into bed together.

My euphoria burst when I remembered that even though I was separated, I was still married with two children who loved their dad and had no idea that their parents' marriage was in jeopardy.

Sex. I'd spent the last few weeks making love to another man. How cavalier I'd been, reveling in the arms of someone who wasn't my husband. Even though Ronnie and I had agreed to a separation, I never could've imagined starting a relationship.

Being at camp was like living in a bubble—no outside interference, no news of the world. All conversations were centered around camp. Was it because I was so immersed in the Woodlands culture that I got carried away and acted on the attraction I had for Teddy?

What if Ronnie found out? Yes, Ronnie had been a jerk, but he didn't deserve to have his wife cheat on him even if we were estranged. Would it even be considered cheating? I didn't know—it wasn't something I had ever thought about. I was in uncharted territory.

What I did know was Ronnie loved his family—he just hadn't made me, Zelda, or Hazel his priority for a long time. That didn't necessarily make him a bad person . . . maybe just a misguided one.

I took a pillow and squeezed it into my stomach, trying to quell the turmoil I felt. I had a niggling suspicion that Ronnie was having a dalliance of his own. There was something a little too familiar about his relationship with Jana. Could I possibly be inventing this scenario to alleviate my conscience? If it were true, would I be upset? Would we call it even and move on as a couple, or would we end our marriage, preferring our lovers?

My relationship with Teddy made clear what was missing between Ronnie and me. Teddy treated me as his equal and partner. Even with counseling, would I be able to put my marriage back on track? Did I even want to? If we didn't share two daughters, I would walk away.

# 32
# Lost

I was kayaking between water activities, watching the Cubs who were kayaking with me, sailing, or waterskiing. When the period was over, Mindy offered me a ride in her golf cart. I preferred to walk, but I was in a wet bathing suit and wanted to change before the next activity. She'd just dropped me off when my radio crackled, "We have a lost swimmer. Lexi Silver's division has left the waterfront, and her card's still here. We have a lost swimmer." I recognized Mike's voice.

"Mike, this is Lori. Lexi's my camper. I just saw her walking up from swim with her group. She's fine."

"I cannot call off a lost swimmer search until I see Lexi Silver standing in front of me."

Crap. I ran toward Mindy's cabin and jumped in her golf cart. Thankfully, the keys were in the ignition. I threw it in reverse, almost falling out when I bumped a tree stump the size of a small dog. Maneuvering backwards I called out, "I'm borrowing your golf cart."

I reached Lexi's cabin as she stepped onto the porch.

"Hey, Lexi, jump in here with me."

"Why?"

"You didn't return your swim card, and all the lifeguards are searching for you."

"Can't you tell them I'm with you?"

"I did but they need to see you in person. Hold on tight." I floored it.

I sped down the hill. When we hit the straightaway, I radioed Mike, "Lexi is almost there."

"Good, my lifeguards are exhausted."

Lexi asked, "Why are they exhausted?"

"They've been searching for you underwater."

"They think I drowned?"

"Yes."

Lexi burst into tears.

I reached the beach, shouting, "I have Lexi. Lexi is here."

I hit the brake, but the cart didn't slow down. I turned toward the beachfront to avoid hitting Mike. I stomped the brake again, turning the wheel, which sent us skidding into the lake. I threw my arm around Lexi to make sure she didn't fall out. Why weren't there seat belts in these damned things?

Three lifeguards swam over and stopped the cart from sinking any further. Di pulled out a sobbing Lexi.

"Lori, shove it over," Mike said.

I'd have preferred to get out, but Mike blocked me, so I slid to the passenger side as he got behind the wheel.

"Okay, men, I'm in reverse. Tell me when to hit the gas."

How embarrassing. I couldn't believe that Mike had to come to my rescue, and this time in front of the entire waterfront staff. They all watched as Mike easily maneuvered the cart out of the water and safely onto the sand.

Mike pulled the key out of the ignition, saying, "Really, Lori, again?"

I put the whistle in my mouth and blew.

# 33
# The Big Dance

The next night at the dance party I spotted Teddy, alone in the far corner leaning against the wall, his arms crossed in front of him, a mischievous smile on his face.

I was sure that my excitement level at the thought of dancing with Teddy like we had at the lake house far exceeded how stoked the campers were for this night.

The DJ was set up on a platform surrounded by flashing lights and blinking electronic equipment. The only illumination in the building was from the pulsating lights reflected by the disco balls hanging from the beams.

Walking across the enormous field house, I caught the essence of sweat socks, bug spray, and something sickeningly sweet that I couldn't place. A few of the older boys sauntered by, and my eyes watered. Cheap cologne.

"Welcome to the boy's indoor gym, one of the finer establishments here at Woodlands," Teddy said.

"Just so you know, my dance card isn't yet full, so if you're interested, you should pick a number."

"Do you think it would cause a scandal if we danced together all night?"

"Absolutely, but it would be so much fun."

He leered at me. "You tease me, wearing your *break and enter* skirt—I may not be able to keep my hands off your arse."

"A risk I'm willing to take." I held his elbow and walked us to the center of the room.

"Stacy's Mom" came on, and I laughed.

"What's funny?"

"I'm a mom that has it going on."

Grinning, he whispered in my ear, "Lucky me," then dipped me.

Before the next song began, Bethany cut in. It was a good thing.

Even though I was enjoying a perk of my job, dancing with the hot soccer coach, I needed to concentrate on my duties. I found a group of Cubs dancing together and joined them.

As we danced, I felt electricity surging through the building to the beat of the song. The lights flashed, the music thumped, and the air was filled with anticipation. There had been so much hype building up to this event that I wasn't expecting much, but all the excitement was legit.

Sarah, one of the Cubs, was skulking on the sidelines. She had refused to attend the party, so I coaxed her by promising I'd be her date. I grabbed both of her hands and started swaying to OutKast.

I saw Dylan the camp photographer snapping shots.

"Come on, let's dance like Dylan was taking our photo."

She reluctantly moved with me into the throng of sweaty dancers. As we swayed to the music, I looked around, trying to pick out my daughters. It wasn't easy to locate them with the blinding strobe lights. I found them dancing with their friends about five feet away from each other, huge smiles on their faces. Hazel wore a sparkly tank top, her hair framing her face. Someone had French-braided Zelda's hair—I needed to learn how to do that. I loved being here with them, witnessing how much fun they were having instead of being at home waiting for a letter, like everyone else's mother.

Abby had the night off along with half the counselors, but they stayed at camp—that was how big a draw the dance was. She shimmied over to me.

"We just got back from our lobster dinner and ice cream sundaes, and now I'm ready to boogie the night away."

"Where're Maggie and Roger?"

"Getting some face time with Tony."

"Have you seen your kids?" I asked.

"Checked them out as soon as I got here." Earth, Wind & Fire blasted from the amps. "Come on, you and me, let's hustle."

As the night wound down, I noticed a group of boys walking over to where Hazel danced. It was about time they mingled with the girls—the party was going to end soon. It was a phenomenon that all the fun started when things were about to wrap up. The leader of the pack started talking to Hazel and I felt a sense of pride that my daughter was singled out. I watched as he moved closer to her and then, without warning, he reached out and pulled down her skirt.

I stood there, staring, registering what happened. The shrieks from Hazel and her friends jarred me into action. Hazel pulled up her skirt, red-faced and crying, while the boy went back to his buddies, grinning and receiving high fives.

My brain raced—should I see to Hazel or grab the boy by his neck? I decided to go after the brat and pull every hair out of his dim-witted head. I ran toward him and saw Teddy heading toward the boy from the opposite direction. When I got a clear view of my target, I stopped short. Zelda had reached him first, hands rolled into fists. The strobe lights blinking overhead made every movement look surrealistically slow as Zelda pulled her arm back and punched him, sending all eighty pounds of her into his unsuspecting gut. The boy bent over, crumbling to the floor, holding his abdomen.

I wasn't the mom who yelled from the bleachers at sporting events, but I pumped my fist in the air shouting, "Yes!" in solidarity with Zelda.

I had never been prouder in my entire life.

A crowd started forming, so I grabbed Zelda's and Hazel's hands and led them outside. We heard Bob yelling above the music, "Nothing to see here, go back to dancing."

There was a key left in a golf cart. The girls slid into the front seat with me. I pulled out without looking back.

"How great was it that Zelda beat up that dumb kid?" I asked.

"Did you see him fall down in front of everybody?" Hazel's tears had turned into a full-on belly laugh. When she caught her breath she said, "I was surprised and then angry. I wish I got to punch him or *pants* him, but Zelda got him good."

Zelda shook out her hand. "It hurts punching boys."

By the time we pulled up to my cabin, the three of us were crying from laughing so much. We fell onto the bed and cuddled.

"I'm incredibly proud of both of you and happy to know that you've got each other's backs."

"Are we in trouble?" Hazel asked.

That was a good question. "You know what? I don't care. All I know is that I have the bravest and most wonderful kids in the world."

I was savoring the moment—it seemed like the girls were also. Then my radio went off, spoiling everything.

"Lori come in for Bethany, Lori come in for Bethany."

"Lori here."

"Your location please?"

"Driving a golf cart with a Chipmunk and a Woodchuck back to their bunks and then seeing to the Cubs."

"Okay, meet me and Mindy after you've finished."

"Mom, you just lied," Hazel said.

"Yeah, well, you just mooned the entire camp, and Zelda just slugged a kid. What can I say, no one's perfect."

# 34
# Let's Make a Deal

It took me half the summer to figure out that if I bribed the girls with candy, the cleanliness of the bunks improved. I had just finished my daily walk-through and was on my way to the office when I saw a red convertible driving toward me.

A silver-haired man was wedged behind the wheel of the Porsche that stopped in front of the office. He was having difficulty extricating himself from his expensive car. The steering wheel sat low on his legs, making it difficult to maneuver.

It was uncomfortable watching his large frame slowly, excruciatingly emerge from the matchbox-sized car. I took out my clipboard, looking away, making it less embarrassing for both of us.

"Hello. I'm Chip Howe, here to see Jack."

"Lori Kramer, one of the division leaders."

"Lori. You're just the person I wanted to meet."

He was as tall as he was round. If I remembered correctly this must be the man Mindy and Bob said was part owner and the CFO of several camps.

Before I could find out why he wanted to meet me, Jack came flying out of the office.

"Chip, great to see you. I see you've already met, uh . . ."

Jack stood with his mouth gaping open. He'd patronized

me last Sunday and chastised me yesterday, but at that exact moment he couldn't remember my name.

"Yes, Jack, I've already met Lori." It was amusing, watching this giant of a man roll his eyes like one of the campers. "I'd think you'd be able to remember the name of the person who saved this camp and your ass."

Beads of sweat formed on Jack's brow. Although I enjoyed watching him squirm, staying with them didn't seem prudent.

"Nice meeting you. I'm off to join the Cubs."

"I hope you'll have time to talk later," Chip said.

I patted the radio on my hip. "You know how to find me."

I made my way to the tennis courts where a round robin tournament was taking place among the Cubs. I cheered the girls on, hoping to see if the instruction during the first half of the summer had paid off.

The call from Chip came during rest hour, asking me to meet him at the back door of the office. He was sitting behind the wheel of Marilyn's golf cart and waved me over.

"Slide in. Join me for a drive around the camp. It's been a while since I toured it, and since I pay for everything, it's good to take a gander now and again. Plus, I want to get to know you better."

He drove us toward the lake.

"I've been hearing good things about you from Bob, Bethany, and Mindy—your quick actions saving Nate. How you stepped into Bethany's role as head counselor. I've even gotten positive feedback from Ted, and he's a hard man to please."

*Not if you know how*, I thought. I hoped my blush would be construed as modesty.

"Bob was practically gushing over you."

"Why?" Because I poured him a gin each night?

"Lots of reasons, but he thinks you're a badass, standing up to Jack."

"I'm impressing you by being disrespectful to my boss?"

He laughed. "You've got a good bullshit meter, and you're obviously not afraid to speak your mind—two important attributes in business."

At the lakefront, we pulled up next to Mike, who wore an orange Speedo. The contrast between these two men was so extreme they could've posed for before and after photos.

"Chip! How's it going, big guy?" Mike slapped him on the back. "Haven't seen you in my territory in years." Only Mike could get away with calling the man who signed his paycheck *big guy*. "I see you've met our heroic division leader."

"Yes, I asked if she'd accompany me on a drive around camp so I could see for myself," Chip said.

"Lori can tell you how I've been her personal hero this summer, saving her twice, so far, but there's still another couple of weeks to go." Mike winked at me like we were a thing.

Chip ignored Mike's boorish behavior. "Everything good for you? Equipment? Counselors?"

Mike stood at attention and saluted. "Everything's in tip-top form."

"At ease, my good man. Carry on." Chip pulled away, driving toward the ski dock. "He's a bit of a pompous ass, don't you think?"

I laughed in response. I didn't want to come across as judgmental and undermine my real concern: Jack.

We stopped at the ropes course, where Chip had a similar conversation with Harry, the head of ropes. Next was Di at sail, and lastly, we stopped and watched some water-skiers.

We turned around by the ski dock, and Chip said, "Everything about this lake is beautiful."

"I agree. I walk down here every morning—it's so calming and serene."

Chip pulled over and pointed to a house across the lake. "Through those trees you can make out a porch. That's where the previous camp directors, Herman and Estelle, live."

A quiver shot through my body thinking about sitting naked on Adirondack chairs, sipping coffee, and holding Teddy's hand. "Does that mean once you work here, you never leave?" I asked.

He laughed. "You've got a quick wit. I've heard that about you."

"I've heard great things about you too," I said. "Tell me how you got started working with camps." I could tell he was flattered; he sat up straighter.

"I've been in the camp business for about twenty years. This camp is one of my favorites. It's beautiful. I mean, look at that lake, the mountains in the distance, and the foliage. Who wouldn't want to spend their summers here?" He took a deep breath, then continued, "I want to personally thank you for saving that child. Would you consider being an assistant director next summer?"

"I'm not planning on coming back," I said. "I won't work with Jack again."

Chip looked at me and nodded. "Well, there may be some changes here. The other partners and I have been talking. We've gotten complaints from parents, the staff doesn't respect him, and the camp is running on, what's the word I'm looking for . . .?"

"Toxicity?"

"Exactly. So, you know."

"Firsthand, very well."

Chip shook his head. "What you probably don't know is, Herman had a heart attack a few years ago and decided to retire on short notice. Who could blame him? Anyway, we needed to find a new owner." He faced me with a sad smile. "Here's a funny sidenote. We brought the Bergers on as partners because Jack had an MBA in human resources."

I tried holding back a nervous giggle but failed.

"I've been fielding offers from people interested in buying the camp."

I blurted out, "I'd like to buy it. My business partner and I would like to buy the camp and run it."

"Who's your partner?"

"Ted Mooney." As soon as I said it, it sounded ridiculous. How could a soccer coach and a first-time DL buy a camp?

Chip smiled. "That makes some sense. Mooney's probably worth about twenty mil."

"What?" If I hadn't been sitting down, I would've fallen over. That couldn't be right. Why wouldn't he have told me?

"This isn't a surprise to you, is it?" he asked. "He's your business partner. You must know about his assets."

Not his financial ones. "Sure, yes, of course, I do."

He looked out at the lake. "If I'm not mistaken, this is your first summer working at Woodlands, right?"

"Not only that, it's my first-ever experience at a sleepaway camp."

"So, what you're saying is that in less than two months, you learned all about running a camp and became good enough friends with Ted to go into business with him?"

I smiled. "When you put it that way, it does sound far-fetched, but yes."

"I have only admiration for a person who knows what she wants and goes after it. And I want someone who knows and appreciates the camp, and Ted is certainly that person. Let's meet, me, you, and Ted to discuss the offer." He looked at his watch. "In about an hour."

I knew I should call Ronnie to discuss buying the camp, and I should do it well before the money conversation. I also knew that when Ronnie became a partner at his firm, it was suggested that our assets be put into my name in case he was personally sued by a disgruntled client. That translated into collateral for a loan.

But the person I wanted to speak to was Teddy. I'd never radioed him, but I didn't know any other way, and I had less than an hour to find him. I was about to press the talk button when I heard "Kramer" shouted in a British accent behind me. He always seemed to appear when I needed him. My impulse was to fling myself at him and scream, "We did it!" Instead, I said, "I just went on a ride with Chip. I hope it's okay with you that I set our plan into motion, our fantasy, our dream, of owning the camp together." I had trouble reining in my excitement.

He grinned. "Brilliant! I wish I could spin you around right now, but our celebrating will have to wait until tonight."

We talked strategy. "Remember, we give nothing away, and we listen," Teddy concluded. "All we have to do today is toss our hat into the ring, so they know we're serious."

Chip pulled up. "I hoped I'd find you together. Hop in."

He steered the golf cart onto the main road that led out of camp.

"Remember earlier I pointed out Herman's house? I have a set of keys. We can talk privately there."

Teddy and I looked at each other. How many spare keys were floating around? Mental note—bolt doors.

We sat across from Chip at the dining room table. The meeting was less about the cost of the camp and more about how to push the Bergers out while leaving them a semblance of dignity.

When the meeting was over, Chip said to me, "Remember, this is top secret, no gossiping over campfires or cocktails."

"Why are you telling me and not Ted?" I'd insist on being treated equally.

"I've known Ted a long time, and I know he's not one to talk. We've just met."

"I trust Lori implicitly," Teddy said.

Chip looked from me to Teddy and back again. "In that case, I trust you too."

After we shook hands and walked out the door, I looked back and said, "There's something about this house. I can't quite put my finger on it—like it's an auspicious place to start a new venture."

Teddy smiled. "Yes, a good omen."

"Personally, I think it's an architectural piece of crap. Herman and Estelle couldn't agree on a style, so they used them all. There's no accounting for taste," Chip said.

Back on the main road leading to camp, our radios crackled. Jack's loud and annoyed voice screeched from the radio. "Has anyone seen either Ted or Lori? I repeat, I'm looking for Ted and Lori. If you see them, send them to me immediately."

We'd been gone for over an hour, and I hadn't let anyone know that I was off radio. I was pretty sure Teddy hadn't either.

"I'm so not in the mood for him," I said.

Chip chuckled. "I may have gotten the two of you in hot water. Let's walk into the office together and really make Jack sweat."

"Ted here, Lori and I are on our way." He clicked off the radio. "That should keep everyone guessing."

"Rumors are gonna fly," I said.

"You both have the right attitudes," Chip said. "I hope all the pieces fall into place because from what I've seen today, you'd make a good team to spearhead Woodlands into the future."

35

# Tantrum

Marilyn had a surprised look on her face as the three of us walked through the back door of the Bergers' office, but the alarmed look on Jack's face when he saw us was worth whatever bullshit he'd fling at me.

Chip spoke before Jack could compose himself. "Sorry, buddy, I needed to borrow these two for a bit. But don't worry, I brought them back unscathed. If you're going to be irate with anyone, it should be me."

Jack hesitated a moment. Even he could see how unprofessional it'd be to berate us in front of Chip. "I need to know where my key people are at all times."

Since when was I one of his key people? Probably since this morning when Chip pointed it out.

"If you don't need me for anything else," I said, "I'd like to check on—I almost said 'my campers,' but Jack has made it perfectly clear to me that all campers are his—the Cubs." I didn't wait for an answer and walked out the door. I could feel Jack's eyes boring a hole through the back of my skull.

Teddy fell in stride with me as I walked toward the canteen, out of view of the office.

"You know that Jack won't bother with you, but he'll ream me out later," I said.

"Don't let him get under your skin. Focus on what we put into motion today and how soon he'll only be a sad memory," Teddy said.

"The gossip, the innuendos, the questions . . ."

"I have complete confidence that you'll impeccably handle anything thrown your way."

Ronnie had never said anything like that to me. I smiled. "Thank you."

"You were brilliant today. You impressed Chip. I can't wait for next summer when we're running this place." We were behind the theater when Teddy placed his hand on my shoulder and whispered, "I can't wait to celebrate tonight."

"When will I stop blushing when you look at me that way?"

His face lit up. "I'm hoping never."

It was already choice period, so I went to my room, threw on a bathing suit, and caught Mindy starting her golf cart.

"Come on, I'll drive us down," she said.

I braced myself for the first round of questions.

"What the hell did Jack want that was so important?" Mindy asked.

"I think he knew I was with Chip, and it made him nervous."

"What did Chip want?"

"To hear my version of what happened the day of the carnival," I said.

"Why was Ted with you?"

"I wondered that myself. I got the impression they're buddies, so maybe he was there to vouch for my integrity." I wasn't lying, but I wasn't completely transparent either. Before she asked another question, I did. "Tell me what you know about Chip."

"Not much. I know he's the brains and the money behind the camp and that he intimidates Jack. I can imagine how anxious Jack was to find out you were with Chip. Jack was probably having a conniption, wondering what you'd tell him."

If Jack only knew.

Later that afternoon, Jack was outside his office waiting for me to walk by.

"Lori, Marilyn and I would like to speak with you."

Even though I expected it and knew he wouldn't be around much longer, he was still my boss. I foolishly hoped that, with Chip still at the camp, Jack wouldn't bother with me. Against my better judgment, I followed him into the office, bracing myself for a confrontation.

"Shall I radio Ted?" I asked.

He looked at me like I was a simpleton.

"I thought that since you're angry that we were off radio, you'd want to reprimand us both. Or is it easier to yell at a woman without a six-foot-two man standing next to her?"

"What's Ted to you? Has he become your protector?" Jack's sneer was menacing.

"I hadn't realized that I needed protecting."

He gawked at me. "That's not what I meant. You always mix my words and use them against me."

He was off balance. Good. "Why did you want to see me?" I asked.

"What did you and Chip talk about?"

I crossed my arms. "Our conversation was private."

His hands balled into fists, and he began to rant. I should never have stepped into the office where no one could witness his tirade. I took a step back and leaned against the file cabinet, next to the useless Marilyn. If he went to hit me, I could duck, and he'd punch the metal drawer instead.

"How dare you speak to me that way you, you, you bitch! Since you've been working here, you've been nothing but trouble."

"Who the hell are you to . . ."

Talking over me, he came closer and leaned into my face. I could smell rancid coffee on his breath and saw the sweat on his brow. "If I could, I would kick your sorry ass out of *my* camp. You may have fooled Chip and everyone else here, but I will not allow you to make a sucker out of me." He sprayed me with spittle.

I looked to Marilyn for help, but she was staring at her keypad.

Jack continued ranting. "You walk around here like you own the place. You do not, *I* do. Me! I've told you all this before, but no, you think you're above everyone else. All I hear every morning is Lori is so smart, so quick, so witty, the campers love her, she's a team player. Well, you are not on *my team*. I've got your number—you lie, you cheat, you drown my expensive equipment, and because of your negligence a camper broke her arm. And don't get me started on your trouble-making kids. You do everything to make me look bad while all along it's you who's incompetent . . ."

Mindy and Bethany almost knocked me over when they burst through the front door. Bob and Teddy came through the back at the same instant. Marilyn remained passively at her desk.

Bob put himself between Jack and me while Teddy placed his hands on Jack's shoulders. Jack tried shrugging him off, but Teddy held on firmly.

In a stern but calm voice Teddy said, "Jack, you need to take a step back."

Jack blinked and looked around, grasping that his leadership team were in the office. He stepped back from me, unclenching his fists. He was breathing heavily, his face still red, and he glowered at me with pure loathing.

No one moved for what seemed like an eternity.

Jack shrugged and said, "Take your hands off me."

Bob still blocked Jack, so Teddy let go. No longer feeling threatened, I threw my shoulders back and positioned myself between Mindy and Bethany.

Jack snarled. "What the hell are you all doing here?" He looked at me as if I'd invited them.

It turned out I did need protection. No one had stood up for me weeks ago when Jack had verbally attacked me, but they all showed up now.

Nicole was at the door. "Your argu . . . discussion was broadcast out to the entire camp."

The color drained from Jack's face as he snapped at Nicole, "How'd that happen?"

Nicole walked to where the camp PA system sat between Marilyn and Jack's desk.

Nicole shrugged. "The switch was on."

Jack was seething. He slammed his palm on his desk and said in a low growl, "All of you, get the fuck out of my office."

We filed out the front door. Bethany waved us to follow her across the road to her room.

Teddy put his arm around me. "I'm here for you. Whatever you need."

"I know." His nearness was reassuring. Hopefully his gesture would be construed as friendly.

When we all were inside, Bethany closed the door, pulled the blinds, and asked, "What the hell just happened?"

"I think I've become some kind of scapegoat for all the bad shit that's happened this summer," I said.

"I think you may be right," Mindy said.

"But why me?" I asked.

"Maybe because you're new, so you're an easy target," Bob said.

"I think it's because whatever good you've done this summer made Jack look bad," Teddy said.

Bob placed his hand on my shoulder. "Are you alright?"

"I guess I'm as good as I could be under the circumstances. Thank you all for showing up when you did. When he gets like that, I'm afraid he's going to punch me," I said.

"Yeah, it's scary when he loses his shit," Bob said.

"All the traits you want in a camp director—bad temper, no connection with the campers, and no respect for or from the people who work for him," I said.

"It took Lori a little over a month to figure out what it took me years to live through," Bob said. "No wonder he's afraid of you."

"Me? He's the one who's scary."

"I've got a totally different question. Who do you think switched on the loudspeaker?" Mindy asked. "Can Nicole do it from her desk?"

"She could, but I can't see my wife doing something vindictive like that," Bob said.

"Do you think Marilyn would have the chutzpah to do it?" Mindy asked.

We all snickered at that.

Bob shrugged. "I think she'd be too afraid of the consequences, but wouldn't it be ironic if she did?"

The door swung open, and Gilda flew in, sweating and out of breath. She pressed her back against the door. "If I tell you something, you need to promise it doesn't leave this room."

Everyone nodded in agreement.

She took a deep breath. "I turned the PA on. I wasn't going to let Jack bully anyone else. Last summer it was me, now it's

Lori. I couldn't live with myself if I didn't do something." She gasped for air. "I taped the entire tirade and gave it to Chip. And then he folded Jack into his tiny car and drove him out of here."

# 36
# The Laundry Shack

"When I heard Jack screaming at you over the loudspeaker, I couldn't get to you fast enough."

Teddy leaned against the laundry shack, his arms firmly wrapped around me, his head resting on mine.

"I felt immense relief when I saw you. I really thought Jack was going to slug me."

"Finally, I was there when you needed me." Teddy took my chin in his hand. "You do know that if he'd laid a hand on you, I would've flattened him."

"You would've, wouldn't you?"

His kiss was urgent, forceful, like he needed to show me the strength behind his words.

"Things are really falling into place for us," Teddy said. "Poor Jack really shot himself in the foot today."

"Poor Jack, my ass. He deserves whatever his partners dish out. Speaking of which, our meeting with Chip was momentous. But you have some things you've been keeping to yourself. I realize I'm not one to talk about lies of omission."

"Lies?" Teddy asked.

"You never told me about your financial situation."

"You never asked." He smiled. "I had a dot-com that did well. I sold it and made enough money to live comfortably for the rest of my life. But then I had to think about how to occupy myself. The answer was easy . . ."

I finished his sentence. "Coach soccer."

"Yes, and I like that you hadn't asked about finances. My ex was a beautiful gold digger wrapped in expensive designer clothes, which I bought her."

Did he have to add beautiful? It made me feel self-conscious. My grays were showing. I'd wanted to go to town to buy some root touch-up, but with Bethany gone, it wasn't possible. Aside from sunscreen moisturizer, I didn't wear makeup. I wore boxy gym clothes, well, when I had clothes on. It was ironic that I was jealous of his ex when I was the one who was married.

"While we're being completely honest, there's more that I haven't told you," he said. "I have full custody of Max. I'm a single dad in the full sense of the word."

"That explains so much. The shopping. The cooking."

"I pride myself on how well I take care of my son."

"And me." He'd had plenty of opportunities to tell me. "Why hadn't you mentioned it?"

"I hate talking about her and I didn't want to tarnish our time together by bringing her up. Here's the short story. I really wanted children, she didn't. I started a divorce petition, and she played me and became pregnant. She used my child to extort me. But honestly, I was happy to pay her off, so I could have Max to myself."

"That's so sad. Does Max get to see her?"

"They go out for dinner once a week and on a yearly extravagant vacation—on me."

"She doesn't mind that Max leaves the country for the entire summer?"

"Mind? She's probably yacht-hopping through the Mediterranean as we speak. She gets a free summer vacation without a single responsibility. No, she doesn't mind. But enough about her." He was grinning when he said, "I would much rather concentrate on you." He glanced up at the stars, and when he looked at me there seemed to be a shift in his demeanor. "Is there something you have to tell me?"

I thought for a moment. "You may be the only person I've ever been completely honest with."

Teddy took a deep breath. "Before we signed on the dotted line, Chip warned me that you may be having a thing with Mike."

I hadn't realized just how much Teddy's irrational jealousy had grown. I'd first seen it after Mike saved me from the bear. Then Mike had gloated about rescuing me when I drove into the lake. Now with Chip telling him that Mike saw himself as my personal protector, I could at least see why he was questioning me. But that didn't mean I had to put up with it.

I scoffed. "I hope you told him that couldn't be possible since we both know I have a thing for *you*." I unwound myself from him and continued, "Mike made it sound like we were involved, and no, I didn't say otherwise. I didn't want to dignify it with a response. We happen to work at the same camp. I've shattered my already broken vows of marriage to be with *you*. I'm not proud of it, but up until this very moment I thought *you* were worth it." My hands were on my hips, and I glared at him the same way I did when I reprimanded my children. "Let me make this perfectly clear—I do not ever want to talk about this again." We silently stared at each other until I said, "Tonight we were supposed to be celebrating, but instead you're accusing me of cheating on the person I'm cheating with. This is absurd."

Teddy opened and then closed his mouth.

"You know what? I don't need this. I don't need to complicate my life with someone who doesn't trust me." I walked away.

"Lori, wait."

I turned around, my arms crossed in front of me.

"You're right. If I've acted as if I don't trust you, that's the furthest thing from the truth. It's my issue. I have to let go of the animosity I feel toward Mike. I thought I was past it, and then when Chip brought him up . . ." I was about to say something, but Teddy continued, "Lori, please don't walk away from our plans." He hesitated. "Or me . . . I'm truly sorry."

I didn't say anything right away. If I had any doubts, this was the time to hit the brakes. I looked him in the eye and said, "It's not just about the Mike bullshit. We need to trust each other. I get that you might not think I'm an honest and ethical person because of, well, my circumstances. But I am." I wiped away a tear. "What we're doing, our relationship I know is morally wrong but yet when I'm with you everything feels so right."

Teddy opened his arms. "Lori, I only have the utmost respect for you—"

I cut him off. "You know we cannot move forward with a partnership if there isn't trust."

Teddy wrapped me in a hug. "I'm sorry that I inferred in any way that I don't trust you because it couldn't be further from the truth. At this point in my life, you may be the only person I do trust." I allowed him to kiss me.

I pulled back, looking into his eyes. "Do we understand each other?"

"We are perfectly in sync in both mind and body." He picked me up, spinning us around. "I'm chuffed to be your partner and I'll never doubt you again."

37

# Infirmary

I was with Maggie and Abby sipping Dunkin iced coffee under the ceiling fan in arts & crafts, trying to escape the August humidity. It was rest hour, and we were enjoying our afternoon pick-me-up.

"I was thinking how good it feels not to have to look over my shoulder or second guess what I'm doing," I said.

"It's true, I feel freer, lighter. Dare I say, I'm the most relaxed I've been since we got here," Abby said.

"Nothing's changed for me. I never had any face time with Jack," Maggie said. "But Roger's happy not to be his errand boy anymore."

We turned when we heard the screen door slam.

"Marilyn, hi! How can I help you?" Maggie asked.

Abby and I looked at each other. We both had uh-oh expressions on our faces—caught in the act of doing nothing.

Marilyn had an unnaturally big smile on her face. "I hoped you could set me up on the potter's wheel. I haven't done it in a while."

"You do pottery?" Maggie asked.

"I used to love throwing pots more than anything."

"Would you like an iced coffee?" Abby asked.

"No, I'd be up all night if I had one now, and I had the best night's sleep . . ." Her face turned red.

Abby and I exchanged another knowing look. Over the course of the summer, we'd discussed in detail how miserable their marriage must be.

Since I didn't want to be reprimanded for sitting down on the job, which was exactly what I was doing, I got up and said, "Well, I'm going to check on the Cubs to make sure no one's melted. But before I go, how're you holding up?"

Marilyn twirled her hair around her finger. She seemed lost in her thoughts and then said, "So far, so good, I guess."

"Good to hear. See you later," I said.

Abby followed me out the door. "She does seem like a different person today."

"I was afraid she'd see how relieved I am that her husband's not here," I said.

"Are you kidding? She's the one that's relieved," Abby said.

There were murmurs of Marilyn sightings all day. With Jack MIA, she became a completely different person. She smiled. She spoke with the entire table while we ate, not only in secretive tones with Mindy and Bethany. She even surprised Mindy and me by joining us at the lake to kayak.

Mike personally helped Marilyn pick out a life vest and a Funyak. He was courteous and respectful, not only to Marilyn but to Mindy and me. When Marilyn paddled off, I said to Mike, "Look at you, being chivalrous. Showing off for the boss?"

"What can I say, I offer different talents to different women." He winked at me.

"I set myself up, didn't I? Don't answer that."

Smirking, arms akimbo, Speedo the same neon yellow as my Funyak, he watched as I paddled away.

The three of us met up at the sweet spot in the middle of the lake.

"I can't believe that it's taken me more than half the summer to take advantage of this beautiful place. I love being on this lake." Marilyn exhaled loudly, as though she'd been holding her breath until that very moment.

I knew I shouldn't say anything while she was enjoying some serenity, but that wasn't who I was. "What took you so long?"

Mindy flashed me a look that said, *Shut up and don't spoil this*. I wasn't looking to make trouble, but Marilyn had never come to my defense or even given me a word of encouragement, just some subpar sushi and a plate of brownies.

Marilyn looked up at the clear blue sky. "When I'm at camp, I feel so much pressure to be at my desk to deal with parents, vendors, and . . . my husband."

"Visiting Day has come and gone. Enrollment is healthy for next summer. It's literally smooth sailing for you until the end of camp." Mindy held up her paddle for emphasis. "You should take time to appreciate your hard work and the surroundings."

Marilyn smiled. "That's why I'm here."

I decided to let her relish her day in the sun. But I didn't have to remain in her company. "I'm going to paddle to the ski dock to watch the Cubs knee boarding."

"Wait, Lori, before you go, I want to apologize on behalf of Jack." Marilyn looked sad. "The way he's treated you has been rude and inconsiderate."

I took a deep breath and looked her straight in the eyes. "I can wait for Jack to apologize himself. If you wanted to apologize to me, I'd be willing to listen."

She stared at me, the paddle across her lap and her mouth gaping open. Mindy had a look of astonishment on her face. Nothing was said for an uncomfortably long time.

"Okay, then I'm off to do my job."

A few nights later I was slicing limes for G&Ts when Mindy said, "I heard that Jack's coming back tomorrow."

"I hope whatever he's been up to the past few days helped to calm and center him," Bethany said.

"I'll drink to that," I said and held up my cup.

"It's great that he's feeling better and all, but since he's been gone, have you noticed how everybody's been smiling? It feels like, you know, the way camp's supposed to be," Bob said.

"Like we all got a Get Out of Jail Free card," Gilda said.

Teddy was nodding in agreement. "Every single person in this room is great at their job. If Jack could only appreciate that he assembled a group of clever, motivated people, he would be so much less stressed, and we would all be better off."

"It's true, we're a well-oiled machine." Bethany swirled her jungle juice.

"I hope all of you, my drinking buddies, my comrades, my friends"—Teddy looked around the room acknowledging every person—"will return next summer. I have a feeling it'll be even more memorable than this one."

Mindy laughed. "Oh crap, I hope not."

After lights out, Genie followed me out onto the porch. "Lori, I need to talk to you."

"Sure, what's up?"

Genie moved close to the railing so we couldn't be heard. "I think there's something wrong with me."

"What do you mean?"

"I was with Connor on the golf course last night and, well . . ."

"Are you okay? Did he hurt you?"

"No, nothing like that, it was actually beautiful and romantic."

I found it difficult to believe having her body humped into a putting green was pleasurable.

"Really?"

"Well, yeah, it was a magical night, the moon was out, and there were like a gazillion stars."

"That's great, but what's wrong?"

"I'm pretty sure there's something in my vagina."

"Did he use a condom?"

"Of course. Do you think it could be gonorrhea or herpes or syphilis or leprosy?" Genie asked.

"I'm one hundred percent certain it's not leprosy. The STDs I'm less sure about, but I don't think it'd incubate so quickly."

"What should I do?"

"Come with me and we'll figure this out."

"Where?"

"To the infirmary. Let's get your insides checked out." I put my arm around her.

When the health care center came into view, Genie stopped and squeezed my arm. "Will you come in with me while I'm examined?" She looked so young, innocent, and frightened in her boxer shorts, hoodie, and Ugg boots.

"If you want, I'll even hold your hand."

"Promise me you won't call my mother?"

"You're eighteen. I legally can't call your mother."

"I'm not eighteen until the end of the month."

"I still won't call your mother."

"Thank you."

I thought back to my first encounter with Genie and how she'd walked away from me when I offered her my assistance.

Her coming to me for help was huge—for both of us. I put my hands on her shoulders. “Come on, let’s do this.”

Dr. Jenny held the tick in her tweezers. She dropped it into a Ziploc bag and used a red Sharpie to draw a circle around it.

“Are you giving that to Genie as a souvenir?” I asked.

“No!” Dr. Jenny said. “I’ll hang this up so everyone can see how tiny they are. These little buggers can cause so much damage.”

“Eww, it gives me the shivers thinking that was inside me.” Genie hugged herself. “Mother Nature really screwed with me . . . well, Mother Nature and Connor.”

# 38
# Vices

I was pouring myself a cup of dirty-water coffee when Abby asked, "Lori, where do you go every night?"

"What do you mean?"

"Come on Lori, I'm not an idiot. I hear the whistles before you leave the cabin after we get back from Mindy's. Where do you go?"

Maggie and Roger were closely examining the cream in their mugs. *Tread carefully*, I thought. "I'm sorry. I didn't realize I was keeping you awake."

"I'm a very light sleeper."

The three of them were staring intently at me. All I could think was, the jig is up.

"I go out for a smoke."

"I didn't know you smoked," Maggie said.

"I did when I was in high school. I've taken up two nasty habits since I've been here, gin and nicotine." I held up my thermos. "Caffeine's year-round."

"Who's the whistler?" Abby asked.

I was doing my best to sound casual. "Ted."

"Aha!" Roger spun his finger in the air. "Everyone over on boys' side is trying to figure out who Ted's been seeing, and it seems like he's been seeing you."

"Wait. No. It's nothing like that. We smoke, unwind, and commiserate about our days."

It had been naïve of us to think we could keep our secret. I knew Abby well enough to suspect that her questioning me like that was her way of letting me know people were gossiping.

"All I'm saying is, Bob and the DLs have been teasing Ted. Seems like he went from being a sad sack to being one happy camper," Roger said.

"We've been smoking together since orientation. I don't know what's happened recently to have made him less grumpy."

I could add another vice to my list. I'd become quite a good liar.

# 39
# Color War

"Color War breakout is tomorrow," Teddy said.

I covered my ears. "Shhh! I want to be surprised."

"You're adorable." He kissed me. "But seriously, I probably won't be able to meet you the next couple of nights. I need to be available to help the captains and won't be able to sneak away."

"You mean your job is getting in the way of our romance?"

"Hmmm, yes, our romance will unfortunately have to take a short break, but I've thought of a way of making up the time."

"You've learned how to stop the clock?"

"Unfortunately not but I've figured out how to make it work in our favor."

I adored how his crow's feet crinkled when he smiled.

"Stay with me an extra night in the lake house."

"I admire a man who has a contingency plan."

The next day everyone was abuzz due to the imminent arrival of Color War. Even though this was my first sleepaway experience, I knew Color War was the highpoint of camps across the country.

By dinner, the dining hall was vibrating with anticipation. Looking at the innocent faces of the Cubs, I smiled. Leah no longer cried every time she saw me, and Sarah had made one real friend. To my astonishment, I felt a burst of pride.

At Flagpole, Bethany stopped midsentence when we heard a thunderous noise approaching from the distance. The sound grew louder. We looked up to see a helicopter hovering above us. The flag whipped furiously, ponytails flapped, and everyone was screaming but you couldn't hear them over the roar of the blades.

A cloud of what looked like huge white snowflakes showered down on us. We were bombarded with ping-pong balls with the words Break Out written in neon green announcing the start of Color War.

As the helicopters flew off, the Swans went into a frenzy. Bethany stood at the flagpole, bullhorn in hand, trying to give directions, but she couldn't control the chaos. The Swans ran behind the cabins and all the girls followed. I looked at Abby, shrugged, and ran after my group. Genie led the pack.

The basketball courts were up a short but steep hill. I impressed myself with how easily I kept up. I thought about how my civilian friends would regale me about their summers spent at exotic beach locations while I'd never worked so hard in my life. The ironic part was that I was having a blast.

Panting, I reached the basketball courts and saw the Swans jumping and shouting, "One, two, three, four, we want Color War."

Bethany pulled up with Mindy and Marilyn in a golf cart, carrying a portable amplifier. After a few minutes, Bethany was able to calm the campers down and take control.

"OMG, I'm so excited. I love Color War." Genie was beaming.

"I bet your Swan summer you were a captain," I said.

"Yup, and my team won. We had dynamite songs."

"Which you wrote."

Genie made jazz hands, "You know me, I'm a Broadway Baby."

Marilyn announced the team captains and co-captains, and the Swans went wild, screaming, hugging, crying, and then tackling the newly appointed leaders.

The team names were announced to more squeals—Winter Greens and Summer Whites.

You could practically smell the charge of electricity crackling through the air. I was covered in goosebumps when Zelda jumped up beaming and joined the Summer Whites, slapping hands with her teammates. By the time Hazel's name was called, I was a blubbering mess.

"Did I catch you misty-eyed earlier this evening?" Mindy twirled the ice in her wine glass as I squeezed a lime into my gin & tonic.

"Don't tell me the woman who had her kids' bags packed and one foot out the door was sentimental," Bethany said.

"Okay, I'll admit the whole girl empowerment thing was special. I wasn't certain that I'd made the best decision to stay at Woodlands until the bitter end, but yeah, watching my daughters' excitement was gratifying."

Gilda asked, "So now that you're within spitting distance of finishing an entire summer, are you signing up to rejoin the cult next year? Have you drunk the Kool-Aid?"

Part of me wanted to tell them that not only had I bought into the cult, I was in negotiations with Teddy to mix a whole new recipe for bug juice. I held up my cup. "You know I only drink gin."

"Come on, you know what I mean."

"I've drunk gallons of bug juice and become a Camp Woodlands disciple." I held up my plastic cup. "Thank you for supporting me through all the nonsense, so I could make it to the other side. Cheers."

Bethany grinned. "I'm looking forward to working with you next summer."

Mindy held up her iced red wine. "Here's to next summer and the best part of camp—Color War!"

After my morning walk in the drizzle, I stopped in the dance studio to stretch. In front of the full-length mirror was a disheveled woman wearing baggy sweatpants with the camp's zip code plastered across her butt. I tilted my head, pulled my hair apart, and saw four different shades of disgusting. Brown and gray roots at the base, the middle was what was left of the auburn color I paid top dollar for every six weeks, the ends were strawberry blonde. I was almost forty and was walking around with a multicolored bush sprouting from the top of my head. On the one hand it was difficult to believe how unkempt I'd become but also liberating not worrying about how I'd looked for the past two months. But I'd book a hair appointment before I left camp.

What did Teddy see when he looked at me? If I asked him, he'd say something suave in his beautiful accent, like, "All I see is the beauty of your heart."

Hooking my slicker on the ballet barre, I bent over and mussed my hair so it wasn't matted against my scalp. I pulled my loosely hanging shirt back, tying a knot at the base of my spine. I'd lost at least ten pounds. I struck different poses trying to find the naïve woman who'd walked into Woodlands almost two months ago. The face staring back was set on a long neck and straight back with shoulders that seemed broader. I smiled looking at her, and in return I received a smirk of someone who had a self-assured air about her.

I strode into the arts & crafts studio and poured myself some dirty-water coffee. "I could really use a day at a salon. Do you think Marilyn would mind if I took some time off? I'll drive into town for a day of beauty and relaxation—a massage, dye job, and a mani-pedi. Wanna join me?"

"Desperately. I haven't been this slovenly . . . ever," Abby said.

"Come on, ladies, you can stand a few more days of looking like schlumps. Everyone knows by now that Abby's not a natural blonde and Lori isn't a real redhead," Maggie said.

I fluffed my hair. "Auburn."

Roger was scanning the day's schedule. "Today's big Color War event is the marathon relay."

"Speaking of marathons, we're at the end of ours. Even with all our bellyaching, it flew by." Abby dunked a biscotti.

"It's like having a baby . . . each day is an eternity and then, in a blink of an eye, they're old enough to go to camp . . ."

Abby continued my thought, "With their mothers."

We laughed.

The relay was the last of the Color War competitions. There were different legs of the race: kayaking, an egg toss, kicking a soccer goal, backflipping on a balance beam, jumping rope, and passing a water bucket to fill a tub. My personal favorite was chewing a piece of Bazooka and blowing a bubble. Intentionally, there was an activity that every camper could successfully accomplish, regardless of their skill set. The last leg of the relay was a two-mile race that started at the ski dock, continued up two steep hills, and ended at the campfire site, where all two hundred and fifty girls would gather, waiting. The first runner from each team to arrive tagged a person designated to start a fire. The flame had to burn through a rope that was strung three feet above the blaze.

Everyone's reward for the afternoon's efforts would be s'mores.

At breakfast that morning, Jordana, one of the two Color War captains, approached me as I scooped granola onto a yogurt parfait. "Lori, my team voted to have you as the DL starting our fire."

"I'm flattered, but if you want to win you should pick someone else. I've never started a campfire."

"Nope, we all agreed. We want you." She beamed at me.

"I don't want to disappoint you and the entire Green team."

"You won't. Besides, if you can't get a flame going within ten minutes, someone is allowed to help you."

"You're sure about this?" I asked.

"Absolutely."

Watching her walk away, I prayed for rain.

Mike was at the campfire site when I arrived. He was wearing a pair of wellies, hip-hugging ripped jeans, and a hoodie zipped up just enough not to keep you guessing what lay underneath. At his side was a fire extinguisher.

"Don't tell me," he asked, "they picked you to start the fire?"

Before I could respond, I heard Zelda before I saw her. I turned as she said to Tara, "This is perfect—our team's gonna win. My mom doesn't know how to make a fire."

I was done doubting myself. I would no longer allow Ronnie, my kids, Mike, Jack, or anyone else to make me feel incompetent.

Slowly the bleachers surrounding the campfire pit filled up. My radio screeched—it was Bethany letting us know that the runners were on their way.

Zoe from the Green team made it through the clearing first. We ran toward each other so she could tag me. Matches in hand, I dropped to my knees, lighting the torch I'd fashioned out of newspaper and a branch. I touched it to the kindling I had bundled into four neat piles surrounding the logs. There was a slight breeze working in my favor, and it blew sparks onto the propped-up branches that I'd formed in a teepee over the logs. The brittle twigs caught fire quickly. I placed my torch directly on the wood at the base, ensuring that the fire would ignite the logs and keep the branches above burning.

Thanks to *The Boy Scout Handbook*, I had successfully built a fire that blazed brightly and burned the rope as the last runners came into sight.

The heat from my fire warmed me from the inside out, and the crackling sound was pure music. I'd never felt more accomplished.

"You may have the qualities of a camper after all," Mike said.

Bethany lifted my hand above my head and announced, "The Green team wins."

I felt incredibly proud. Zelda was at my side and said, "I'll have to tell Dad you learned how to make a fire, but why did you have to do it for the other team?"

The next day after breakfast, Girls Camp met up by the campfire area for the Burying of the Hatchet ceremony. I shouldn't have been surprised to see Mike standing next to a small hole, one hand leaning on a shovel. He wore tight jean shorts and a white collared shirt, and for once, not an ounce of unnecessary skin was showing. I couldn't make out what he was holding. When I got closer, I saw it was an actual ax.

"They're literally going to bury a hatchet?"

"I'm here to make sure no one hurts themselves, and I wouldn't expect one of you prissy DLs to dig the hole."

"So, they sent a big strong man to do it."

He stood straight and saluted me. "At your service."

The hatchet was painted white on one side and green on the other, and it would be buried green side up because the Green team had won.

The captains faced each other as the rest of the camp watched from the benches. They hugged, and Bethany asked them to kneel while she gingerly handed them the hatchet, which they placed in the ground. They each took a pile of dirt in their hands and tossed it over the ax.

Bethany led the group in singing the original Color War songs written by the Swans. They all knew the words—it didn't matter which team you were on. When they finished, Bethany led everyone in a song that I'd never heard.

She started singing, "Twenty plus years at Woodlands," while looking at Mindy.

Then Mindy sang, accompanied by Bethany, "Friendships and memories in a circle of sisterhood that never ends. Come join me, those who have been here for ten years." There were no takers. "Nine?" Finally, Genie popped up for seven years, and she belted out the song and invited all the Swans who had been at camp for six years to join in. By year three, most of the campers swayed arm-in-arm, and then the rest of us joined in.

The singing continued until everyone held hands in a friendship circle. I was holding hands with Maggie and Abby. If someone had described the scene taking place, I would've thought, *How corny*. But being part of a living, breathing friendship circle was poignant and inspiring. Watching Zelda and Hazel, I laughed and cried simultaneously.

I had thought that unpacking the trunks was hard, but I was wrong—repacking them was worse. The campers weren't allowed to help and were all outside playing and exchanging email addresses and phone numbers.

Amber called me over. “Lori, I’m so sorry, this is all my fault,” she said.

“Why, what’s wrong?”

I followed her over to Chloe’s cubby where Genie was standing. Next to Chloe’s bunk was the floral roller bag she had brought with her on the bus.

Genie said, “Hold your nose.” And she unzipped the bag.

The acrid ammonia stench of fifty-six days of urine filled pull-ups permeated the cabin. It was far worse than any underground subway passage I’d ever walked through. Coughing, I covered my eyes as they began to water.

“Quick, close that. Chloe’s mom had told me she was a bed wetter, and I had asked her to send along extra sheets and underwear. She must’ve also packed pull-ups.” The troubled look on the faces of my most responsible hard-working counselors made me laugh.

“You think this is funny?” Amber asked.

I was laughing so hard, I had to sit down. “We were outsmarted by an eight-year-old.”

Once they realized I wasn’t angry, they saw how funny it was and joined me. When we calmed down, Amber asked, “So what do we do?”

“Nothing. I’ll take the bag to where they’re collecting the garbage and leave it there.”

“What if she asks for it?” Amber asked.

“I doubt she will, but you can always say that Lori took care of it. I’d bet she’ll be relieved.”

“So, we’re good?” Amber asked.

I brought them in for a group hug.

# 40
# Mic Drop

Everyone gathered on the baseball field where the end-of-camp Awards Ceremony was taking place. Even though the humidity was oppressive, there was a palpable excitement in the air—the boys sat on the bleachers by first base, facing the girls sitting at third. The benches were filled with happy campers ready to cheer on their friends and their accomplishments. A makeshift podium had been set up in the middle on the pitcher's mound.

When it was over, Bethany took the microphone and said, "We have one last award of distinction to bestow on a very special person, and it will be presented by Zelda and Hazel Kramer."

I was sitting on my soccer-mom chair next to Abby, chatting and cheering on the campers when I saw my children take the microphone.

"What's going on?" I asked Abby.

"Beats me."

I looked across the field and caught Teddy's eye. He shrugged.

"The special person award is for going above and beyond your duties and for saving a camper's life," Hazel said.

Zelda grabbed the mic. "And being the best mom. Lori Kramer, please accept your award."

I was dumbfounded. Abby had to pull me out of my chair and give me a little push. I pulled my shoulders back and strode toward the proud faces of Zelda and Hazel.

Bethany had tears in her eyes as we embraced. Then my kids hugged me, handing me a loving cup made from clay. It was glazed a shiny emerald green and was hefty for something the size of a small soup tureen.

The crowd shouted my name, over and over. Zelda handed me the microphone.

I gripped it tightly to steady my nerves. Everything seemed to be happening in slow motion. I scanned the crowd and saw the Cubs jumping up and down. Mike and Anya were off to the side, fists pumping the air. Bob and Teddy wolf-whistled. I was surprised to see Chip next to them, clapping and grinning.

It took me a moment to appreciate what was happening. I thought of Gary Cooper in *The Pride of the Yankees*, echoing his thanks across a baseball field. I held the mic and said, "I want to thank everyone here for making this the most exciting and rewarding summer for me and my kids." I held the loving cup over my head. "We've come to love Woodlands." I looked at Zelda and Hazel, who were smiling and nodding. I stopped to choke back tears.

In my peripheral vision I saw Teddy and Bob running toward me, yelling and pointing. I turned the other way and saw Jack barreling toward me with a wild gleam in his eyes. Instinctively, I stepped back as he lunged at me, tripping over the microphone wire and falling flat on his face. He seemed confused—like he didn't know how he'd ended up on the ground. When he managed to stand, he snatched the microphone from my hand and shoved me. The loving cup fell and shattered at our feet. He looked down at the broken shards and then at me, sneering, seemingly happy that he had broken my trophy. I glared at him, hoping he felt the repulsion I had for him.

He screamed into the mic, "This is *my* camp and *I* decide who gets awards and Lori and her troublemaking kids are not worthy." He was red in the face shaking with fury. He pointed his finger in my face, not aware or not caring that the entire camp was watching.

I hissed into his ear, "Let's see who's worthy when you're out on your ass, and I'm running the camp." I grabbed Zelda's and Hazel's hands and left him standing there with his mouth gaping open.

Jack went completely ballistic, wildly waving his arms while shouting into the mic, his words incomprehensible. I half expected foam to gurgle from his mouth—he was acting like a rabid dog.

Bob and Chip were trying to wrest the mic from him.

"What the hell are you doing? I'm not the problem, that bitch Lori is." He was trying to shake loose from Bob's grip. "Get your fucking hands off me."

"Why was Jack cursing at you?" Zelda asked.

"I don't know."

"He smashed the trophy we made for you." Hazel was trying not to cry.

I hugged them. "Thank you for the beautiful trophy and for what you said about me. I love you both so much. I'll explain everything later, once I figure it out. Go join your groups."

Teddy appeared while I was with Maggie and Roger, who was unplugging the speakers. "I wanted to make sure you were okay before I see to Jack."

"A little shaken but yeah, I'm fine."

"I'll check back with you later." Teddy ran toward Jack.

Maggie, Roger, and I saw him at the same time: Dylan, the camp photographer, had been videoing the Awards Ceremony, and Jack's outburst had been broadcast live to the families.

"Hey, Dylan, you should stop taping," Roger said.

Dylan had a sardonic grin on his face. "Are you kidding? Jack treated me like crap all summer."

"Talk about digging your own grave," Maggie said.

I barely heard the radio over the commotion. "Hello, is anyone out there? Please, someone pick up for Nicole."

"This is Lori."

"Lori, good, what's going on out there? The phones are ringing off the hook."

"Short answer, Jack lost his shit during the ceremony while the parents were watching on video."

"Jesus!"

"Nicole, this is Gilda. I'm on my way to help."

"Good. Thanks. Nicole out."

The mood of the camp had been chill—all kumbaya. But once Jack let the vulgarities rip, any semblance of decorum was lost in the August haze.

The bleachers emptied. The older girls and boys flirted while the rest of the campers played in the outfield, running the bases, chasing each other, and cartwheeling. Spontaneously, the entire camp was having a joyous free-for-all. It reminded me of the first day of camp, the kids descending from the buses filled with excitement and anticipation for the summer ahead, and now it was the culmination of the camaraderie and shared experiences on this, the last day.

Maggie and Roger started packing up the stereo system, but I asked them to plug it back in and play something danceable.

When the music began, Abby and I started singing and bopping on the pitcher's mound. A bunch of counselors joined us, and soon we were in the middle of an impromptu dance party. It was a perfect diversion to keep the kid's focus away from what had unfolded before them . . . and their parents.

Teddy caught my eye as Abby and I danced to "I'm a Believer."

He joined me, grinning. "I see how you've single-handedly kept the camp running while the assistant directors are dealing with Jack."

"What about you? Aren't you an assistant director? What've you been doing?"

"Watching and learning from a pro. Well done, Kramer." He actually clapped.

"Thanks. I'm going to end the party after this song. The kids have to shower and get ready for the Banquet."

"Good idea. I'll walk with you—first I need to check on a couple of things."

When he was out of earshot, Abby said, "You two seem to have some kind of connection."

I shrugged and picked up the mic. "Attention Woodlands Campers. It's time to get ready for tonight's Banquet."

Roger put on the Miami Sound Machine and the campers conga-ed their way off the field.

Teddy caught up with me on the road. "Let me take that." He hoisted my chair over his shoulder.

"I have to tell you something. I may have messed things up for us," I said.

He stopped and looked at me. "What could you have possibly done?"

"I taunted Jack about me running the camp. I know it was stupid, but I couldn't help myself. I hope you're not angry."

He chuckled. "Angry? On the contrary, your timing is excellent. You inserted the knife, and Chip will twist it."

"One more thing. Nicole's flooded with phone calls from parents who witnessed Jack's behavior. There may not be any returning campers next summer."

"I told them broadcasting live was a stupid idea."

"But you know, I think it may work to our advantage," I said.

"How?"

"Chip was talking about us being interim directors, but after what happened today, he'll be begging us to buy the camp. No outsider will want to touch it. My only concern is, do we want to own a disgraced camp?"

"It won't be easy, but I think the two of us together can turn this around. I have the utmost confidence in your abilities to succeed at anything you set your mind to."

## 41

# Banquet

Maggie had turned the dining hall into a winter wonderland. There was a five-foot-tall snowman made from wire and papier-mâché, complete with a corncob pipe and two eyes made of coal, greeting us as we walked through the door. The buffet tables were covered in cotton snow and glittering snowflakes hung from the ceiling. Cardboard cutouts of pine trees surrounded by candy canes and red, green, and silver-foiled chocolate kisses stood on each lazy Susan. Maggie was dressed in a white fur boa and tiara and held a wand topped with icicles. It was still as hot as blazes outside, but with the air conditioner blowing, you could almost pretend to feel the cold emanating from the decorations.

Chip appeared at my table. "Sorry ladies, I need to borrow Lori."

As I stepped away, I caught the confused looks passing between Bethany and Mindy.

Teddy was already outside leaning against a golf cart, his arms crossed and a wry smile on his face. I admired how comfortable and confident he looked.

"Where're we going?" I asked.

"To the lake house," Chip said.

I saw Teddy momentarily squirm.

"Why?" I asked.

"To discuss the transition," Chip said. "What Jack did today, well, there's just no way to salvage it. We had to stop answering the phones, or we would've lost a good chunk of next season's tuition. We're in damage control right now."

"Will naming new directors be enough?" I asked.

"Bob and Mindy are working on a letter to put up on the website, apologizing for Jack's behavior and letting parents know that someone will be in touch with them before the end of the day tomorrow."

When Chip opened the lake house door, there was one majestic sunflower sitting on the kitchen counter next to a bowl of cherries and a bottle of champagne. I smiled.

"Huh, someone's been here, using the house," Chip said.

"I must confess, it's me. Herman and Estelle allowed me to use their digs while on vacation." Teddy's cheeks had a slight blush.

Chip slapped Teddy on the back and said, "Glad to see you back in the saddle, my friend." I couldn't see Chip's face, but I assumed he threw in a wink.

I whispered in Teddy's ear, "Giddy up," as we walked into the dining room, and he blushed more deeply.

Chip was at the head of the table, and Teddy sat across from me.

"My partners are invoking a stipulation in Jack's contract, which states that if either party is not happy or has just cause to step away from the contract, they can do so. We probably had enough reasons to enforce the clause before today's fiasco," Chip said. "We intend to name the two of you as interim directors."

"Interim directors is bollocks—Lori and I want to own the camp." Teddy's arms were crossed.

Chip smiled. "I was hoping that's where this conversation might go."

"We'll need to review the financials," Teddy said. "We can draw up an agreement stating we'll be running Woodlands with the intention of buying it when it's free and clear to be sold."

"That seems fair enough," Chip said.

My chest constricted as my panic rose. I had no immediate funds ready to make an offer—but my fantasy was rapidly becoming a reality.

"I'll gather the paperwork for the past five years so you and your attorneys can evaluate the information, and we can come to an equitable agreement." Chip sat back and took a deep breath. "It's in everyone's best interest to move this along as fast as possible." He pressed his fingertips together, smiling at us.

"The way I see it, Jack's antics have gone viral, turning Woodlands into a joke," I said. "The numbers for re-enrollment are precarious at best. Filling the bunks next year will be a massive undertaking." I let that thought hang in the air.

Chip took the bait. "What're you saying?"

"If you're hiring us, we need to discuss two things. First, our salaries for next year, keeping in mind how hard we'll have to work to fill five hundred beds. We're basically going to have to rebrand the camp. Next, a discounted purchase price for the camp to be put in the agreement."

Chip chuckled. "Shrewd."

Being married to an attorney had some benefits. Teddy beamed at me.

"Can we put our plans into effect as soon as we agree on the terms?" Teddy had spent time thinking this through.

As had Chip. "Absolutely. That's what we want."

We were leaving the house when Chip said, "Maybe you should put that champagne in the fridge."

This time I saw the wink.

Chip dropped us at the dining hall.

"Is this really happening? Are we actually buying a camp together?" I asked.

"The way you outlined your terms, I thought it was a done deal."

"I wanted to make sure to get a sweet deal, especially since we'll be taking on a risky investment."

"True, and it will be so much sweeter doing it together."

I stopped and looked at him. His smile was irresistible.

I wasn't afraid. I knew I'd be good at it, much better than the Bergers. My plan all along had been to look for a full-time job, something to fill the void in my life. Putting the question of financing aside, did I want the responsibilities of running a sleepaway camp?

I thought I'd enjoy the challenge of rebuilding, owning, and operating Woodlands. And I needed to prove to my family and myself that I was capable and resourceful. Not to mention, I'd have my own source of income.

I returned his smile. "Yes, I'd like to own the camp with you. But I don't like the idea of Chip and his people as partners in *our* camp."

"I agree and I've given that some thought. At first, we'll need them. I'll ask my attorneys if they could draft a clause that phases out the silent parties over a short period of time so that within a few years we own everything outright."

"I like the way you think, Mr. Mooney," I said.

"Me? What about you, playing to his financial concerns, undercutting the camp's worth? That was genius." He put his hand out. "I look forward to our partnership."

I took it and said, "And I look forward to drinking champagne in bed with you."

# 42

# Burning the Numbers

A sea of ponytails was forming at the base of the hill in front of the gymnastics shed. It was the meeting spot where each DL handed out three-by-three wooden rafts, each with a candle mounted in the center. As the Cubs streamed past me, I counted forty-eight heads for the fifty-sixth night in a row, pleased that one of my biggest fears had never happened: Trip day aside, I hadn't lost a camper.

Becky had broken her arm on my watch, but Teddy had assured me that at least one camper broke some part of their body each summer. He told me he'd had three consecutive summers when a camper had either broken a toe, an ankle, or a leg during soccer. "Don't worry, it happens, they're young, and they heal." He had laughed. "And they'll always remember you."

Following them down the sandy path lit by a full moon framed by twinkling stars, I watched clusters of Cubs arm in arm with their heads leaning into each other, probably realizing that after tonight they wouldn't be waking up next to each other for another ten months.

Zelda's and Hazel's groups were far ahead of mine. I was lucky to share this night with them, but camp was about friendships. Even if I caught up to them, I wouldn't intervene and ruin the intimacy of their bonds.

I pushed the reality of having to leave Teddy to the back of my mind. I wanted to be present for my campers and counselors.

I had walked this path several times a day, either briskly in the early morning or later in the day with my bunks at a more leisurely pace. Tonight felt different. It was mesmerizing, watching the girls slowly amble down the pathway. Faces in shadows, the six-foot-tall reeds snapping on either side, frogs croaking, crickets singing, and the murmurs of the campers formed a melodic ambience. I was swept up by the surge of energy in the air and felt like I was in the only place in the world that mattered.

I caught up to the front of my bunks so I could walk with Abby who was at the rear of her group alongside Maggie. I wanted to experience the last night of camp with them.

"Have you ever been struck by a moment you know will stay with you for the rest of your life, and you'll see things differently because of it?" I asked.

They agreed and we linked arms.

"I love that we got to share it together. I consider our friendship the silver lining around all the chaos we lived through. Without the two of you, I'd never have made it till tonight."

"We were just saying the same about you. Like we've known you forever," Maggie said.

By the time the Cubs rounded the bend, the lake was ablaze with candles floating in the inky blackness of the water. The big dipper sparkled clearly in the night sky—it seemed as if we were enveloped by light from above and below. I stopped in my tracks, amazed at what I saw and how I felt. As if I'd stepped into a place of worship. Suddenly, the sand I'd walked on all summer grounded me in a way that felt spiritual, ethereal.

I stepped aside, making sure that I saw the Cubs'—*my campers'*—reactions when they got a glimpse of the spectacle on the lake. I saw the shimmering lights reflected in their eyes, and each girl, including the counselors, looked enthralled.

Soft singing off to my right added to the aura. Their sweet voices deepened the feeling that this evening was enchanted.

Bethany and Mindy made sure all the candles were lit and each Cub held a tiny flame in their hands.

Bethany told them, "Don't forget to make a wish before you send your candle into the water."

The girls bent down to release their desires along with the others already melting into the night.

Standing with Mindy and Gilda, Bethany asked the DLs to form a circle. "I want to say something now that we're all together on this last night of camp. Thank you for all your hard work this summer. I know it wasn't always easy, but I want you to know that I truly appreciate each one of you." Bethany looked us in the eye. "Let's float our candles together in the name of friendship."

At that moment I felt so much love for Bethany and these other women who'd stood by me all summer. I wanted to personally thank each one for getting me through these intensely wacky months. My thoughts were about to gush out of my mouth when Mindy said, "Bethany, I swear, sometimes you're such a sentimental fool."

The other ladies snickered but my feelings aligned with Bethany's. I gave her a one-armed hug, making sure not to singe her hair, and whispered, "Thank you for your leadership and guidance, but more importantly for your friendship and telling me it would be a mistake to leave camp."

Tears streamed down Bethany's face. "Thank you for keeping my family whole and for picking up the slack."

She took my hand and led us to the water's edge. Abby, as always, was on my left. Bethany squatted and I was on my knees. We were ready to release our candles.

"I'm thanking the camp gods for letting me make it through one more summer intact." Mindy floated her candle.

"I'm grateful for an entire summer of no housework, and for not having to pay two camp tuitions." Gilda pushed hers into the lake.

Bethany, Abby, and Maggie let theirs float away in silence.

The aspirations I had for Zelda and Hazel had come to fruition. I'd watched them mature, becoming more resilient, more confident, but most importantly I knew that they'd look out for each other. Their love and respect for each other and for me was apparent.

I probably should wish for my marriage to be repaired, but there was no denying it, my desire for Teddy had blossomed into love. In Teddy speak, I was completely besotted.

Who had I become that I'd even consider walking away from a fifteen-year marriage for a man I'd known for two months? Was that personal growth or insanity? There was no one I could confide in at camp. I thought of telling Claire. If she was close enough to give me a vibrator then she was definitely close enough to confide in. But calling her wasn't an option until I could answer the questions she would invariably ask such as, "What about your girls?" Plus, all our college friends adored Ronnie and thought we were the ideal couple. What a joke that was.

I released my candle into the lake as if it were a coin tossed into the Trevi Fountain, wishing to return next summer to continue the love story I shared with Teddy.

"Hey, ladies, get it together. Marilyn's ready to burn the numbers. We need to head over," Gilda said.

All of Girls Camp watched Marilyn as she touched the torch to the lighter fluid soaked rags that were arranged on a chain link fence in the shape of the numbers representing the year.

"This doesn't look like it's going to end well," Maggie said.

Mindy pointed. "Over there, a little bit behind Marilyn, Mike's got a fire extinguisher."

Sure enough, Mike was ready as usual to save the day, wearing the equivalent of a Speedo for after-hours: crotch-hugging jeans, bare feet, and a camp hoodie with the zipper only a third of the way up his torso. No shirt.

"Look at him, dressed like some kind of Greek god. Really, who's he trying to impress?" Abby asked.

"Over there, near the bushes," Bethany said.

There was Anya with a look of pure adoration and lust, gazing upon her summer Poseidon. My Adonis was somewhere across the camp.

"It's enough to make you want to puke," Mindy said.

I couldn't put it off any longer. The news about the camp ownership was going public, and I wanted Ronnie to hear it from me directly, not by email.

I made the call from the privacy of Bethany's room. "Hi, Jana, it's Lori. Can I speak to Ronnie?"

"He's busy right now preparing for an extremely high-profile case. Can I take a message?"

"This is really important. I need to speak to him right now."

"Are the girls okay?" Jana asked.

Was she screening my call? "Yes, the girls are fine, but I need to speak to him."

"I don't think you appreciate how important Ronnie's work is to him and to the firm."

She had to be fucking kidding me—lecturing me about my husband and keeping him from me. I decided now was a good time to see if my suspicions about Ronnie and Jana were correct. I snickered into the phone. "Jana, does he tell you his wife just doesn't understand him? Did he tell you that when you were sipping Ouzo, overlooking the Mediterranean?"

There was an audible gasp and then silence. I could practically hear her heart thumping through the receiver. She finally said, "Give me a sec."

I must have really flustered Jana because she didn't press mute. "*Your wife's* on the phone," she said. "You told me not to tell anyone you took me to Greece. How did she find out?"

I couldn't make out Ronnie's muffled response. Jana tersely said, "I'll transfer you, but he told me to tell you to keep it brief."

"Ronnie here."

"No, 'Hello, Lori, how are you?'"

"I don't have time right now. Can it wait? I have a deadline."

"Quickly then: I'm buying the camp." I made a split-second decision. "And I'll need to stay here longer. You'll take the girls on vacation without me. Good luck with your deadline."

"Lori, wait. What?"

"What part didn't you understand?"

"You said you're buying the camp?"

"Yes."

"That makes no sense. I won't allow that. Nothing you said makes any sense."

"It makes perfect sense to me. You'll take the girls on vacation while I stay at Woodlands so I can do—what's that word you always use?—reconnaissance."

"I have to go. Can we talk about this when you're home?" He sounded annoyed.

"Perfect, so we'll talk in a week or so. Don't forget to pick your children up from the bus. Have fun at the beach." I hung up.

My brain was humming—Jana and Ronnie's affair had just been confirmed. I'd pondered this scenario, and there it was—like a slap in the face.

I wasn't innocent. This wasn't a case of being the wronged woman, since I spent my days counting the minutes until I'd be kissing Teddy. Would I admit to my affair and then work on repairing our marriage, or would we both walk away? If our children weren't involved, my answer would be easy.

Was I even upset that Ronnie was screwing his secretary? It was such a cliché. That made me the bored housewife shagging the soccer coach. My actions were as horrible to him as his were to me, only he didn't know it—yet.

Zelda and Hazel. I kept thinking about Chloe and how she'd fallen apart after Visiting Day. She was a happy camper until her parents refused to show up together. I'd never want to cause my children that level of misery.

Teddy. Yes, I loved him, but we'd made one rule together—when the summer was over, we were over. Would that change if I decided to walk away from my marriage?

Surprisingly, I wasn't crying, even though all the truths I had brought with me to camp were tumbling down, out of control. The inevitable earthquake would split the foundations of our children's lives, with me on one side and their dad on the other.

If Ronnie bothered to call me back, I wouldn't take the call.

As I had done for the past one hundred and sixty meals, I looked at the four tables of Cubs, counting off each camper. I remembered how nervous I'd been about meeting and taking care of these forty-eight girls. Now, as I watched them finishing the conversations that began on that very first day and were still going strong, I smiled.

"Leah, you must be happy. Don't you get your puppy today?" I asked.

"So excited."

"Tell me, were you really homesick, or did you just play your parents?"

Leah turned beet red and giggled. I laughed and gave her a hug.

Sarah was animatedly chatting with Jada. They had started hanging out the night of the dance when Sarah finally broke out of her shell.

I placed my hands on their backs and asked, "Will you get together during the winter months?"

Sarah put her arm around Jada. "Definitely."

Kacie stood up and gave me a hug. "Lori, I'm going to miss you. If I write to you, will you write me back?"

"Of course."

"Jamie, I know you weren't a fan of rollerblading, but what was your favorite part of camp?" I asked.

"Learning how to use a potter's wheel."

"Do you think you'll be back next summer?"

"I'd rather go to an arts camp. I don't really like sports, especially skating." She gave me a small sad smile.

"I'd miss you, but I'd understand."

I made sure to touch each child on her back whispering something personal into her ear.

# 43
# Inspection

Abby and I were in our rooms, chatting across the hall as we packed up the last remnants of our summer. I'd accumulated a lot of *stuff*—taped to the mirror was a watercolor landscape of the camp that Jamie made for me. On top of the dresser were neon-pink feather earrings from Hazel and a lopsided piece of pottery that was supposed to be a mug from Zelda. A tall glass vase held the sunflowers from Teddy.

I thought back to what a nervous wreck I'd been when I met Abby, unsure of my responsibilities. Leaning on and commiserating with her and Maggie had made everything tolerable.

"I can't believe we survived the entire summer," Abby said.

"And that we're still standing and . . ."

"Sane?" Abby finished my thought as she had since our first day.

"I know that some would question our sanity, but yeah, sane works."

"What do you think's going to happen with the camp next year? Are you coming back?" Abby asked. "I'm not sure if I will."

I walked into her room. "It all happened quickly, and I've been dying to tell you, but I didn't want to burden you with it."

She stopped folding T-shirts. "What's going on?"

"Chip asked me and Ted to be the interim directors next summer." I decided not to add anything about purchasing the camp until my name was on the contract. "But you can't say anything until it's publicly announced."

"You and Ted?" She looked at me suspiciously. "Do you really want all that responsibility?"

"Before I came to work here, I was looking for a job, and this opportunity fell into my lap."

"Is it year-round?" she asked.

"Yes, and I can do it from home so it should fit into my life."

"Hiring you as a director is the smartest thing anyone's done this summer."

I hugged her. "And yes, to answer your question. You're definitely coming back. I can't do this without you."

The first thing I'd want to do would be rehiring all the senior staff. I needed my allies by my side. I'd privately spoken with each Cub counselor after Carrie had told me they believed I didn't think they were doing a good job. Soon after that, I felt like we melded into a united team. I would rehire each of them—even Jasmine. It had taken almost half the summer, but once she fell into a routine it all came together for her. I smiled. I guessed the same could be said of me.

We were interrupted by Marilyn. "I've come to inspect your rooms."

Abby and I looked at each other.

"I hope you're not wearing white gloves," Abby said, "because I never had time to dust. Come to think of it, I barely had time to sleep."

"Oh, it's nothing like that. Just want to make sure things are in order."

I panicked. I didn't think I'd be within a hundred miles of the camp when my room was checked. I pushed my duffel bag over the stained piece of carpet. I glanced at the curtains. What if Marilyn noticed they weren't her grandmother's?

She went into Abby's room first, clipboard out, scrutinizing—she even opened the closet. I tried not to care, but my heart pounded. The obedient girl my parents raised wouldn't damage property, steal, lie, or worse, cheat. My stomach flipped—who had I become this summer? I'd completely turned my life upside down and inside out.

I hated doing the daily bunk inspections, even though they were necessary, but this inspection was degrading. I made a mental note, *Never treat the staff as if they were children.*

"Everything looks good in here. Can you sign this form?" Marilyn asked Abby.

"What am I signing?"

"That we both inspected your room, and everything was left the way it was found."

Abby signed. "Here you go."

"Thank you for all your hard work this summer." Marilyn gave Abby an awkward hug.

"Okay, Lori, your turn." Marilyn flipped a page and stopped to stare at the window above the bed, twirling her hair mindlessly around her index finger.

"These curtains . . . I forgot how pretty they were."

When Marilyn left, I let out a gasp. I'd been holding my breath the entire time she was in my room.

I met up with Zelda and Hazel as they waited to board the bus home. Their cheeks had dried tearstains from saying goodbye to their friends. My stomach dropped, thinking about the conversations and tears that would ensue once the four of us were home together.

I'd spend the next week concentrating on my career. Once that was in place, I'd hopefully have a clearer picture of what I wanted my future to look like.

"You should have your dad take you for sushi tonight," I said.

"I've already thought of that. We'll miss you, Mom," Zelda said.

"I'll miss you too,"

They both threw their arms around me.

"Dad's letting you stay?"

If it were the other way around, Zelda would never have asked that question.

"You know how sometimes we have plans, and your dad can't make it because something came up at work? Well, this is like that."

"But it won't be any fun without you," Hazel said.

"I had you all summer. Now Dad gets his turn to have alone time with you. It'll be like when you guys go skiing, except now you'll have Dad to yourselves, all day, every day."

Thankfully, the bus driver turned on the engine.

I gave them one last hug and kiss and waved to them as they rode off. When the buses had gone, I looked up and saw Teddy smiling at me from across the road.

I asked, "Do you have time to go for a walk?"

"That's the best offer I've had today . . . so far."

We stopped at the wooden fence that overlooked the lake.

"I told Ronnie I was buying the camp."

"How'd that go?"

"Not well."

Teddy didn't respond. We quietly stood next to each other. I started walking down the path, and he matched my pace.

"I don't need to leave tomorrow morning," I said.

"What changed?"

"I figured if I'm going to own a camp, I should start learning what that entails. Plus, I should see if I'm compatible with the person I'm buying the camp with." I looked at him and saw that his smile matched mine. "I told Ronnie he should take the girls on vacation without me."

We walked in silence for a bit. The kayaks, paddles, and life jackets that had hung on a wire between the trees were gone. Teddy took my hand. We passed the ropes course; all the climbing apparatus was padlocked in the shed. Teddy draped his arm around my shoulders. The sails were detached from the sunfish and the boats were upside down on the pier. Teddy's arm dropped to my waist, pulling me close.

I wanted to tell him about Ronnie's affair, but I enjoyed how his body gravitated to mine the further we walked toward the isolated edges of the camp. I didn't want to say anything that might spoil the feeling.

When we arrived at the ski dock, we walked to the middle of the platform.

"Since the first time I kissed you, I knew I wanted to kiss you every day for the rest of my life," Teddy said.

His long arms wrapped tightly around me, holding me like he would never let go. His kiss was as exciting as the first time, but now it was deeper, more meaningful. I returned his fervor, melting into his arms, forgetting about any existence beyond the sensation of his lips on mine.

There was one rowboat left in the water tethered to the dock.

"I have an idea," Teddy said. "I'm going to row us over to the house."

He helped me into the boat and oared us to the middle of the lake.

"This time next year, all this will be ours and we'll have finished our first successful summer." He beamed at me.

"How can you be so confident?"

"Because I have you in my corner."

I couldn't help smiling at him. "Are you trying to sweet talk your way into my shorts?"

"Those aren't just words. It's true. Together, we make a great team. But I do expect to be in your shorts . . . shortly."

The boat drifted while we basked in the sun and each other. I began singing one of the campfire songs and making the accompanying hand gestures.

"A boy and a girl in a little canoe with the sun shining all around and as he paddled his paddle you couldn't even hear a sound, so they talked, and they talked . . .".

He listened indulgently to my off-key singing and reached over just as I sang the kissing part of the song, and the boat started to rock. He tried balancing it, but that made things worse, and it tipped, sending both of us splashing into the lake. Laughing, we held onto the boat, catching our breath.

"I know I'm tone deaf, but you could've just asked me to stop."

With one arm draped over the hull, he glided me toward him. "You can serenade me anytime, anywhere."

I gave him the kiss he desired.

After several ungraceful and unsuccessful attempts to get back in, we kicked the boat under the weeping willows, leaving it on the shore. We left our sneakers in the sun and stripped off our wet clothes, throwing them into the dryer.

He chased me up the stairs and grabbed me around the waist, throwing me over his shoulder and spinning us around the bedroom. We collapsed onto the bed laughing.

We were in my favorite place, in bed, with my head on Teddy's chest.

"What are you thinking about?" he asked.

"I don't want to say goodbye."

"These past few weeks. You. Us. Today. Singing to me, falling into the lake and then into bed. Talking, sharing, laughing. I've never felt so alive, so happy. This is what life should be, what I want with you . . . every day. Lori, you've become everything to me."

My heart stopped and every hair on my neck stood up. He had reached inside me and found my inner thoughts.

"What I'm saying, Lori, is that I'm in love with you."

I looked into his eyes. "Teddy, I love you too." We sealed our confessions with a kiss. "But what about the rule we made, when the summer was over, we were over?"

"I've already broken several of your rules and you didn't throw me out of bed. Rules are meant to be broken, especially that one."

"Throwing you out of bed would've been a colossal mistake." I snuggled closer. "I need to tell you something."

"I'm listening."

"Ronnie's been screwing his assistant."

"Are you sure?"

"He took her to Greece."

I could tell he was working through what I said. A wry smile appeared on his lips but was instantly gone.

"The audacity . . ."

"Said the man I've been having sex with all summer."

"Don't exaggerate, it's only been half the summer." He kissed the top of my head. "Have you confronted him?"

"No. I thought that was a face-to-face conversation."

"I could kill him for hurting you if I weren't so happy to hear that he's been a scoundrel. The way I see it, he's made it easier for us to be together."

I tensed. I'd been fantasizing about this scenario, but now that it was becoming real, I was petrified.

He held me securely. "I hope your feelings mirror mine."

"If it were just you and me, there'd be no question. But we

have children. Are we willing to turn their lives upside down?"

"We have great kids. I already have a relationship with yours, and I know you and Max will adore each other. One thing I learned after my divorce is that children are resilient. We'll help them navigate through it all."

"There are so many hurdles. Where would we live? What if our kids don't like each other, or us?"

"I know it won't be easy. We'll take care of any issues one at a time. We'll figure it out together. We can do this. Look how much we've accomplished in one summer."

"You've put a lot of thought into this."

"It's all I think about."

"When you're holding me, my world is perfect. But when I'm alone, everything becomes more . . . complicated."

"That's okay because my plan is to never let go of you."

I kissed him with all my heart, and he returned it with an urgency that made almost all other thoughts vanish.

Teddy skillfully paddled us back to the camp side of the lake. It was late afternoon, and the sun's golden rays made everything seem to glow. One of those things was Teddy's rugged tan face. I looked into his piercing green eyes and thought, *Yeah, I could look into them for the rest of my life.*

He had on his impish grin as he stood and shouted, "I love you!"

His voice echoed on the water.

Laughing, I said, "Stop. Someone will hear you."

He cupped his hand around his mouth and yelled louder, "I love Lori Kramer!"

I tried pulling him onto the seat but he somehow managed to get me up and toss me into the water, jumping in after me. We laughed and kissed, gasping for air.

# 44

# No More Bug Juice

Gilda and I walked into the dining hall for the end of summer celebration dinner and stopped to take a glass of wine from the tray by the door. "No bug juice tonight." She tapped her glass against mine and said, "Cheers to making it to the last night of camp."

We joined our friends. Teddy was walking toward us. We had already set into motion our commitment to a work relationship. But just a few hours ago, he'd told me he wanted more, that he was willing to do whatever it took for us to be together, including uprooting his son and moving across an ocean to be with me and blend our lives, our families.

However our relationship evolved, I'd always be grateful to Teddy for helping me rediscover what I had slowly lost over the past fifteen years—my true identity, swallowed up while focusing on being a wife and mother. But more than that—my ego had gotten a huge lift. With Teddy's encouragement, the best of me had surfaced once again.

Owning the camp would fill a void, a hole I hadn't known was there. I was excited about the prospect of sharing everything with Teddy, as partners, as equals. I already knew he was a great collaborator, and together we would make Woodlands the best it could be for the campers and the staff.

I contemplated what a future with Teddy would look like. I knew for sure that we would always respect each other.

Gilda was watching me closely.

"What's going on between you and Ted?" she asked.

I put my arm around her. "I promise you'll find out before the night's over."

"What do you think the odds are that Marilyn and Jack join us for dinner?" Bethany asked.

"I'd say four to one for a no show, but the smart money's on those who don't give a rat's ass," Bob said.

Gilda took a sip of wine. "No betting necessary. Chip drove Jack out of here in his Range Rover hours ago. Marilyn followed in the Porsche."

Teddy mimed washing hands. "Good riddance."

Platters laden with catered food had been placed on the lazy Susans. While I ate, I decided that after dinner would be the best time to announce the plans for next summer. I was surprised I wasn't nervous walking to the center of the room.

"May I have your attention please?"

No one responded. Teddy stood, put two fingers in his mouth, and let out an ear-piercing whistle that stopped the room. He beamed at me, waiting to hear what I was going to say.

"We all witnessed Jack's outburst in front of the entire Woodlands community." I waited for the jeers and hisses to subside. "You're probably wondering what damage was done to Woodlands' reputation, and what that might mean for all of us next summer." I had everyone's attention. "I want to introduce you to the new leadership of Woodlands."

I paused, watching the reactions. Bethany and Mindy looked completely perplexed. I was sure they wondered why I'd be making the announcement. Teddy stood off to the side, hands in his pockets, grinning.

"Ted, please join me."

Murmurs and whispers floated through the room.

I placed my hand on his shoulder. "Ted and I will be purchasing the camp as co-owners and directors before the year is out."

There was a moment of stunned silence, and then everyone was on their feet, cheering, whistling, and clapping.

We were bombarded with congratulations and questions.

Gilda crossed her arms. "I knew it! I knew there was something going on between the two of you!"

Teddy placed his arm across my shoulders, giving me a conspiratorial smile. "Yes, we're business partners."

I was immediately surrounded by the women who had helped me navigate the summer and become important to me in a very short time. It was mind boggling to think how much my life had changed since I first drove under the Woodlands sign. My people, my friends were hugging me and offering their congratulations.

"Where were *we* when you and Ted became such good friends that you decided to buy the camp together?" Mindy asked.

I smiled at each expectant face. "I'll explain everything and answer your questions tomorrow over breakfast at the diner."

# 45
# The Last Breakfast

The first things I noticed when I walked into the diner were beautiful new curtains and a security camera. I should've felt a twinge of guilt but instead it just made me smile. *Teddy will think it's hilarious.*

We pushed two tables together without asking because we were five take charge women—some might call us assertive, okay pushy. But we had just finished eight weeks taking care of two hundred and fifty girls and we knew how to go about getting things done.

The same waitress, the one with the blonde bouffant who served Gilda and me breakfast weeks ago, poured hot coffee into the large clean white mugs as we settled in. "Do you gals know what you want, or do you need more time?"

"Give us a minute," Gilda said, then in her blunt way turned her attention on me. "Congratulations on buying the camp with Ted but I don't believe for a second that you two haven't been *schtupp*-ing all summer—right under our noses."

Gilda was holding court sitting at the head of the table. I was on her right, Abby as always on my left, and Mindy and Bethany sat across from us. Maggie and Roger had driven out of camp at 5:00 a.m. to get an early start on their drive to join Tony at his grandmother's and eventually make their way home to Florida.

Looking everyone in the eye I said, "I haven't been honest with any of you. At the beginning of the summer, I wasn't going to unload on a group of people I'd just met, but now after a solid two months of building what I'd like to think of as lasting friendships, I'm ready to let you in on my personal dramas." I took a deep breath. "No messy details . . . all you need to know about my husband is that he's been screwing his assistant."

All eyes were wide and mouths were open.

"I was feeling anxious those first few days during orientation and reignited an old smoking habit." I looked at Bethany. "Yes, you did catch me that day Becca broke her arm."

She smirked. "I knew it."

"That night I found Ted behind the laundry shack with a cigarette in his hand, and we became secret smoking buddies, and everything blossomed from there."

"Look, she's blushing like a schoolgirl talking about her first crush," Bethany said.

I brought my coffee up to my face, trying to hide behind it.

"You fell in love while nobody was watching?" Mindy said.

"Well put," I said.

"What about your husband?" Gilda asked, "Does he know?"

"I told him I was buying the camp," and added, "but I thought confrontational conversations should be done in person."

Abby seemed proud of herself when she said, "Maggie, Roger, and I figured it out a couple of weeks ago."

Gilda added, "Nicole and the other office ladies noticed that Ted changed his days off to match yours, so there were speculation and rumors flying about."

"The last thing I thought would ever happen when I made the decision to work at Woodlands was to fall in love." I shrugged. "Or buy a camp for that matter."

"Two life-changing events," Bethany said.

"Two life-changing events," I repeated.

"What about Zelda and Hazel?" Abby asked.

"They're my biggest concern. I have a reprieve in having to tell them. They'll be away with their dad for a week while I stay here with Ted, learning how to run a camp."

The waitress returned to take our orders. As soon as she was out of earshot Gilda turned to me and said, "This is probably none of my business—"

Mindy cut her off. "Since when has that stopped you from asking?"

"Never. Do you have the funds to pay for Woodlands?"

"Really Gilda, money is not a conversation for polite company," Mindy said.

Gilda picked up her coffee mug with her pinkie sticking out. "I hadn't realized I was in polite company."

I let out a nervous giggle. "It's fine—finances are my second biggest concern. But I'm pretty sure I have that figured out. All assets are in my name. I just need to figure out how to access them without Ronnie having any *interests* in my owning of Woodlands."

"Rumor has it that Ted has a boatload of money from the sale of his company. Can't he give you a loan?" Gilda asked.

Mindy said, "Good grief." Before dropping her head into her hands.

"Believe me I've thought about that, but we'll be business partners, we are romantic partners, and then I'd be indebted to him. One of the reasons I wanted a separation in the first place was that my husband thought since he worked and I didn't that he had control over our finances. I've wanted a job where I'd make my own money and therefore my own decisions. I promised myself that I would never be under the thumb of anyone again."

Since money was a topic that made people uncomfortable (well, except for Gilda), my friends focused on their omelets.

After a few bites Bethany thankfully changed the subject. "Wait a minute, everything we've talked about is coming together in my brain. You're gonna be my boss next summer." She waved her hand. "All of our bosses, that is if you deem us worthy of re-hiring."

"Of course I want all of us working together next summer. I couldn't do this without all of you."

Gilda said, "Hey, boss, in that case can I have a raise?"

I laughed. "It'll be the first agenda item discussed with my business partner."

The conversation turned to rehashing the escapades of the summer. I smiled and laughed when it was appropriate, but my mind was on my daughters and my future. Well, not my immediate future. I was very excited about my week getting to know Teddy better. It was sort of like being on a honeymoon but also the opposite of being on a honeymoon—we had a lot to discover about each other.

The five of us ate slowly, not ready to say goodbye. When we finally meandered outside, I got a little teary and said, "I was always jealous of people who went to sleepaway camp, but now I finally have my own camp stories and even better—camp friends."

"Ha, thirty years late," Gilda said as she hugged me.

# 46
# Day Is Done

By midday, the camp had emptied except for the maintenance crew and key staff. I smiled to myself—I was now *key staff.* Teddy and I sat opposite each other at the office conference table. He flipped the pages of the contract, making notations, engrossed in what he was doing. I couldn't focus. I was thinking, *Did Ronnie bring sunscreen or pack enough underwear for the girls?* One reason I had wanted Zelda and Hazel to go to camp in the first place was to learn responsibility. This was their first test. But the real question was: What was Ronnie telling them about my absence? I had to let it go.

I was not looking forward to confronting him about his affair—or telling him about mine. At least owning Woodlands would give me an income and the security to make the best decisions for Zelda, Hazel, and me.

I started re-reading the same paragraph for the third time, but the words blurred. I knew that once I read it through, I'd sign it and begin my new career. I looked up. Teddy was watching me.

"You seem like you're a million miles away."

I held up the documents. "I can't seem to concentrate."

"Let's go for a drive and get some fresh air."

I appreciated that he was always thinking about how I felt

and made me his priority. I slid into the golf cart next to him, and I held the hand draped over my shoulder, my leg rested against his, my other hand on his knee—he took it and kissed it. That would never get old.

We drove leisurely around camp, stopping at the tip of the property. We were looking out over the lake when an unnerving thought popped into my head. Would our love be sustainable while we lived an ocean apart?

"The first thing you ever said to me was that Woodlands was your slice of heaven. It never would've occurred to me that you and this camp would become my paradise." I looked into his eyes. "Do you think what we have only exists in the bubble we created at camp?"

We got off the cart and he took my hand, leading us to the bench facing the water. "My feelings for you aren't limited to these two hundred acres. Where we live doesn't matter." He squeezed me into him, smiling. "I'll be calling you every day—we do have a business to run." He slid off the bench onto his knees in front of me, so I looked directly into his sparkling green eyes. He held my hands. "Lori, I love you, and now that I've found you, that we've found each other, I'm not going to lose you."

"I love you too . . . but . . ."

He stopped me with a kiss. "We'll figure it out together. Whatever you need, whatever it takes. We'll make *us* happen."

I sighed. "I love you Theodore Charles Mooney the third."

His roguish grin appeared. "Oh, no, that will not do. Please call me Teddy."

# Book Club Questions

1. Did you relate to any characters in the book? Why?
2. What feelings did this book evoke in you?
3. Did the book remind you why you loved sleepaway camp? For those who didn't have the good fortune to attend camp—as a child or an adult—did the author place you in the middle of camp?
4. Was Lori's interaction with her daughters relatable? How different is your parenting style compared to Lori's?
5. What were your feelings about Lori's relationship with her husband Ronnie?
6. If you were in Lori's situation, would you have succumbed to Teddy's charms?
7. How did you feel about Lori and Teddy's chemistry and compatibility? Did you root for them or not?
8. How did the author balance the romance with other elements of the book—dealing with her bosses, with the campers, with the counselors?
9. How do you think Lori handled her relationships with her bosses? Jack and Marilyn? Bethany?

10. What did you think of the secondary characters? Did you like them? Mike? Genie? Jasmine? Maggie & Roger? Abby? Gilda? Mindy?

11. Did the situation Lori found herself in seem realistic to you? Did the characters' motives seem reasonable or a little far-fetched?

12. Which character did you like best? Least? Why?

13. Which of the other characters would have made an interesting protagonist?

14. What do you think Ronnie wanted to talk to Lori about?

15. Did you agree with how Lori handled herself after finding out that Ronnie was unfaithful?

16. Was there enough romantic *heat* in the book?

17. What do you think of the title of the book? How does it relate to the contents? What title would you have chosen?

18. Did the theme of second chances resonate with you?

19. Did you find the end of the book satisfying? What do you think the plot of a sequel would look like?

20. When the book becomes a TV series, who would you cast?

21. If you could ask the author one question about *Summer Husband*, what would it be?

# Permissions

FLY ME TO THE MOON
(In Other Words)
Words and Music by Bart Howard
TRO-© Copyright 1954 (Renewed) Palm Valley Music, LLC, New York, NY
International Copyright Secured Made in U.S.A.
All Rights Reserved Including Public Performance For Profit
Used by Permission

IT'S NOT UNUSUAL
Words and Music by Gordon Mills and Les Reed
Copyright © 1965 Valley Music Ltd.
Copyright Renewed
All Rights Administered by BMG Rights Management (US) LLC
All Rights Reserved Used by Permission
*Reprinted by Permission of Hal Leonard LLC*

HELLO MUDDAH, HELLO FUDDAH! ( A Letter from Camp)
The melody is from the opera La Gioconda by Amilcare Poncheilli.
Lyrics are by Allan Sherman and Lou Busch
Copyright 1963
Reprinted by Permission of Sentric Music

A BOY AND A GIRL IN A LITTLE CANOE
The song is credited to various Indigenous People of the Americas

# Acknowledgments

The writing of *Summer Husband* would not have been possible without the unwavering support of my husband, Steven Schreiber, who has always believed I could do anything I set my mind to. To my daughter Jenny, who said way back in 2013 to stop talking about writing a book and go do it. To my daughter Zara, who said in 2019, when the school I worked at closed, "This is the universe telling you to finish the book." To my daughter-in-law, Jordana, a voracious reader who encouraged me and couldn't wait to read my book. I also want to include my grandsons who, like their mothers, love to read—but they'll have to wait until they go off to college to read my novel. Saying thank you doesn't seem to be enough for what you all mean to me. I am grateful and blessed to be a part of our family.

A very special thank you to best-selling author Jennifer Belle. I am proud to be one of your Hell's Belles since 2013. I am thankful for your advice, guidance, and the fact that you never gave up on me or allowed me to give up on myself. I also want to acknowledge the other new and fledgling authors in the workshop for allowing me to be part of their creative process and for the brilliant edits they suggested for my manuscript—I couldn't have done this without your support: Penny Arcade, Meryl Branch-McTiernan, Donna Brodie, Joi Brozek, Tess Clarkson,

Andy Delaney, Angela Dorn, Mel Jennings, Brandie Knox, Stephanie Krikorian, Joanie Leinwoll, Judy Marlowe, Barbara Miller, Matthew Ochs, Maria Pramaggiore, Leslie Ross, Katie Sammis, Marilyn Simon Rothstein, and Lisa Smith.

To Brooke Warner of She Writes Press, who took a chance on me: I will be forever grateful to be part of the talented group of authors you have assembled. Addison Gallegos, my project manager/editor, guided me through the arduous process of publishing *Summer Husband* and bringing it out into the world. Thank you both.

Ed Dansker, who became my first "Ed-itor." Ed always said he couldn't wait until the book was finished. I'd answer with, "Neither can I." Ed continues to be an unwavering supporter and champion of my writing journey. Thank you from the bottom of my heart.

Carrie Hochstadt Lenga for continually nudging me until I caved and gave her my working manuscript. Her feedback sometimes pissed me off—but she was always right. Thank you for over forty years of friendship that has crisscrossed the world.

Linda Kunesh, who inspires me and always makes me laugh, from the first time we met one June morning over a cup of the best coffee I'd ever had until this very day. I appreciate your artistic visions and inspiration and all the reading and re-reading of the manuscript. Thank you from the bottom of my flat feet.

Julia Lindon, who shares the love of sleepaway camp with me. As soon as we met over gin & tonics, she asked to interview me for her podcast, *Happy Campers* (Episode 28, "Amazing Amy Goes to Camp"). As she so well put it, I never met a person whose first time at sleepaway camp was as a fully formed adult. My dream is that Julia will be the showrunner when *Summer Husband* becomes a TV series. (A girl can dream, can't she?!)

To my camp BFF's, I toast to our friendship with a gin &

tonic. Your support has meant so much to me. Here is the roster of my camp friends, alphabetically: Lowella Abikoff, Will Agnew, Michele Barbato, Stephen Board, Debra Carrion, Cynthia Foran, Cindy Gardner, Hinda Goldman, Jeremy Goldman, Shawna King, Mel Lee, Barbara Leeds, Florrie Nebiolo, Marissa Rahn, Dave Rosser, Tom Troche, Phyliss Weinberg, and Barbara Weisman.

To my lifelong friends who have continually asked about the book and have shown me love and encouragement through its lengthy process: Joanne Bennett, Yasmin Hurd, Susan Goldberg, Alyssa Sadoff, and two newer trusted friends Jana Goldfarb and Allie Tabak. Thank you.

My Binghamton University buddies who agreed to participate in my first book club meeting prior to my publishing deal with She Writes Press: Jody Ferrer & Stan Honig, Diane & Howie Fine, Paula & Dave Kornberg, Merrill Feldstein & Seth Lucash, Val & Andy Zeigher. With honorable mention to Rich & Rhonda Weiss, who were unable to attend. Thank you.

I owe much gratitude to my beta readers. They gave honest and invaluable feedback. Doris, Hannah and Isabel Eisenach Katie Flannagan, Debra Gelband, Mona Green, Staci Kirschner, Ken Ricken, Lisa Schreiber, Mimi Schreiber, Lisa Rosado, Carol Sisson, and Diana Wallerstein.

Karyn Schoenbart, who shared tales of her publishing experience both pro and con and was generous with her sage wisdom. She also introduced me to the Authors Guild—a wonderful source of information. I highly recommend becoming a member if you want to publish a book. Elyse Gilman, Esq., for reviewing my contracts and for sharing the wonderful role of grandma with me. Thank you both.

I am privileged to be a member of a book club for the past twenty-five plus years. I want to thank the brilliant and accomplished women for their insights and knowledge of all things books that we've shared over the years. I hope *Summer Husband* will make the list of possible books to discuss and that you will give it 7 points out of the 28 allotted.

# About the Author

Photo credit: Henry Castro

**Amy Lorowitz**, a lifelong New Yorker, grew up in Brooklyn and graduated from SUNY Binghamton. She has spent her adult life living in Manhattan with her husband, only leaving New York for a three-year stint in Tokyo, Japan. She's a proud mother of two daughters and Nana to two grandsons.

*Summer Husband* is Amy Lorowitz's debut novel.

www.amylorowitz.com

## Looking for your next great read?

We can help!

Visit www.shewritespress.com/next-read or scan the QR code below for a list of our recommended titles.

She Writes Press is an award-winning independent publishing company founded to serve women writers everywhere.